ALSO BY MARGOT HARRISON

e Made It All Up

he Glare

he Killer in Me

ONLY

SHE

CAME

BACK

A
W
T
T

ONLY SHE CAME BACK

MARGOT HARRISON

LITTLE, BROWN AND COMPANY

New York Boston

Little, Brown and Company
Hachette Book Group
1290 Avenue of the Americas, New York, NY 10104
Visit us at LBYR.com

First Edition: November 2023

Little, Brown and Company is a division of Hachette Book Group, Inc. The Little, Brown name and logo are trademarks of Hachette Book Group, Inc.

Little, Brown and Company books may be purchased in bulk for business, educational, or promotional use. For information, please contact your local bookseller or the Hachette Book Group Special Markets Department at special.markets@hbgusa.com.

Library of Congress Cataloging-in-Publication Data
Names: Harrison, Margot, author.
Title: Only she came back / Margot Harrison.
Description: First edition. | New York : Little, Brown and Company, 2023. | Audience: Ages 14 & up. | Summary: When true-crime fanatic Sam discovers her former classmate is the prime suspect in a potential murder case, their newfound friendship reveals there is more to the case than anyone knows.
Identifiers: LCCN 2022058568 | ISBN 9780316536080 (hardcover) | ISBN 9780316536295 (ebook)
Subjects: CYAC: Murder—Investigation—Fiction. | Missing persons—Fiction. | Interpersonal relations—Fiction. | Mystery and detective stories. | LCGFT: Detective and mystery fiction. | Novels.
Classification: LCC PZ7.1.H375 On 2023 | DDC [Fic]—dc23
LC record available at https://lccn.loc.gov/2022058568

ISBNs: 978-0-316-53608-0 (hardcover), 978-0-316-53629-5 (ebook)

Printed in the United States of America

LSC-C

Printing 1, 2023

To my dad, Harvey Sollberger, who raised me
on the creepy legends of the old Southwest

COMPILATION OF LEAKED SECURITY FOOTAGE POSTED ANONYMOUSLY ON AUGUST 4 AT 5:05 PM

She walks out of the desert painted with his blood.

It's July 28, 6:30 PM, in a convenience store on a sandy two-lane highway in New Mexico. I've never been there, but you can see it on Street View. It looks like the last gas station for miles around, a few red-and-white pumps and a squat building in a seething sea of sun and sand and dirt.

We see her walking up to the counter: a tall, lanky girl with platinum-blond hair in a ponytail, wearing a tank top and shorts and a sweatshirt tied around her waist. She takes her time, head held high.

The sweatshirt is his. She left all the rest of her gear—their gear—back at the campsite. The cops and park rangers will have to recover it later.

From the cam behind the counter, her expression looks serious, as if she's giving a presentation in school. On the way back to Los Alamos in the state police cruiser, she'll pass out from fatigue and dehydration. But here you can't tell how close she is to the edge.

You also can't see that the sweatshirt is stiff with dried blood. You can't see the additional traces—much of it rubbed off after five days—that still show on her hands and forearms and collarbone.

The stains are faint enough that the clerk probably thinks she's seeing only the remnants of windblown sand. "Can I help you?" she asks, used to dealing with hikers and campers who look ragged after a few days or a week in Lost Village National Monument.

The girl speaks so softly the clerk asks her to repeat herself.

"My boyfriend is in the park, out past Lonely Mesa. No one's answering his phone. You have to help him. I think he's dead."

POLICE SEARCH FOR MISSING INFLUENCER IN LOST VILLAGE NATIONAL MONUMENT

Los Alamos, NM, July 29
By Lani Sandoval for the Associated Press

The disappearance of a young "survival guru" with hundreds of thousands of YouTube followers has rocked the rural towns surrounding Lost Village National Monument and raised questions about the lengths to which social media influencers will go for a viral post.

Callum Massey, 24, disappeared from the site where he and his girlfriend, Kiri Dunsmore, 18, were camped on the west side of Lonely Mesa, 22 miles from the park entrance in a rarely traveled area.

On July 28, Dunsmore entered the Phillips 66 service station in White Ledge, on the edge of the park, wearing a sweatshirt covered with dark stains, according to employee Lyla Garrison-Cruz. Dunsmore told Garrison-Cruz, and later the state police, that on July 23, she and Massey had left the campsite separately to gather firewood.

When she returned to the campsite, Dunsmore said, she found Massey's bloody sweatshirt. Panicking, she barricaded herself in a cave on the mesa for the night.

The next night, July 24, Dunsmore posted a video using Massey's account. She would post three more short videos before hiking out of the park, eventually hitching a ride in a family's RV. While she spoke only vaguely of Massey's disappearance in the videos, they alarmed some viewers of the feed. In one video, she pointed out what she claimed were a stranger's footprints in the campsite. Dunsmore's parents began trying to reach her on July 25, according to a press release from the National Park Service's Investigative Services Branch (ISB), but she did not pick up their calls.

Both young people are residents of Vermont, where Massey built a large following with videos portraying his "ultra-minimalist, apocalypse-ready lifestyle." On June 5, the couple left on the road trip that eventually brought them to Lost Village. There they planned to hunt for the notorious German's Gulch treasure, which has fascinated thrill seekers since it was reportedly buried near Lonely Mesa in 1908. In videos shot along the way, Massey described the trip as a test of his desert survival skills. The last video in which he appears was posted on the morning of July 23.

Massey is the son of Jared Massey, a vice president at Brauer Pharmaceutical, and constitutional lawyer Amanda Tripp-Massey. The couple reside in Annandale, VA, and are well known in Washington, DC, social circles.

At a press conference this morning in Los Alamos, Park Ranger Randy Michaels said he had seen no recent reports of suspicious activity in the park. Emily Garza of the ISB, which investigates crimes within the National Park System, asked for volunteers to aid in the extensive search for Massey.

Asked why Dunsmore did not use her phone to call for help from the park, or answer her parents' calls, Michaels said the young woman was malnourished and dehydrated when she was found.

"This was a gal who was shaken and not thinking clearly," he said, noting that the park's more rugged areas are challenging even to survival experts. "We think these two young people did not know what they were getting into. These kids on social media, going for the perfect photo op, sometimes they forget to watch out for their own safety."

When asked if Dunsmore was a person of interest in Massey's disappearance, Investigator Garza declined to comment.

Darkness.

Then a flash of light on a tear-stained white face. Trembling lips. Bright, scared eyes. The camera darts away to give us a blurry view of a rounded, clay-walled chamber that looks barely large enough to stand up in.

She keeps the camera there, off her face, and talks:

"Everybody's wondering where Callum is today, right?" A nervous giggle. "Right. I hope you're okay out there, Cal."

Her breath catches. "I hope you aren't too lonely, but I guess you wouldn't be. You're so much stronger than me. Stay strong. Stay safe." Pause. "I know you told me not to sleep in these caves. They were spiritually important to the people who lived here, like, seven hundred years ago."

Another raspy sound—a laugh? "And I respect that! But I'm so scared, Cal, and I'm alone. I know you think I don't listen to you, that I don't care about you and the things you try to teach me. But I do."

Thirteen seconds of silence, except for her breathing.

"Can I tell you a secret, Cal? I didn't always believe you when you said the world was ending, but now I feel it's true. We dropped off the edge of the planet, and nobody's left but you and me. Or maybe just me."

1

The first time the video popped up in my feed, I recognized her straightaway.

But not the name, because I'd known her only as Katie, never as Kiri. And all the posts in my feed were screaming "Kiri's Eerie Cave Video" and "Does Kiri's Story Hold Up?" and "What Was Really Happening with Kiri and Callum?"

I recognized that face, though, and that voice, low-pitched and wispy, from more than a year earlier when Katie Dunsmore sat behind me in junior English.

Katie was a girl who took up space, maybe six feet tall with long legs and broad shoulders—a girl who looked like a Valkyrie even in those days, when her hair was mousy brown, but who seemed to try to minimize her Valkyrie-ness by hunching over and crumpling into herself. She ran track and sat alone in the cafeteria or with some teammate friends. No boyfriend or girlfriend that I knew of.

We paired up for the final project in that class because there was nobody else for us to pair up with. Katie focused on the work, which was fine with me, and I don't remember a single in-class conversation about anything else. No nudging, no private jokes, no texts that weren't about meetings and deadlines. She made a label for our joint portfolio—strange, fey hand lettering wrapped in intricate flowers and vines—and when I complimented it, she said, "I used to want to be an artist, but I can't do perspective."

On the last day of school, Katie gave me a ride home. Pulling up at my place, she said, "We aren't that far apart."

For a second I thought she meant we were both shy, or both anti-social, but then I realized she was talking about where we lived. Geo-graphically, it was true. But when she told me her address—"The very last house on Dumont Street in Queen City Park"—I felt the gulf between us. My mom and I live up by the highway in a rental duplex with mangy vinyl siding and a view of Kinney Drugs and the neigh-borhood sports bar where people get rowdy on weekend nights.

If Katie's saying we were close was a shy way of asking me to hang out, I didn't take the bait. Back then, I spent all my free time taping and editing my podcast about serial killer Drea Flint, thinking I could be the next true-crime sensation. By the time I realized I had nothing new to say and no subscribers except my friends and my mom, it was summer. I ditched the podcast and started working at the multiplex and met Regina Chen—Reggie. She made my life more exciting, so I basically blew off fall semester. I barely cared that I was tanking my grades until later, after the January night when everything went to pieces.

I didn't graduate with honors the way Katie probably did. I spotted her after the ceremony on the UVM campus green, one arm around a man who was probably her dad and the other around a hot guy with black hair tumbling in his eyes. I noticed Katie's new hair color and threw her a wave. If she saw me, she gave no sign.

The hot guy was Callum Massey—you can see the graduation pics online—but I didn't know that. I'd never heard of him until he went missing.

It's a strange thing to go looking for random distraction, lying in the dark with your phone because it's too hot to sleep, and to find videos describing your English project partner as an "ice queen" and a "murderous femme fatale" and a "stone-cold killer."

I watched video after video, starting with Kiri/Katie's videos from the park. They were hard to watch, because she didn't make a lot of sense and moved the phone so the angles made me seasick, but it was *her*. It was Katie. And everybody was talking.

Murderer. Victim. Killer. Survivor.

After that, I went down the rabbit hole: the local and national news reports, the top influencers' takes, Callum's videos, especially the ones with Kiri in them. There were a bunch from their road trip and Lost Village National Monument, some a whole half hour long.

I watched the road trip videos over and over: Katie driving on heat-hazed highways toward glowing pink horizons, her skin burnished gold. And this is going to sound weird, but I was jealous.

I'd spent the summer pedaling the four blocks between home and my job through molasses-thick air, helping my friends pack to leave town for fancy colleges and knowing that all I had to look forward to were shitty blockbusters and smoke breaks outside a half-abandoned movie theater. Every night I scrolled through videos in the dark, here in my mom's apartment where the moments were sticky and endless and even the crickets sounded like they'd given up on the possibility of change.

Meanwhile, Katie was frolicking in the spray on the Jersey Shore. She was climbing the Washington Monument; running her fingers through the tassels of midwestern cornstalks; munching on authentic tamales at roadside stands; watching sunsets with her head on her boyfriend's shoulder. It made me itch a little, imagining myself so close to someone. Imagining her head on *my* shoulder, her long hair tickling my cheek.

But even though Kiri was usually the one on-screen, the story still belonged to Callum. It was his channel. He was the one behind the camera, making everything look good.

Then Kiri walked into that gas station. And the story became hers.

When I was twelve, the whole town was plastered with posters of a college girl named Kelsey Detwiler who'd gone missing after a night out. Weeks later, they found her strangled body in the woods, and after a month, they caught the killer—a guy who'd lent her his phone, then followed her back to campus. He was a family man with a loving wife and two daughters, and everyone who knew him said he was kind and generous—he attended church every single Sunday, so he must be, right? But my dad became a churchgoer, too, after spending years as a raging, ass-kicking drunk and walking out on us when I was nine. These days, he acts like he invented human goodness.

I hate hypocrites. If you're going to be a waste of space in this world, own it.

After what happened to Kelsey, I couldn't stop thinking about all the evil out there—the fine, upstanding family men I passed on the street who might secretly be rapist-murderers. I craved more stories about killers, so I ate up library books and went down Wiki rabbit holes. When Mom and I took the long drive to see my dad, we listened to murder podcasts, and that made it easier to tolerate my stepmom's sanctimonious eyebrows and knowing that I could never be as sweet and picture-perfect as my half siblings.

Stories about serial killers get depressing, though, because most of them are insecure creeps who try to make themselves feel bigger by hurting women (or whoever else they can get away with hurting). Even the cleverest killers, the ones who lead elaborate double lives, basically just do variations on that same ugly MO.

Every now and then, though, I found a story about a woman who tried to even the score, and those were my favorites.

What makes a woman want to kill? I don't think it should even be a question—don't we have plenty of reasons?—but because it's more rare, everyone wonders.

Sometimes being spurned by a man pushes a woman over the line. Sometimes it's money. Sometimes despair. And sometimes she just wants payback for all the crap she's had to put up with. My favorite example was Drea Flint, a twenty-one-year-old who started out by killing her stepfather, then joined up with an older boyfriend and cut a bloody swath across the Southwest, robbing a bunch of guys and leaving five truckers and a gas station attendant dead.

"Cut a bloody swath" is sensationalist language, my friend Lore would say. Lore was happy to watch *Hannibal* and *Natural Born Killers* with me, but look at crime scene photos? No way. And in junior year, when I told Lore about my podcast idea, they got all uptight about my "obsession." Was I a murder hound? A police groupie? Did I know that murders of pretty white girls get disproportionate attention?

I knew all that, of course. I also knew that most murders aren't mysteries at all, and the ones that do go cold rarely get solved. My podcast was not about being an armchair detective. I just hated how people talked online about Drea Flint, treating her as if she were sicker and more disgusting than her boyfriend, though he was just as abusive as the other men in her life. Nobody seemed to care that her stepfather used to beat her, or that her teachers remembered her as a talented poet, or that she couldn't seem to shake her addiction to sleazebag guys who told her what to do. I wanted to tell all of her sad story.

In the end, I just didn't have enough to tell. Or maybe the problem was how I told it, with my wobbly voice and crappy home recording setup. I was another clueless kid desperate to be part of the conversation, and when I realized the whole thing was embarrassing, I stopped. Soon after that, I met Reggie, so I didn't mind being just a true-crime consumer. We'd swap our most horrendous murder stories at the Grand Nine, trying to gross or freak each other out and usually failing.

It gets boring just collecting stories, though. Deep down, I still wanted to be the one to tell a story no one else could.

By the time I'd watched all the essential videos in the Callum/Kiri saga, it was nearly 2:00 AM. But it was tough to sleep when everybody online was buzzing.

Was Kiri involved in Callum's death? She had to be, right? (Have you seen those vids?)

Why'd the cops even let her fly back to Vermont? Shouldn't they have held her in New Mexico for more questioning? What if she made a break for the Canadian border?

My fingertips itched, I wanted so badly to write my own comment. *I know this girl! We went to high school together!* After all my years of true-crime obsession, finally I knew a person of interest.

But what did I know, exactly? That Kiri/Katie was shy? That she used to have brown hair? I cringed at the thought of posting that.

So I just lay there between the sweaty sheets, scrolling and scrolling, listening to the happy laughter and zydeco beats that wafted across the parking lot from Molly B's Bar & Grill. I switched from feed to feed, finding the influencers who had the most active comment sections, waiting for one of Katie's friends or teammates to post *real* insider info. My shift the next day didn't start until noon.

The more I read, the smaller and grubbier I felt. Between junior year and now, Katie Dunsmore had grown larger than life.

Maybe she'd gotten some earlier attention on the YouTube channel, but it was nothing compared with this. Whatever happened in the desert had made her every action and motive worthy of dissection—the tilt of her head, the way she wore her hair when she boarded the plane back to Vermont, the tone of voice she used to say, *I think he's dead.*

It was partly because she was pretty—but not in a good way, people kept saying. *Her eyes are so dead*, several insisted.

So many people were already trying to spin the story the way they read it.

Her eyes? What about his?!

Callum's an inspiration. If you don't see that, you need to wake up.

Callum's a perv. If Kiri didn't ice him, she should've.

But if Katie really was a killer—I couldn't assume that, of course—how had she become one from the person I had known? What was her story, and would she ever be able to tell it on her own terms?

People kept reposting the same still of Kiri and Callum standing arm in arm in the late desert sunlight. With matching dark sunglasses, gleaming teeth, and brilliant smiles, they were a movie poster. They felt immortal.

Aliza Deene of Murder Most F**ked Up, my favorite true-crime source, posted a video encouraging people to stop jumping to conclusions and wait for more evidence. That was typical Aliza: Instead of going for the most sensational angle, she tried to understand what made criminals tick. But it did no good: Everybody already had a take, had their assumptions.

She's obvs mentally unstable.

He's six years older. Classic grooming.

That doesn't make it okay to kill him.

We don't even know he's dead!

She's a sociopath. I can always tell.

Last call came and went at Molly B's. At nearly three, I couldn't take all the voices buzzing in my head anymore (*look at her hair, look at her smile, look at her bitch face*), so I got up quietly and locked the apartment and wheeled my bike down the steps to the pavement.

Aside from the groan of the four-lane highway just up the road, my neighborhood was dead quiet. Classic Burlington. There aren't many houses around here, just warehouses and city utilities sitting in big patches of concrete and pools of orange light. I took the left turn away from Burton Snowboards and along the park, then into the woods, until I came out in a tiny neighborhood that curves around the lakeshore.

Katie's house was as nice as I expected. It wasn't right on the water, but it stood up away from the street with a good view: two stories, clean and modern, surrounded by placid globes of light. There was a window under the second-floor gable, facing the lake. Maybe that was hers.

I stood there in the middle of the street, holding my bike, thinking about how alone Katie—Kiri—must have felt in the desert and how alone I was now. Just me and the keening katydids and the dull *clang, clang* of a boat's mast as the waves sloshed it back and forth. The winking lights on the far side of the lake cast a hazy glow that showed me the outlines of the Adirondacks.

Had I been *envying* Katie because she was famous for possibly committing a murder? Out here in the fresh air, closer to where she was hiding out, I didn't feel good about that.

But it wasn't like I had anything better to do. Should I be getting my beauty sleep so I could scoop popcorn for kiddies tomorrow? Reading community college catalogs? These days, "waste of space" kind of described me.

A mass of trees rose behind Katie's house; the yard must back onto the park. I'd probably seen this house a million times from the other side, walking the trails, and never realized it was hers. Never had a reason to care.

I snapped a photo, careful not to use the flash. If I were an even bigger waste of space, I might have posted it: *Hey, guess what, y'all? I'm outside Kiri Dunsmore's house right now!*

Instead, I kept it for myself. A wild plan was already forming in my head, and that plan required me to be more subtle. More cunning.

I hadn't been able to tell Drea's untold story because I didn't know her. She'd died by suicide in prison, and all my sources were second- and third-hand accounts. But Katie's story—I was close to it already, and maybe I could get closer.

Two days later, on my day off, I dug out some old running gear, biked to the park, locked up the bike, and "jogged" the trail behind Katie's house. I'm no runner, so the best I could actually do was fast-walk most of the way.

When I reached the stretch of woods that I suspected adjoined her backyard, I did start running (slowly). It was a good thing, because up ahead stood a young guy wearing city clothes—nice jeans and a leather jacket—and talking into a headset. He leaned against one of the boulders on the other side of the trail. I ran past him and around the curve, forcing myself not to glance in the direction of *her* house.

Probably media, doing exactly what I was—monitoring the area for sightings. He was still there the second time I came around the loop, but not the third. I left the trail and did hamstring stretches while I chanced some glimpses through the screen of trees: a garden bright with zinnias and tiny tomatoes. A deck draped with colorful beach towels. A big slider window.

I did several more loops, dripping with sweat despite doing more walking than actual running. By then, it was nearly dinnertime, and the park was emptying out. I lingered opposite the house for twenty minutes, long enough to see flashes of TV inside and a skinny bald guy (Katie's dad?) pacing the lawn, having an inaudible phone conversation.

But no Kiri—*Katie*. I kept having to remind myself to use the name I'd known her by, because Kiri wasn't someone I knew yet, even if I wanted to think I did. Katie was my English classmate; Kiri lived on screens and might be a murderer.

Come out, Katie. Come out.

Should I text her? She was still in my contacts, but her inbox would be full of media people and old friends suddenly wanting to reconnect. I needed a reason, something plausible that had nothing to do with the case. I racked my brain.

Lore texted to ask if I wanted to hang at the waterfront. I texted back that I had community college enrollment paperwork to do.

You're stalking her. You're better than this. I could just see Lore saying that, shaking their head sadly. On the other hand, Brenna, my step-mom, wouldn't be sad at all. To her, everything I'd done today would be proof of my unfitness for salvation in her high-class heaven, right in line with my punk T-shirts and my mom's tattoos and the fact that I'd been watching R-rated movies since I was ten.

Sometimes I wonder if Brenna knows that Dad used to hit Mom while I cowered under the covers. Sometimes I wonder if she thinks it was Mom's fault for not being the amazing wife that Brenna thinks she is.

Screw her. Screw everyone. I wasn't hurting anyone by scoping out a backyard.

On my way out of the park, I detoured to the mouth of Katie's street and saw two news vans, one local and one national, with their anten-nae stretching up into the sky. The reporters in those vans wanted candid pics and sound bites that they could twist into a juicy narrative about an unhinged little rich girl. I already saw it happening when I scanned the headlines.

What I wanted was so much harder to grasp. Her story. In her own words.

The next morning before work, I ran the loop in the park again. This time, I found only one van on the street and no headset guy lurking in the woods. The curtains were drawn across the slider window of Kiri's house. No one came into the yard in the ten minutes I dared to stay.

The frenzy was dying down. The #kiridunsmore hashtag wasn't trending anymore, knocked out by some meme about a tortoise. Maybe it was time for me to let it go, too.

But that night, the feeds exploded with new intel.

The blood on the sweatshirt was the same type as Callum's; DNA results were pending. The medical examiner said Callum could have bled that much and survived, but it was unlikely without prompt medical attention.

As for the footprints of a stranger that Kiri claimed to have seen around the campsite in one of her videos, investigators found no trace of them—or any useful prints at all. In the days between Callum's disappearance and Kiri's arrival at the gas station, there'd been a rainstorm in the desert. The amateur detectives online were busy comparing Kiri's video to earlier footage of the campsite, trying to establish whether the footprints she pointed out in the sandy soil had already been there before Callum disappeared.

Just like that, #kiridunsmore was trending again.

That girl is a dirty lying h-bag.

Callum was big and jacked, tho. No way she killed him.

Maybe she got him by surprise.

I tried to care about Callum Massey being dead. By this time I knew every angle of his face, every plane of his ripped chest. I knew how his voice sounded when he was schooling his loyal viewers on building a chicken coop or making your own venison jerky or finding a safe way to eat a cactus. Patient, but with an edge.

It was the edge I didn't like. It made me think he was holding things back. And you heard it most often when he was addressing Kiri, as if he didn't quite trust her to get things right.

The next day, instead of dawdling over breakfast with my phone, I put my runner disguise back on and grabbed the bike. I was halfway to the park before I even considered what I was doing (*stalker stalker stalker*), but by then it didn't seem worth turning back.

This time, I wouldn't pause by her house any longer than it took to stretch my hamstrings. Just a quick check.

I ran faster this time, legs pumping and lungs straining. Knowing it was Callum's blood on the sweatshirt made everything seem a little more dangerously real. But with no weapon and no body, would they have a case against her?

What if I just texted her and told her I was producing a podcast? *I know you're not what people say you are. Let me tell your story.*

Good luck with that. My breath came short as I reached the curve where the boulders loomed opposite her backyard. At this point, any reporter in the country would leap at the chance to interview Kiri. But she hadn't given any interviews, probably on the advice of her high-priced lawyer.

I was so busy scolding myself that I barely noticed branches thrashing to my left. But I stopped short when a figure burst through the trees from Kiri's backyard and dashed past me onto the trail.

Her feet were bare. Her cheeks were red, her hair knotted up and falling messily around her face, strikingly blond in the morning sunlight.

I stood stock-still, not breathing. I expected her to keep right on running, and I don't think I would have had the guts to try to stop her. But when she reached the boulders, she paused to look around, her eyes wild, and her gaze caught on me.

I gulped. What if she thought I was one of *them*, like the guy with the headset?

But no, she wouldn't think that. She knew me. "Katie?" I asked tentatively.

She frowned. For an instant, I thought she couldn't place me—or maybe she wasn't used to hearing her old name. Then—"Sam?"

"Been a while." I tried to smile. Everything Lore had ever said or might say about me—*murder tourist, voyeur, stalker*—ran through my head, and my cheeks stung. But Kiri wouldn't notice that. I wouldn't let her. *She's a friend I haven't seen in forever. That's all.*

Kiri glanced back the way she'd come, a nervous dart of the head. "I, uh—this is gonna sound weird." She took a step toward the boulders. "But if those people ask you, could you maybe say you didn't see me?"

Then I heard them, too—the voices of a man and woman. I could see them coming toward us through the woods from the backyard, the woman's high heels slowing them down. She had long black hair as smooth as suede, and she didn't sound happy.

"Worth a try," the man said, readjusting the burden on his shoulder—a camera with the red-and-white logo of a local TV station. They were looking at each other, but any moment they might glance our way.

I didn't think. As Kiri took another step toward the boulders, I realized she meant to hide behind them, and I grabbed her hand.

"They'll find you there," I said. "Come with me."

2

I veered off the path and led Kiri down a semi-overgrown trail toward the lake. She followed, but she kept glancing backward, and I said, "Don't worry. We'd hear them. No one can see us here."

Kiri. No matter how many times I reminded myself, I couldn't seem to think of her as Katie anymore.

I pushed aside a tangle of hemlock and stopped on the edge of the cliff. There was the lake, sparkling sapphire eighty feet below us. The shoreline stretched to one side, dark and fuzzy with pines. The gabled roofs of the suburbs looked like toys.

Kiri reached the jagged lip of the cliff and stopped short. She grabbed a tree trunk, as if she expected a strong wind to pull her over.

Was she actually scared? I'd seen her climbing up all kinds of rock formations in Callum's videos. "You're not going to fall," I said, and sat down and slid myself off the edge.

Maybe I was showing off a little. I'd been coming here for years, sometimes with Lore and sometimes alone, so I knew there was a protruding ledge below us. My feet found it easily, my hands steadying me against the rock face.

Kiri cried out. Keeping hold of the ledge, I looked up and saw her peering down at me, eyes wide and face white.

When she saw I was fine, perfectly stable on the ledge, her cheeks turned red. She laughed in a strange way, like a hiccup. "I'm so stupid. You scared me."

"Oh God, I'm sorry!" My own cheeks burned; it hurt to see that look of fright on her face and know I'd caused it. I had to remember that she might be fragile. I hoisted myself back to the top and sat beside her, our legs swinging over the cliff. "Are you okay?"

Kiri laughed again. Her eyes were wet, yet her smile looked genuine, as if I'd released something that had been coiled tight inside her. "I should probably, um, explain everything."

"You don't have to, really," I said too quickly.

"I don't?" Kiri played with a strand of hair that had fallen out of her knot. The soles of her dangling bare feet were dirty, the nails unpainted.

"No." I tried to pretend that she was still Katie-who-ran-track, Katie-from-English-class, and not Kiri sitting alone in the dark cave, Kiri emerging from the desert with a bloody sweatshirt knotted around her waist. If only I could decipher the tiny shifts in her eyes, her expression, her body language, I might learn what everybody wanted to know.

What *I* wanted to know.

She said in a higher, anxious voice, "Is it going all around school? Are people talking about me?"

"We're done with school, remember?"

"Oh, God." Again the nervous laugh. "I don't know why I'd say that. I saw you at graduation. I just imagine you at school because that's where I always saw you."

Because you've moved on from school, and I haven't. "It's okay," I said, trying to sound the way Reggie might in this situation—breezy, just on the edge of snarky, like I was above caring whether anybody's name was a trending hashtag. But I couldn't meet her eyes. "I get it. Time is weird that way."

"But you have to know," she said in a lower voice. "About all the..."

This was the crucial moment. Real podcasters, the ones who tell the untold stories, know how to make people trust them.

"Those reporters are vultures," I said. "Can't your parents call the cops on them?"

She relaxed. A fraction, but I felt it. "My dad keeps threatening to. But they're pros. Usually they stay on the street, but my parents were out, so I guess they got brave and snuck up along our property line. I went out to do yoga on the deck, and suddenly that woman, she was just...in my face. Asking me things."

She tugged the knot loose and ran her fingers through her hair. It fell around her shoulders the way it did in Callum's videos—a pale gold cloak for her face, catching the light. Her roots were showing.

I wondered why I hadn't noticed in English class that she was beautiful. Was it the icy-blond dye job that made the difference? She'd shed any trace of softness since I last saw her, and while her new, hard physique was a little forbidding, it also emphasized her features: brow and cheekbones jutting above her full lips and cleft chin.

Barbie doll, I heard Reggie say dismissively. But she would've seen it, too. She would have crushed on Kiri like nobody's business.

"I should've just gone back inside." Her voice trembled. "I don't know what made me bolt. They've been calling and texting ever since I got off the plane, but I guess that wasn't enough for them."

I wanted to know what questions the reporters had asked her, but that would put me on their side, not hers. What would Reggie say in this situation? And then I had it: the airy tone and the words: "Asshats. What's their deal? Do they think you've done something *wrong*?"

Kiri's head swiveled toward me. Her eyes were big and dark, such a startling contrast with the hair, and her brows were dark, too.

"Do *you* think I've done something wrong?" she asked.

I forced myself to hold her gaze. "Well, I'm not scared of you, if that's what you're asking."

I remembered a series of interviews with a serial killer I'd heard. The FBI agents put him at ease by never hinting they thought there was anything wrong with him. "I mean, like, you're the quietest person I've ever known," I said. "The worst you could do is drag me off to play a board game or something."

Her face relaxed into a smile. "Ha. Well. You might be surprised."

I gazed up at the sky. "People just say things. The media. I kind of ignore it, honestly. Most of it's not the truth."

"I don't know what people are saying anymore." Kiri parted her hair—loose, it fell past her shoulders—and started to braid it on the left side. "They took my phone, the investigators." She pronounced each syllable carefully, as if she were a child saying the word for the first time. "My dad won't get me a new one. And my mom changed the Wi-Fi password so I can't go online at all. They say it's for my own good."

"That's fucked up," I said. "You're an adult."

"Well, they're still paying the bills." Kiri undid her braid and redid it, leaning her head to that side. Then she started on the second pigtail. "What are *you* doing this month, Sam? Packing for college?"

She wanted to change the subject. I could do that. "Nah. Working at the Grand Nine. I'm going to start CCV in the fall and try to transfer out next year."

"CCV? They've got some good programs, right?" There was the slightest condescension in her tone. If I hadn't been the one going to community college, I might have sounded the same.

I kicked the cliff with my heel. Couldn't help it. "I screwed up the first semester of senior year. Got a couple of Ds."

"You?" She sounded genuinely shocked. Maybe she remembered me as a nerd, which I guess I was before I met Reggie. I was such a child then, thinking my podcast journalism would make me the next big thing. I wanted desperately to prove to my dad and Brenna that I was destined for better than a crappy apartment by the highway.

Then Reggie came along and taught me that I could have good things right now. That I could be someone who stayed out late, mixed a crack whiskey sour (even if the taste made me puke), and leapt from cliffs and came up scream-laughing. That I could fly.

Until that winter night when I went to see Reggie at Tierney Brenner's place and left buzzed and crying so hard that I hopped a curb and wrapped my mom's Hyundai around a lamppost. My BAC was close to the limit, and I was lucky I didn't get charged and lose my license, or so Mom kept telling me.

Reggie quit the theater after that, and I hadn't seen her since.

So, maybe I also had stuff I didn't want to talk about, even if Kiri's stuff was of national interest. "I'm going to transfer," I said. "Maybe to UVM."

Kiri's second pigtail was done, but she hadn't secured the ends, and both of them were unraveling. "I was supposed to go to UVM," she said. A strip of stomach showed under her tee, hard and flat and golden—the abs of an athlete or a model-influencer, not a regular person like me.

"Aren't you still going?"

"No." After a moment, she said, "When the world is ending, college is a waste."

The world was ending. That was what she'd said in her cave video, and Callum liked to talk about the "coming collapse" in his videos, too. "Wow," I said. "That's . . . intense. But I guess I know what you mean."

We turned our heads toward each other at the same time, and our eyes almost met again, but I looked down.

"My mom changed the password because I kept reading stuff," she said. "About, you know, me."

My mouth went dry. "It's messed up the way people obsess about shit that's none of their business."

Reggie could have said that and 100 percent meant it. She liked murder stories, but she didn't give a flying fuck about trending anything. She *was* the trend. I tried to say it the way she would have, but I wasn't sure I sold it.

When I looked up, Kiri was still gazing at me. "You said they're vultures. Well, that's how I feel: like a corpse in the desert being picked dry."

A corpse in the desert. A hum rose in my ears, as if the very air around us were vibrating, and my throat closed. Was this a test? Did she want me to think about Callum's corpse, to ask about Callum's corpse? Or did she *not* want me to?

"I'm sorry," I said. "That fucking sucks."

She winced—maybe she didn't like my language. Then she smiled, and I found myself looking right at her white, even teeth.

"That reporter, just now," she said. "She asked if I thought Callum was dead."

His name fell like a stone between us, hard and heavy. For the first time, it occurred to me to wonder what I would actually do if she confessed to me. Not that it would ever happen, but—would I keep her secret? Should I?

"*Do* you think that?" I asked, looking into Kiri's eyes.

She gazed back. "I can't be sure. But I think he is, yeah. If he wasn't, he would come back. He wouldn't just hide and let people...suspect me. And all those news people, they don't know the whole story."

My heart gave a lurch. She *was* testing me. If I asked for too much now, she would turn around and walk away; she would never trust me again.

"The feds know everything, though, right?" I asked. "You told them everything. I assume they just aren't releasing it all to the media."

"I told them most of it." Kiri pulled up her legs. Scrambled to her feet. "I should go back. Mom freaks if I leave the house for more than a short run."

Was that it, then? Had I passed or failed? I led the way back up the path through prickly juniper and buckthorn, panting on the steep slope. When I heard a sharp intake of breath behind me, I remembered her bare feet and held the bushes back for her.

"Careful to step over that log." I held out my hand, and she took it. Hers felt so delicate, but I could see the bitten nails. I tried not to tremble; she would feel it.

At the top, just before we left the cover of the woods, I let her hand go. She said, "Have you ever jumped off these cliffs?"

"Not this one—the water's too shallow." I pointed up the coast. "There's a better spot up there."

"Kids have died doing it."

"Yeah, a couple." That's why I'd been terrified both times, but why were we talking about cliff jumping? And before I knew what I was doing, I burst out with it: "Should I still call you Katie? Or...is Kiri better now?"

She turned to look at me, and I could swear that for the first time in our conversation, she relaxed. "My parents still call me Katie. But Kiri is who I am."

My heart battered my chest wall, though climbing the hill was a contributing factor. "Okay. Kiri, then."

"Will you come see me tonight? I don't go out, but I can have visitors. My folks won't bug us if we stay in my room or the den."

"I have to close at work. I won't be done till one."

"Come then. I'm always up late. If you leave your bike under the tarp in the garage, my parents won't even know you're there. Just tap on the basement slider window that faces the woods."

Her face was turned away from me, but there was a wistful note in her voice. "I get lonely sometimes at night. Scared."

3

Anyone can see that the Grand Nine is a tax shelter. Old Man Brenner, who owns it and a bunch of other movie theaters and real estate in greater Burlington, lives in Florida playing golf with other millionaires. He drops by once a year to pat us on the heads and show off his leathery tan, and he doesn't seem to care that we sell two hundred tickets on an average weekend and sometimes as few as ten on days like Tuesday.

The Grand Nine doesn't have reclining chairs or stadium seating or burgers and fries like the Imperial Ten, the flagship of the Brenner empire, in the spiffy new shopping center on the other side of town. The Ten supports the empire, with lines snaking out the doors for every new DC or Marvel release. The Nine just sits. The carpet never gets changed out and the broken restroom locks never get repaired and the projection booths stink of cigarettes and I kind of love it.

It was Thursday, with a preview of Friday's new blockbuster release at seven, and three of us were working. A few couples came for the preview, followed by a brief rush of moms and dads sweet-talking bawling toddlers on their way to the latest DreamWorks cartoon. Once all the six thirty or seven o'clock shows had started, the great lull began. At the register, I ate stale popcorn and scrolled through my true-crime feeds.

A new case out in California—a pregnant woman's disappearance on a Walmart run—had caught people's attention, but there was plenty of Kiri/Callum buzz, too. Callum's mom had done a tearful interview on a morning talk show. When the host asked if she believed Kiri's story about what had happened in the desert, she said, "I don't believe there was some mystery person who wished ill to my son. Callum wasn't someone who made enemies. Beyond that, I won't speculate."

On my favorite channel, Murder Most F**ked Up, Aliza Deene was doing video analyses of every single vid Callum had posted on his YouTube from the desert, with diagrams and commentary. Everybody had noticed that Kiri and Callum both looked much thinner in the last video than the first, and Aliza called her "horrifically emaciated."

I remembered Kiri crying out when she thought I'd fallen, and a chill seized me around the middle. She'd filled out some in a week; she wasn't skeletal anymore. But the hardness that I'd noticed did give her a haunted look.

I get lonely sometimes at night.

Maybe she didn't trust me yet, but she did want to see me again. I'd made her laugh.

"That girl wasn't eating," Aliza droned on inside my earbuds. "And, given what Callum said about how they were getting most of their food from hunting and gathering in the effing *desert*, is anybody surprised? Now, watch what happens in this scene where Callum and Kiri count out the beef jerky sticks they've got left."

I already knew what happened. Kiri slipped a jerky stick in her back pocket. Callum did a second count, caught the discrepancy, and turned to her with a goofy surprised look: "You got one by me!" She gave him the jerky and made a funny face, too, as if she'd just been testing him to see if he'd notice. But in the moment before she handed it back, her smile slipped. She looked scared.

"Hey, Sam!" Maren Armstrong, the manager on duty, shoved open the gate of our ticket booth / refreshment stand. "Could you go clean Two? I'll take over here."

"Sure thing." I'd been too absorbed to notice that the glorified slasher in Theater Two was over and people were trickling out—in my defense, there were only a handful of them.

I tossed my empty popcorn bag and went to the supply closet for the broom and dustpan, silently thanking Maren for not cussing me out for being on my phone the way Dictator Debra would have. Maren was my favorite manager since Reggie left. The best thing about her was that she'd just graduated from UVM and had an out-of-state job lined up for September, at which point I hoped to be promoted into her place. It was either me or Owen, and Owen was even grumpier with the customers than I was. He mostly worked up top in the projection room, dealing with the balky hard drives the movies came on.

Luckily, the one who made the hiring decisions was Old Man Brenner's boring, balding son, Kevin, and not Kevin's own offspring, Tierney the Dickwad, who sometimes came to strut around the place and play manager. He hadn't been around much since Reggie left, though.

A familiar shudder ran down my spine as I crossed the dimly lit corridor and swung open the door of Theater Two. Reggie was always smart about people, except for guys like Tierney Brenner. A sexy sneer switched her brain right off and something else on.

Still, we had fun last fall, Reggie and Owen and Tierney and I, giving ourselves a midnight preview of the big Halloween horror release.

Just four of us in the biggest theater, passing a flask and giggling help-lessly and falling into each other's laps and yelling at the screen: "Don't go in the basement, shit for brains! Don't go *there!*"

After that, we went to the cemetery, where Reggie and Tierney practically made out in front of me. It was a joke until it wasn't. "It's nothing serious," she told me the next day. "Sometimes I just want a warm body against mine."

No. I wasn't going to think about that dillweed, and I wasn't going to think about Reggie. I was going to focus on sweeping dust and straw wrappers and popcorn from this grimy theater floor while the credits of a slasher flick played to nobody.

I was in the tenth row when the double doors swung open behind me, and a familiar voice said, "Fancy meeting you here."

"Fancy meeting *you*, well-known fan of shitty movies." I bowed to Lore like an old-time usher as I waved them into their favorite spot, right at dead center. "Still addicted to toxic 'butter' topping, too, by the smell of you."

Lore bowed back. Unlike me and everybody else at the Grand Nine, they were dressed like they gave a damn, in a cute floral dress and bike shorts. "I brought my own homemade kombucha, at least."

"Of course you did." Lore plans to weather the collapse of civiliza-tion on an organic goat farm, preferably with the help of a nonhierar-chical femme collective. They foster kittens and refuse to see movies where animals are ever in the slightest peril, but people getting sliced and diced by psychopaths is another matter.

"I'm freaking out about moving into the dorms," Lore said, settling themself and carefully balancing the popcorn in an empty seat. "Puff-ball won't be ready for adoption till late September, and I don't like leaving him. I wish I were staying at home like you."

"It's a half-hour drive. And your dad loves Puffball." I knew Lore didn't mean to rub it in—that they were moving, if only to Middlebury, and I wasn't. It still felt that way.

The two of us have been friends since fifth grade, when we discovered we both preferred hanging out at the rink to after-school soccer. We both took figure skating lessons, though only Lore was good at it. The mean girls at our school who gave Lore shit for their weight never saw Lore on the ice—dipping, swanning, jumping, spinning like a top.

My first month or two working at the Grand Nine, Lore would come by every few days, and I'd sneak them in free and join them to whisper and snark through bad movies. Then Lore decided they didn't like Reggie, though they claimed they didn't have a problem with Reggie herself, just with "who I was around her." In November, the Owen debacle happened, and it was no wonder our conversations were still a little awkward.

Nearly two weeks had passed since we'd seen each other. We kept texting about going swimming, but Lore was always busy buying college supplies and attending "mixers" and meeting cool new cosmopolitan people on their dorm's Discord server, and I had so little going on that I worried if we did meet up, I'd be the most boring person in the world. And maybe that was why I just burst out with it: "Do you remember Kiri Dunsmore from school?"

Lore frowned, seemingly clueless.

"You know. The girl who came back from the desert." She was the headline in our local paper today; I'd seen a copy in the theater lobby. But Lore didn't read papers. "*Katie* Dunsmore. They think she could have killed that YouTuber."

Recognition bloomed on Lore's face, followed by surprise. "The couple who went out West? That was *Katie*?"

"You're behind the times, Lore," a voice boomed from the entrance. "You don't even know we went to school with America's foremost psychopath?"

"Owen!" Lore rose from their seat and bounced up the aisle to give him a hug. "Oh my God," they said, running their knuckles over his bearded chin. "You've sprouted!"

"That's just all-organic ginger. Like you put in your kombucha." Owen ducked his head; he was still a little self-conscious about the facial hair. "I knew you'd be impressed."

"I am! It's just...weird." Lore sighed. "It seems like yesterday we were ten and running the Ninja Warrior obstacle course together."

"You sound like my grandpa." Owen hunched his chin toward his chest and quavered, "Oh my, Myrtle! Where have the years gone? Little Owen is off to college already!"

"Shut up!" Lore said, laughing, which is a surefire way to make Owen *not* shut up.

"And you"—he addressed me, leaning on an invisible cane—"little Samara, who's named after the girl that comes out of the TV, God bless her. No wonder you're obsessed with psychopaths."

"I'm *not* obsessed." Owen knew perfectly well I was named for my godmother, not Samara in *The Ring*. But ever since the debacle—*our* debacle; I shouldn't pretend it was his fault—he'd been extra diligent about teasing me, as if that could restore the easy friendship we used to have.

"You could've fooled me," Owen said.

The credits had ended, and the theater's sound system was playing jangly commercials for local banks and shoe stores the way it always did between shows. "This one," I said, pointing at Lore, "is the one who cares enough about Jigsaw's convoluted psyche to show up alone for the tenth movie in a crappy franchise on a Thursday night."

Lore slipped back into their seat. "I'm not alone. I've got you two clowns to entertain me."

"Clowns?!" Owen glanced around in mock panic. "Where?"

But Lore's gaze was on me. "What were you saying about Katie, Sam?"

"I spotted her today in Red Rocks Park when I was running." I kept my tone featherlight, as if it had been a chance meeting. "I don't think she recognized me. A WPTZ reporter was after her."

Lore frowned. Owen looked more intrigued, his brown eyes fixed on me. "They must really think she killed that survivalist dude."

"Callum Massey's *missing*. They haven't found a body." I leaned on my broom, trying to look casual, like I hadn't been following every aspect of the case. "Anyway, I don't get those vibes from her—like she could kill someone, I mean."

"Way too mousy," Owen agreed.

Lore was giving me the bullish look that always preceded our arguments. "I didn't think you even knew Katie Dudley, Sam. You've never mentioned her."

"Dunsmore," Owen said.

"Whatever! I didn't know her, either. I only ever noticed her for two reasons: She was tall, and she was obviously dieting—part of the salad-and-cottage-cheese brigade."

I thought of emaciated Kiri in the desert, and my stomach lurched. "I did an English project with her. She seemed pretty cool then."

"Mm-hmm." Lore was staring me down. "And your new appreciation for Katie has nothing to do with the murder she's suspected of?"

Oh yes, Lore knew me well. When I asked them for their opinion of my podcast, they said I sounded "kind of gleeful" about Drea Flint killing those truckers. Apparently it was "creepy" how much I empathized with a woman who taught men how it felt to be helpless and terrified. I pointed out that some of Lore's own favorite horror movies were about women getting bloody revenge, and they said, "Yes, but Drea Flint's victims are real people. How would their families feel if they heard you talking that way?"

Which honestly made me feel shitty, but also seemed a little unfair. Why was bloodlust just fine as long as the victims were fictional?

"Katie's not officially suspected yet," I said now, trying for breezy. "We don't even know a crime happened."

"And if one did, the guy probably had it coming," Owen said in his rumbling, unserious way. "From everything I hear about him, he was one of those super-jacked, CrossFit-obsessed, controlling types."

Some people on my feed had similar takes—that Callum was sinister and manipulative of Kiri. Others, who'd been his fans before he vanished, insisted he was shy and sensitive and that Kiri was the possessive one who'd tried to ride his coattails to fame. I didn't see how anyone could look at the two of them and see *her* as being in control, but whatever.

"You're talking about a *person*, not a TV trope." Lore twisted to shake a finger at Owen, using the same argument they'd used on me. "See, that's the problem right there."

"I'm the problem?" He did his bug-eyed innocent face.

"Yeah. Both of you! None of us know the YouTube guy, and here we are deciding whether he deserves to be alive. This is what parasocial relationships have done to us."

"I didn't say anything about whether he deserved to be alive," I said.

"But you're watching all the vids where people debate that in the comments." I opened my mouth to deny it, but Lore said, "No, I know you. You eat this stuff up, Sam. All these people speculating and theorizing and gossiping and…"

Right then, the lights went down. The Brenner Theaters logo blared and flashed to life, followed by the MPAA badge announcing a trailer.

Lore never misses the trailers. "See you on the way out?" they stage-whispered through the darkness.

"Enjoy your bloody mayhem that's totally fine because it's all just 'tropes,' right?" I grabbed my broom and dustpan and followed Owen up the aisle.

As we stepped out into the hall, he asked, "Smoke break?"

"Give me ten."

Fifteen minutes later, we slipped out the back into the dusk, past the dumpsters and across the loading dock into the pines on the south side of the multiplex. Little-known local fact: There's an old, over-grown cemetery wedged between the Grand Nine, the highway, and Olive Garden. If you push through the pines, into a grassy area where sickly light filters in from the Olive Garden parking lot, you'll find a few grave markers, standing and fallen, mostly from the Civil War.

It didn't feel right to sit on the graves, so Owen and I always settled on a fallen log. He rolled a joint, took a drag, and passed it to me.

Smoking is less fun since they made it legal and my mom started talking about healing terpenes and lighting up right in front of me. But I still like doing it in the cemetery—the smoke grainy in my lungs, forming a plume in the cool evening air, as the scent of pine needles blends with the highway exhaust. The stars were hazy that night, drowned in city lights. The traffic was a constant drone, but we were hidden in our own world of mossy granite and spidery inscriptions and death.

After we'd each had a few drags, Owen said, "Lore needs to take a chill pill."

"It's the whole true-crime thing." Guilt was queasy in my gut. "They think I'm *gleeful* when women kill men."

"Sheesh! I'm the one who said the YouTuber had it coming. Anyway, if you run into Katie Dunsmore, it's not like you have to shun her because she's the latest obsession of all those murder hounds."

In that moment I wished I had "just run into" Kiri. But I needed to tell someone, and Owen would be less judgmental. "If I tell you something, will you promise not to tell Lore?"

"Did *you* murder someone?"

"Ha. Nothing like that. But when I said Katie—Kiri—didn't recognize me, I lied. We talked for a little. She seemed lonely. She said her parents don't like her to leave the house."

Owen passed the joint back, the touch of his fingertips sending shivers of sense-memory up my spine and all the way to the roots of my hair. I was acutely conscious of all the parts of him even if I could only half see them in the dark: broad shoulders, narrow hips, knobby knees. Owen is taller than Kiri, way taller than me, and he moves like a puppet whose puppeteer needs some practice, all sudden jerks of loose limbs. It's ridiculous and I love it.

The last time we kissed, back in November, he didn't have the beard yet. Now I wondered how it would feel against my skin...but not enough to find out.

After Reggie decided she needed a warm body to make out with, I figured I should have one, too. She dared me to hook up with Owen, and he was certainly the safest, most natural option. Too bad it got awkward fast.

Something I've learned about myself in the past year is that I like to be close to certain people, physically close, and that's enough. Sex doesn't disgust me, but it also doesn't really work for me, not the way it's supposed to. I get attracted to people, though. Way too many people, I sometimes think.

Lore says I'm asexual. Reggie said I might just not have enough experience yet. Me? I honestly don't know.

"How can Kiri's folks lock her up?" Owen asked. "Isn't she eighteen?"

"Yeah, but her folks have to be paying for her fancy lawyer." There'd been ample discussion on the feeds of Kiri's slick DC-based attorney, Ryan Parmintel, who was the reason she hadn't talked to the FBI since her first interview in New Mexico. "They probably think it's for her own good."

"That's messed up. Whatever she did or didn't do, she shouldn't have to be cooped up all summer."

"It hasn't been all summer." I took a quick, shallow drag and handed the joint back. Soon I'd be on my knees scrubbing the toilets of the Grand Nine, and I didn't want to be stoned out of my mind while I was close to fecal matter. "Summer's not even over. She went on a two-month road trip and spent three weeks of it in the desert. She only just got back." That twinge of envy again.

"The desert in July sounds hellish," Owen said, "especially if she was alone most of the time with Mr. CrossFit. He doesn't seem like a laugh a minute, does he?"

No, Callum didn't, despite his occasional forced attempts to inject humor into his videos. Some posters clearly found his intense gaze sexy, but I thought of Christian Bale in *American Psycho*.

"Whatever happened out there," I said, "they must've gotten pretty bonded. She cares about him."

The words felt bitter in my mouth. You could see it in the videos, though, Kiri's gaze following Callum in the melting way that girls look at guys sometimes—a look that says, *I'll forgive anything you do, just keep loving me back.*

She'd told me matter-of-factly that she thought he was dead because, if he weren't, he would never have abandoned her to face this kind of public suspicion. But I wondered if Callum cared as much as she did.

Owen snorted.

"What?"

"Why do women always have to fall for assholes?"

Guys never called me a "woman." I was always a kid, a girl, "my dude," a buddy. But that was the difference between Kiri and me: You couldn't diminish or ignore her. She was in a different stratum. Whether she was a loving girlfriend or a murderer, she had everyone's attention.

"Boo-hoo," I said. "Nice guys can't ever get a break, can they?"

"Shut up." Owen flicked dry leaves at me. "You gonna tell all the true-crime bloggers about your exclusive convo?"

"*You* shut up. You think I'm that thirsty? It's not like Kiri even told me anything." But she might tonight. The possibility was a Fourth of July sparkler burning inside me, bright and hot and overflowing.

It was better to keep it close to my chest, the way Owen shielded his lighter from the wind. If I told him, he might ask me for a recap tomorrow, or even blurt out something when Lore was around.

"Weren't you scared of her?" Owen asked. "Just a little? I mean, when you think about all that blood..."

I remembered Kiri comparing herself to a corpse being picked clean in the desert. That had spooked me a little. But she was so nervous during our conversation, even crying out when she thought I'd slipped off the cliff, that I couldn't be afraid of her. I hadn't lied to her about that.

"Of course not," I said, getting up. "I don't scare that easy."

4

By ten or eleven on weeknights, the highway traffic dwindles to almost nothing. I coasted along in the bike lane past the bright logos of Panera, Burger King, Lowe's, Hannaford, all dark inside. There was nobody left out here but the long-haul truckers and late-night mini-mart workers and me. A breeze ghosted over my shoulders, bringing the bright green scent of the lake.

Four blocks north, and a wide, arcing left under the yellow-blinking traffic light brought me into the dark maw of Queen City Park Road. I passed our two-story townhouse complex with the fake-cedar siding, giving the pedals a good pump.

The lake smell got stronger as I coasted downhill past the humane society, past warehouses and water tanks and acres of parking lot and the grassy concrete stub of a freeway connector that never got finished.

Then I was in the woods. The fresh wetness wrapped around me, rippling like the water itself. The weather had cooled a little, but insects still keened in the grass. The streetlights threw shadows of moving branches on the road.

At the head of Kiri's street, I jumped off and walked the bike as quietly as I could. Maybe I should have come the back way, through the park, but I didn't usually leave the road late at night. Anyway, if there'd been a camera crew here today, they must have run out of patience, because the place was deserted. Her house was dark except for one upstairs window.

The door of the detached garage gaped open, a car parked half in and half out. When I got inside, I saw why—a tarp-covered wood pile filled the whole back of the garage.

I used the loose end of the tarp to hide my bike, as instructed by Kiri, and went around back to the deck. The house was built on an incline, the rear section lower than the front, and the big slider there must be the basement she'd mentioned.

I crept around the edges of lighted areas, waiting for the air to explode with the barking of a guard dog or the whoop of an alarm. Some Vermonters don't lock their doors, but the Dunsmores seemed more like the type to have a camera trained on every possible entrance.

The backyard was dark except for floodlight that trickled over from the side of the house. The stars were bright out here on the shore, but not bright enough to see by.

Making my way across the deck, I bumped into something that skittered away with a clatter—a table or chair. I swore under my breath, then froze as a strip of light appeared in the slider.

It was Kiri, pulling back the blackout curtain. She slid the door open and beckoned.

She wore a hoodie now, her hair in two tidy pigtails, her feet still bare. She stuck her head out and peered around before she closed the slider, as if she thought someone might be lurking out there.

I followed her into a finished basement that was fancier than any room in our apartment: Berber carpeting, a sectional sofa facing a giant flat-screen, and a wet bar topped by sleek maple cabinets.

Kiri sat down on the sectional in a nest of tangled blankets and pillows. Her posture was rigid, as if she didn't feel at ease even in her home—or with me here. "We hardly ever use this room," she said, as if she needed to apologize. "It's a waste. Want something to drink?"

"Um." I didn't want to hold a glass full of clinking ice cubes, and beer makes me burp when I'm nervous. "What are you drinking?"

"I only drink water. But we've got..." She rose and went to the bar. "Bourbon, whiskey, gin, vodka, rum, tequila..."

"It's okay." I sat down on the only part of the sectional that wasn't covered in blankets imprinted with her body. "Water's great."

"It's seriously okay if you want a real drink." Kiri tossed me a bottle of water. I fumbled it. "You drink with your friends, right? Your friends at the theater?"

"Sometimes." What did she know about my friends?

"Last fall when the new Spider-Man movie was out, I went to the Grand Nine with my dad." Kiri sat back on the sofa and pulled her feet up. Big feet, long and narrow. "He never misses a Spider-Man. Anyway, I saw you behind the counter with that girl, the one with blue hair and the lizard tattoo. I've seen her around town. You and she were whispering and laughing like you knew secrets nobody else did."

Reggie and I were probably a little buzzed that day. She often passed me her flask before work, always with a wink and a crack about corrupting a minor. "I don't remember that," I admitted, wondering why she did.

Kiri tugged the blanket over her feet. "Well, I didn't actually say hi. I got self-conscious and hid behind my dad while he bought the tickets."

That was the shy Katie I remembered. I imagined myself giggling with Reggie, totally ignoring her, maybe even with that melting look of adoration on my face, and my cheeks burned. I'd been such a loser and not even known it, and Kiri—had she actually thought we were worth noticing? Envying?

"I was kind of out of it that fall," I said. "The girl you saw me with, Reggie—she was older." If I opened up about myself, maybe Kiri would feel safe enough to open up, too. I tried to think of PG-13 ways to describe Reggie. "She was really cool, but a little wild. She got me into some stuff I don't think I was ready for."

"Was she the one you jumped off the cliffs with? At the park?"

"She dared me," I admitted.

The nearest lamp was behind Kiri, making it hard to see her expression, but I caught the glint of her eyes narrowing. "It's exciting having a friend like that. Someone who pushes you to be more."

Oh God, it was.

I never talked to anyone about missing Reggie. My mom and Lore would act all sympathetic and understanding while secretly being glad I had nothing to do with her anymore, and Owen—I felt *sure* Tierney had told Owen about that night. Dickwad couldn't keep his mouth shut.

"I mean," I said, "she wasn't some stereotypical bad girl, you know? Reggie's smart. Her folks wanted her to go to college, but she didn't see the point. Every shift we worked, she had a new book, and she was always telling me about cosmology and quantum physics and politics and famous murderers—"

Bad word to use. "We had a whole plan," I babbled on, unable to look at Kiri. "After I graduated, we were going to drive out to California and get jobs in San Francisco. I'd write news-feed and listicle stuff, maybe even be a reporter, and she'd audition for acting gigs and sell veggies at the farmers' market. We'd get an apartment in one of those Victorians in Haight-Ashbury."

Saying it out loud, I realized how absurd the plan had been. I'd need a BA to write for any decent website. And those cute Victorians in the Haight had been bought up by Google employees long ago.

It wasn't even a real plan, just idle talk between us as we printed out tickets and scooped popcorn into bags. But the idle talk bloomed into a golden cloud that bled into my regular life and made it bearable. Sitting in trig, I saw the Golden Gate wink in the corner of my eye. I saw the highways we'd travel out West, the candy-colored California sunsets—just us, together in a whole new world.

"That would be so awesome." Kiri's voice jarred me back to reality, but she didn't sound embarrassed by my ridiculous fantasy. She sounded wistful.

"Yeah, well." I yanked the water bottle open. Tried to seem older and wiser. "Reggie decided I wasn't cool enough for her, and she moved back to Massachusetts last spring."

"Not cool enough?" Kiri looked really surprised. "How?"

Uptight was the main word that Reggie had used on that January night. She'd also mentioned something about my being a "scared little girl." I rolled my eyes, trying hard to telegraph that I couldn't care less. "Whatever. She was kind of a bitch."

Kiri's eyes opened very wide. "But you and she were…together?"

"I guess." It hurt to talk about this, and I wanted to turn the pain back on her. "At our age, isn't that all just about hormones?"

"You really think that?"

She sounded wounded, all right, and I was sorry I'd said it. "I don't know. All I know is, I'm over it." *Yeah, right.*

Kiri tucked her feet under her and propped her elbow on the back of the sectional, face half buried in her palm. "How, though? When someone comes along and turns you into a better person, the best

version of you, and you make all these plans for your future together...
how can it just be over?"

Plans. With Callum. I kept my mouth shut and my expression open.

"We were going to have a cabin and live off the land," Kiri said.
"Just the two of us, maybe on Vancouver Island with those towering
firs everywhere. Every morning I'd get up and smell salt, and the colors would be brighter there than anywhere else."

It sounded lonely, but I imagined it through her eyes—all fluid
light and saturated colors, transformed by love. "That's beautiful.
Couldn't it still happen?"

Kiri dropped her gaze. "I don't know."

We were in dangerous territory, but I needed to know what she'd
meant this afternoon. "With his skills, couldn't he be lost out there
but..."

"Surviving?" Her bottom lip curved.

"I mean, it's a huge place, right? It takes a while to search?" The
parts we weren't saying were sucking the oxygen out of the room. Callum hadn't just wandered off. The sweatshirt, the blood.

And then Kiri burst through the barrier. "When I came back to
the campsite and found the...his sweatshirt...well, you might laugh
if I told you the first thing I thought. There are catamounts in that
park. Cougars."

"Yikes." Here in Vermont, no one's seen a catamount in fifty years
or so.

"I was scared to walk too far alone, so Callum drilled me on what
to do if a cougar showed up. Like, open your coat to make yourself
bigger—but it was too hot for a coat!" She sounded frustrated, as if she
were talking to Callum, not me. "Whatever you do, don't run."

"Did you see many cougars?"

"Only one, far away. When I found that sweatshirt, though"—she shuddered visibly, the tremor gripping her whole body—"that was my first thought. A cougar. But there were no rips, no…teeth marks. And then I thought maybe he planted it there to freak me out. Which made no sense." A feeble giggle. "I mean, the blood. It was getting all over me. But I wasn't thinking straight, and he'd left his phone in the tent, so I thought he *had* to be pranking me and he *had* to come back, so I waited for him. Till night came."

I pictured her out there alone as the sun fell, their tent a white dot in the golden vastness. You could find snaps of the campsite everywhere, drone shots taken by people who'd defied the police tape. Nestled at the foot of a high ridge pocked with caves, screened by juniper bushes, it would be pure desolation after dark.

Then I realized something. "His phone was there? I thought…"

I broke off, not wanting to let her know I'd seen the convenience-store video in which she'd said Callum wasn't answering his phone. If Callum had left his phone at the campsite, that made no sense. And wouldn't the media have mentioned it?

Kiri didn't seem bothered. "Yeah," she said. "I'm getting to that part. I didn't tell the investigators because I didn't think they'd believe me."

My breath caught.

She kept talking, staring straight ahead. "I thought of so many scenarios. Like, what if a cougar came to the campsite, and Callum tried to chase it away from our food and it wounded him, and he left the bloody sweatshirt and went to find me? And the cougar found him first?"

She'd seen human footprints around the campsite, not paw prints. But I couldn't admit I knew that, either—the details would reveal that I'd spent hours obsessing over the case. "That seems pretty unlikely. I mean, how often do cougars attack people? And Callum knew how to handle them, right?"

"I know. I know." Kiri covered her face with her hands. Another shudder rocked her shoulders. "But I was scared, and I had no way to reach him, so I slept inside a cave, the highest one I could reach. It wasn't till sunrise the next morning that I saw footprints all over the campsite— ones that weren't there the night before. We never had guests."

"Oh my God," I said.

"Right?" She spoke faster now, as if the words had been tamped down inside her and she needed to release them. "I started noticing other things that were off about the campsite, then, like a hammer that should have been on a milk crate and was on the ground instead. Nothing that would make you say a struggle happened, just things a little askew."

As she paused for breath, I realized how still I was sitting—my shoulders rigid, my breathing shallow. As if there were nothing left of me but eyes and ears to take her in.

Tell me everything. Show me who you really are.

I made myself uncross my legs and stretch. A motorcycle revved in the distance, a sound from another world.

Kiri had drawn her knees up to her chin. "I just kept waiting," she said softly. "For him to come back. The next night, the moon was full, and I thought my phone would ring and it would be him! Like, maybe he'd just gone to see the bikers who had a campsite a couple miles from ours. I knew I should go there and check, but those guys scared me. One of them had, I swear, a white power tattoo."

I made a mental note: The news reports hadn't mentioned any bikers.

"I tried to make a couple calls, but they kept dropping, and my battery was low, and I wasn't sure how to use his solar power bank.

He always handled that; he rationed the power we used. And then I cried because I didn't know what to do without him. I was so hopeless. I went back up the cliff to the cave."

That's when she made the first video. The one where she said she was the last person in the world.

"You really couldn't make a call go through?" I blurted out. *And yet you posted a video?* She couldn't have been as helpless as she seemed to want me to think.

"I should've tried harder." Her voice was shrinking. "But I didn't want to talk to anybody, especially my parents. They started calling, I'm not sure when, and instead of picking up, I posted more videos. It felt like the only thing to do."

"Why?" Surely she knew the videos had upset her parents.

"I still thought Cal would come back, and he didn't want either of us to make calls from the desert. We were survivors of an apocalypse. We could only rely on each other."

"You were... what?" She'd spoken as if it were the literal truth.

Kiri's head gave a little jerk. "That's what he told me. That's what we told ourselves."

"If it was supposed to be postapocalypse," I said, "then why was he posting the whole time on YouTube and everywhere else? Who was gonna watch?"

She smiled—a tiny smile. "I asked him that a few times."

"Who did you think was watching the videos you posted?"

I braced for her to ask if I'd watched them myself. But she just gazed past me, as if she were seeing the events unfold all over again.

"This is going to sound messed up, but I thought that if Cal was out there, he might see my videos and come back. I was trying to show him that nothing had changed, that I was still surviving the way he showed me how to. When I finally got up the courage to hike out, I wasn't honestly sure if I'd find anybody alive."

"But your parents' calls…"

"I wasn't thinking straight. Is it so hard to believe, though? That the end of the world seemed real to me?"

Sometimes, late at night under the covers with only my phone for company, I felt like the last person on earth, too. The people on my screen? They were illusions created to distract me while the world melted away.

But I had never fully believed it, and I could tell she had. Out there in the desert, she had lost track of the difference between reality and imagination. "No," I said.

"I've seen a therapist a few times since I got back," Kiri said after a moment. "She says a state of near-starvation can make you delusional. All I have to do is eat a balanced diet and practice my breathing exercises, and I'll be fine. The real world will just…snap back around me."

She motioned, her fingers snapping like a mouth, and I said, "But it hasn't snapped back."

"No. It hasn't."

Now I understood why her story had come rushing out of her. Her parents probably didn't want her talking about the desert, but somewhere in her mind, she was still out there. She had never come home.

The realization made something crumble inside me. She was trapped in her own past, and I wanted to get her out of that spiral. But the only way out was through, wasn't it? Whatever had happened, she'd have to face it. I could only try to help.

I forced myself to shift and stretch. To take a sip of water. To notice the framed Formula One racing posters on the walls, the bulbous porcelain base of the lamp, the distant wail of a siren.

Then I said, "This afternoon, you said there was another reason you think Callum's dead. Besides the fact that if he weren't, he would come back and help you."

"I can barely see you." Kiri rose from the couch, stretched—her calves were pure, sleek muscle—and walked across the room to switch on the recessed lights over the bar. I blinked at the sudden glare.

"Too much?" She switched off the lights and lit a second lamp. Then she sat down opposite me and huddled up again.

She said, "I checked Callum's phone when I found it in the tent. The whole time we were out in the desert, he made only one call, to Simon Westlake. On the same day that he disappeared."

"Simon Westlake?" None of my sources mentioned the name.

"Everybody called him West. He was Callum's prep school friend; they climbed mountains in Peru together. I met him in DC at the beginning of our trip, and you wouldn't forget this guy." Her voice had gone hushed, as if someone might be listening. "He was huge—tall, muscly. He had these eyes—I can't describe it! They stared through you. This deep, velvety voice. And a tattoo of a scorpion on his neck. He creeped me out, and Cal didn't seem happy to see him, either. Especially when West popped up the second time."

"The second time?"

"On the road trip. At the last rest stop before we got to Lost Village, Cal and I split up so I could wash my hair in the restroom. But before I could go in there, West appeared from nowhere and put his hand on my arm. Like an ambush! He made me go sit in the food court with him, and he said he was worried about me and I shouldn't go into the park with Cal. He told me a bunch of things about Cal—bad things."

"Like what?" I asked.

"It doesn't matter." Her pigtails swung with the force of her headshake. "They aren't true. Callum told me something about West, too, months before we even met—that West got in trouble once, when they were in school, for being creepy with a much younger girl. So I knew not to trust him. Anyway, Cal came and found us. It turned out West was driving to Arizona to work at a summer camp, and the two of them had arranged to meet up on the road. So from Cal's perspective, everything was normal. As we drove away, I told Cal what West had said to me—some of it. All he would say was 'Poor old West. Gotta have some purpose in his life.'"

"But the phone call," I said.

A hard nod. "Callum only called West the once. But in the weeks leading up to that, West called Callum three times. Texted him, too, just *Hey, checking in* and stuff like that. When I saw those texts, I remembered how Callum looked when I told him what West said to me at the rest stop. He tried to laugh it off, but inside he was shook. I could tell."

"You think West has something to do with...Callum being gone?"

Maybe I sounded incredulous, because Kiri flinched. "I never saw him in the park. I don't have any reason to think he was there."

"But you told the investigators all this, right?"

Kiri lowered her gaze. Her eyes had such heavy lids, it was like drawing a curtain to shut me out. "No."

"Why not?" I didn't hide my shock. "I mean, don't they need to know everything to have the best chance of finding Callum? If you suspect this guy, his friend—"

"I would tell them, right? Because that's what an innocent person would do?"

"I didn't say that." I felt like she could see straight into my mind— the embarrassing memory of that whole week I'd spent wondering whether she'd killed Callum and, if so, why.

Kiri drank the last of her water and tossed the bottle to the floor. On the thick carpet, it barely made a sound. "Now you're starting to understand why people don't trust me," she said softly. "Why people think I killed him."

"I don't think that." I didn't *want* her to have killed Callum. But I crossed my ring finger and pinkie under the edge of the blanket—a little-kid habit I never shook—because I couldn't assume things were the way I wanted them to be. I had to keep my mind open. "I just don't understand why you wouldn't tell them everything you know about this sketchball West. He seems like a slam-dunk suspect."

Kiri glanced at the stairs, then toward the slider. Her hand crept over the blankets and touched my arm, as if she needed me to steady herself.

"I didn't tell them," she said, "because I can't prove that Cal called West on the day he disappeared. That first night without Cal, I left his phone in the campsite while I slept up in the cave, and when I woke up, it was just... gone."

Her fingertips were cool and soft. I stopped breathing, waiting for her to look at me. Waiting for her to take her hand away.

"You think someone took his phone? That night? Someone like West?" The footprints could have been his.

"I don't know. They're probably tracking the phone, my lawyer says—the cell towers it pings off. So if West *did* take it somewhere, maybe it'll lead them to him. Or... to whoever. But I can't tell them about him, see? Or about how the phone disappeared. Because then it's like I'm trying to throw suspicion on him and off myself."

I was starting to see her logic. A lot depended on where the phone's signal was and when, but she was right to fear that her story about an intruder in the campsite wasn't the most convincing. No one had been able to prove yet that the footprints in her video had appeared overnight, as she claimed. "So you just want to let things play out? See what happens?"

Her fingers closed on my arm, squeezing a little. "Now you see."

"So why are you telling me any of this?" The words just slipped out.

Her hand opened again. Slid off my arm and back into her lap. "I guess I trust you. Is that weird? I mean, we barely know each other. We're barely friends."

Don't say it. Don't think it. Don't stop trusting me. "I shouldn't be asking you questions," I said in a rush. "You get enough of that from the cops. And what you want to tell them is your business."

"I know. I guess...I just needed to tell someone." She wrapped her arms around herself. "I know this won't make sense to you, Sam, but I'm scared of him. West. I'm worried that whatever happened in the desert isn't over yet."

By the time I left Kiri's house, it was nearly three. A wind had come up, clouds covering the stars, and the waves were whitecapped and whipping the shore. *Clank, clank, clank* went a boat's mast, far out in the water, as I tore off the tarp, grabbed my bike, and wheeled it out of the garage and onto the street.

We'd agreed that I'd return tomorrow after work—through the park rather than via the street this time, in case any news vans decided to stick around into the evening. I didn't love the thought of hiking through the park this late, but I wanted her to think I was tough, not a "scared little girl."

My brain was humming so hard that I was barely aware of what I was doing. I pedaled back through the dark woods on autopilot, from one pool of streetlight to the next, and all I saw were Kiri's dark eyes fixed on me, willing me to trust her. All I felt were her fingertips on my skin.

She could have been lying to me about the things she hadn't told the police—West, the rest stop, the phone. But she had no reason to think I would tell anyone. She didn't know about my failed podcast, how badly I wanted to know every bit of her story, all the parts that the internet didn't know.

I couldn't just blurt out what I'd heard like a desperate clout chaser. First I had to know it was true.

My mind raced, assembling the clues. New footprints in the campsite. Scary bikers. West, with his shady history, trying to scare Kiri away from Callum by telling her things she refused to repeat to me. Maybe West had some kind of beef with Callum, wanting to ruin his relationship. Or maybe some of the "bad things" West had said about Callum were true.

Kiri might be guilty for all I knew, but after tonight, I couldn't see her as cold-blooded or manipulative. Her nervousness, her desperate eagerness to talk, her admitting that she couldn't just snap out of the survivalist mindset—all of that felt too real. Maybe I'd never been quite that irrational, but I knew how it felt to let someone else define your reality.

From behind me came the steady purr of a car in low gear.

I was just past Burton Snowboards, back out of the woods in the open. A glance over my shoulder showed me a burly black SUV. I hugged the shoulder and motioned for the driver to pass, but they crept on, keeping only a car length behind me.

Hunched over the handlebars, I pedaled faster, feeling the burn in my hamstrings. I suck at telling one make of car from another, but I knew that Tierney Brenner had a black Range Rover. Why would he be dogging me when he'd steered clear of me since January?

The car still wasn't passing, the engine rumbling softly.

Ice flooded my chest as I passed the mouth of Pine Street and the dead-end freeway. There were no houses for another few blocks, only the giant, fenced-off tanks of the Champlain Water District to my right. If this person chose to run me off the road, no one was there to stop them.

No side streets to peel off onto, either, except for Kindness Court, the humane society's driveway, which was up a steep hill with no outlet. I could only keep going.

It had to be Tierney the Dickwad. But what did he want with me?

I risked another glance backward, though it slowed my momentum uphill and made the bike wobble dangerously. All I saw were lights smeared across a windshield and a lump of darkness that might have been a man.

Kelsey Detwiler, the girl who was killed downtown, popped into my head, followed by a fractured collage of all the stories I'd consumed over the years. Did any of them start with a girl on her bike out so late that no one would hear her scream? The stub of freeway, with its tangled sumac and concrete barriers, was the perfect place to dump a body.

Maybe I deserved this. Maybe by fantasizing about telling Kiri's story, I'd called the black SUV to me, summoning the universe to make the story about me instead. One I would know all of but wouldn't be able to tell—not if it ended here.

Eyes straight ahead. Pedal, pedal, pedal.

Past Kindness Court, close enough to Molly B's to hear the thump of a classic cover band practicing after hours, I cursed the incline. *Faster.*

Still the motor purred evenly behind me. Not a single rev. Imagine the self-control it would take to keep your foot so steady on the gas.

Here, inland, the wind was gone and the treetops were still. The air shivered around me—air that had been lazy and lake-smelling and ordinary, now taut and vibrating with danger.

He didn't have to creep behind me. He could just run me down. Or block my way, cut the engine, jump out of the car, pull me off my bike. Cover my mouth. Drag me into the back seat. Lock all the doors and peel out.

For all victims, there must be a moment when the world changes. A sick, sudden wobble of the earth on its axis, when the guy who lent you his phone is no longer a helpful stranger. The guy who showed up at your campsite is no longer a friend.

The rumble of the engine rose to a roar, drowning out the classic rock from the bar. Light blinded my left eye; he was pulling abreast of me. Passing—or making his move to cut me off?

My bike took a sickening lurch onto the shoulder. The blaze of headlights cast long grass and milkweed into relief. One glimpse of a green-and-white license plate, and then I was veering toward the ditch, out of control—and I bit down hard on my lip and put my whole weight on the pedal, wresting the front wheel back into line.

When I looked up again, the SUV's taillights were shrinking to twin glints in the distance. They seemed to twinkle, but that was just my shaking.

I touched the ground long enough to draw a deep breath and pull myself together. The smell of fried food from Molly B's meant that our apartment complex was just a bit farther. I'd made it.

I rode the last quarter mile with my heart drumming madly and my shirt soaked with cold sweat. Maybe it was just a stray reporter who'd seen me sneaking into Kiri's and followed me. But if they didn't want to get out and talk, why would they make their presence so obvious to me?

When I reached home, I leapt off the bike and marched it to the rack, willing it to stay straight this once. Though I couldn't see it from here, I could *feel* the vast, empty Kmart parking lot stretching out behind our building.

If I were following a girl on a bike, trying to find out where she lived, that's where I'd wait for her—in a spot with a view of the intersection.

I had no reason to think the SUV driver was anything but a random creep. But I stopped fumbling with the chain, tossed the backpack over my shoulder, and hustled the bike up the front steps by the handlebars, the front wheel swinging madly. The door locked behind me with a reassuring click. Mom would be pissed to see the bike in the hallway when she got home from her night shift in the NICU, but I didn't care. It felt safer not to linger outside.

Upstairs, I tiptoed across Mom's empty bedroom to peer out the back window. There were a few cars in the Kmart parking lot, but none I could be sure was the SUV.

Its plate had been green and white, but more white than green— not a Vermont plate. Not Tierney, or anyone local. Someone who liked making girls on bikes feel vulnerable. As I curled up in bed, I tried to shake the sensation of being prey.

5

I woke up to a notification for a new video of Callum and Kiri on the road trip.

It was taken in the parking lot of a Waffle House near Tulsa on July 4 at dusk. Somebody raised their phone to film fireworks in the distance, and suddenly, in between faint booms and sprays of colored light, they heard a couple arguing.

Her voice is high-pitched, shrieky. "Let's just go, okay! I'm ready! You win!"

His voice is much lower—the words almost inaudible, but clearly meant to calm her. "You just need to wash your face. You just need to—" and then something else.

The phone swings jerkily across the parking lot to frame them—a tall guy and a tall girl in front of a van, his white T-shirt and her blond hair glowing under the light.

"No, I *don't* need to sit still!" Kiri's hair spills tangled over her shoulders, which are strong and tan and mostly exposed by her tank top. Tears glint on her face.

"Shh," Callum says, and then they both turn toward whoever's holding the phone as it bobs closer to them.

A fuzzy male voice: "Are you okay, miss? This guy giving you a hard time?"

Kiri's face is splotched red, but she wipes away the tears. Her mouth forms a jagged smile. "No, I'm fine, sir. He's my boyfriend. We were just having a disagreement about..."

"Our route," Callum says. Quick as a flash, he reaches into the van's cab and produces a map. "We're driving cross-country. She likes to use the GPS. I like to do it the old-fashioned way."

He unfolds the map and moves forward, out of frame, as if to discuss it with one of the strangers. The phone stays on Kiri. A female voice asks, "Are you sure you're okay, hon? You seem pretty upset."

Kiri grabs her hair, pulls it back into a ponytail, and catches it in a band—brisk, angry motions. "Really, I'm fine," she says, smiling even as her voice wobbles. "He just makes me feel stupid sometimes. But it's because he's so smart."

"Oh, hon," the voice says. The video ends.

"What on earth is that?"

I straightened to find Mom peering over my shoulder and pulled the phone against my chest, as if I could protect Kiri from the world's prying eyes. What I'd seen felt so raw and private. "Nothing. A news clip."

Sunlight spilled through the window over our sink. In daylight, I could see that none of the cars in the Kmart parking lot that I remembered from last night were black SUVs. The events of 3:00 AM had the same murky quality as the video I'd just watched; I could barely be sure any of it had happened, much less what it meant.

What I did know was that I would see Kiri again tonight. The thought made my cheeks hot and tight, my pulse pounding so hard my body seemed ready to fly apart—like those fireworks over the Waffle House parking lot, like a rocket streaking across the sky.

"That girl sounded really upset." Bathrobe-clad, my mom padded over to the sink and ran water into the coffee carafe. "Is she okay? She's not dead now, is she?"

"No." Mom doesn't share Lore's feelings about true crime—she appreciates a good mystery—but if I let her know I had anything but a casual interest in the case, she would start worrying. "It's the guy who's missing, actually. A YouTube influencer. They found his bloody sweatshirt."

"Oh, Lord." Mom measured grounds into the coffeemaker, hair tumbling in her eyes—red-brown and wavy like mine, but touched with gray. "His poor parents must be going through hell."

"You're such a mom," I said, spooning up cornflakes. Somehow it had never occurred to me what Callum's parents might be feeling right now, but I'd better start caring. I would need to tell all sides.

"Right?" Mom flipped the coffeemaker's switch, then sat down and propped her elbows on the bare wooden table. As always after one of her long shifts, she moved with the slow determination of a sleepwalker, smoky shadows under her eyes. "I did a reading for Mrs. Linderholm on Tuesday," she said. "You know, the one who lost her son to an overdose last year?"

My mom's side hustle is giving readings in a ranch house just off the highway with a neon sign that says PSYCHIC out front. It's as tidy and impersonal as a therapist's office, but with crystal balls. When things got bad with Dad, she told me once, connecting with the universal energies helped her center herself. I wished the universal energies could have told her to kick him out the first time he ever laid a hand on her—or the second or third time—but I didn't say so.

She used to say he only hurt her because he loved her too much. If that's true, love is a hell of a thing.

"There are so many sons and grandsons with overdoses," I said. "I can't keep them straight."

Mom shook her head at me. "If you ever have kids, Sam, you'll stop being so flip about it. Mrs. Linderholm's son was missing for two weeks before he was found in a ravine. Waiting for news, wondering...the news was almost a relief. She asked me to ask him—"

"His spirit," I said.

"Right. She asked me to ask his spirit if he was lonely out there. If he was still tied to his body, if he understood that he was dead."

I don't believe in life after death, but a shiver feathered its way down the bare backs of my arms. On my phone screen, Callum had been calm and in control. Now he might be a bloody shell buried in the sand or hidden under scrub brush.

Or maybe he was alive, riding through an unknown landscape in a car driven by a man with a scorpion tattoo on his neck. If West really was involved, who was to say he'd killed Callum?

Kiri had been so upset in the Waffle House parking lot. Such a mess. Maybe Callum had had enough of her and faked his death, using his old friend as the ticket to a new life. It was an ugly thought, but sometimes men do just cut and run—*hello, Dad.*

As the coffee perked, I scrolled through the comments on the video—hundreds already. This was a bombshell, the first hard evidence that something was wrong between Callum and Kiri. Predictably, at least a third of the comments said Kiri looked "like a psycho." Another third said she was obviously the victim of Callum's abuse.

"What did the guy's spirit say?" I asked as Mom got up to pour her coffee. "Was he lonely?"

"You know my clients' readings are confidential, Sammy. But, as a rule, spirits aren't lonely or confused unless they have unfinished business with the living." She bent to look over my shoulder again, the rich coffee scent wafting from the cup in her hand and making my stomach grumble. "What are you reading? Is this about the missing influencer? Why are people so obsessed with him?"

"People like to solve mysteries." I scrolled faster as the comments started to repeat themselves: **That bitch needs to be arrested. Someone should've called the cops on Callum. She was unstable. He was controlling. A tragedy. An outrage.**

Mom straightened, the smell retreating. "But once you solve the mystery," she said, "what's left? Usually just somebody like Mrs. Linderholm, caught in that spiral of grief while everybody else moves on."

Aliza Deene was doing a live reaction to the Waffle House video, rubbing plummy blush on her cheekbones while she explained her take:

"I know some of y'all want to believe that Callum Massey was a saint. But if you analyze how he's trying to calm Kiri down in this clip, how he's trying to minimize her pain, you see all the classic signs of a controlling personality. And notice how, when bystanders step in, he continues to try to control the narrative. You heard how hysterical Kiri was. You really think they were fighting about whether to use the *GPS*? Not a chance. This was a serious, potentially relationship-ending argument. So yeah, Callum isn't being honest. But there's more to the story. If we look at this shot right here, right *before* Kiri says that Callum makes her feel stupid—"

"Hey." Owen's hand was waving in my face. "Earth to Sam. Is Maren around?"

I batted him away and set my phone on the ticket counter, plucking out an earbud. It was another dead afternoon at the Grand Nine, all the four o'clock shows playing to a handful of customers. "She's on her half."

"Well, when she gets back, tell her we got a problem with our copy of *Stations in the Night*. Every ten minutes or so the whole image turns red like somebody dropped a bucket of blood on it."

"Um, nice visual. I thought you were the kind of enlightened cinephile who appreciates the expressive use of color."

"Expressive, my ass. That movie's a piece of shit." Owen leaned over the counter. "Popcorn?"

I snagged a prefilled bag from under the heating lamp, trying to keep my attention on what Aliza was saying in my left ear:

"Now, I know some of you don't agree with my diagnosis of Kiri as having histrionic personality disorder—"

"That's bullshit," I said aloud.

"What is?" Owen eyeballed my phone. "Oh, that again. These people need to get lives."

"Are you talking about me?" I handed over the bag. "You know you're basically filling your stomach with salt-covered cardboard, right?"

"Nice visual, and no, I didn't mean you." He watched Aliza tracing a perfect arc of black eyeliner. "So, what's this expert's theory? Does she think Katie Dunsmore's a killer?"

"What would she know about it?" Too late, I realized how annoyed I'd sounded. Aliza kept running the same clip in slow motion: Kiri raising her wet eyes to look earnestly into the face of the person holding the camera, or into the camera itself.

Yes, she *was* looking into the camera. But what was that supposed to prove? If someone's filming you, isn't that a natural place to look?

Now Aliza was off on a weird tangent about Kiri's voice, comparing a bunch of different audio clips. No wonder she was overanalyzing things when she knew so little—nothing about the cougars, or the appearing and disappearing phone, or the disarranged campsite. Nothing about West.

"Oh," I called as Owen turned to go, a kernel already caught in his beard, "I meant to ask—have you seen Spawn around lately?" Spawn of Brenner is one of our many names for Tierney.

Owen shook his head, shoveling another handful of popcorn down his gullet. "Nah, unless you count the time I saw him downtown, coming out of Nectar's—that was back in the spring. Think Dickwad's lost interest in us."

He may call him "Dickwad" now, but Owen used to be a Spawn fanboy—gushing over Tierney's tricked-out truck, watching with googly eyes as Tierney flirted with Reggie. Sometimes I wonder if he was thinking, *What would Tierney do?* the whole time he was hooking up with me.

Of course, I'd been just as bad with Reggie, making her into my role model. I remembered Kiri's surprise when I told her I didn't have those feelings for Reggie anymore. *When someone comes along and turns you into a better person ... how can it just be over?*

Was that how she felt about Callum, even now? That he'd inspired her to be her best self? Watching the video clips and hearing her words echo in my head, I felt as if something cold were slipping down my spine.

Owen trudged back into the entrails of the multiplex, and I sank onto the stool and rested my head on my folded arms, trying to pay attention to the voice in my earbuds. Trying *not* to think about seeing Kiri again tonight.

What would Aliza Deene do for two exclusive interviews? Sell her soul, probably. But Aliza hadn't heard the desolation in Kiri's voice as she confessed that, in her mind, she was still lost in the desert and never coming home.

No, Aliza knew nothing about Kiri. Her monologue cut through my thoughts, her voice sharp as a blade:

"So, we have a young woman here who's extremely skilled at performing on camera. Who weaponizes her big eyes and 'poor little me' voice to get sympathy from everyone around her. Don't get me wrong—Callum Massey reads like a narcissist, and I fully believe this relationship was abusive on both sides. But when Kiri drops that innocent little comment about Callum making her feel stupid, in the Fourth of July video? Yeah, I'm calling this, folks—she's self-consciously playing the part of a victim. She's preparing a defense. I think that's when she knew she would kill him."

6

When I left work, a strip of light still clung to the pines on the western horizon. Mom had a shift again tonight, so I couldn't ask her for use of the car for safety reasons. I stopped at home to change into dark clothes and grab a flashlight and pepper spray, then pedaled as fast as I could toward the lake.

I looked out for black SUVs on my way to the park, reminding myself that Vermont isn't a dangerous place, statistically speaking. I'd biked this route a thousand times, at all hours; last summer, Lore and I swam in the park at least once a week, staying late on the beach to count shooting stars.

Anyway, I couldn't focus on a vague threat when Aliza's betrayal had shot my veins full of adrenaline. It wasn't that I expected her to assume Kiri was innocent. But to call Kiri a faker when Kiri's eyes were full of tears? It was as if we'd watched two different videos.

Or was I just too gullible? The thought made me want to hit or punch someone; if Mr. SUV had come along just then, I would've pepper-sprayed him in the eyes with pleasure.

Light rain was falling. At least no one was parked on the strip outside the trailhead. I locked my bike to the rack and walked briskly into the woods, flashlight off to avoid calling attention to myself.

Streetlights are few and far between in the park, but the distant glare of the town reflected off the pale gravel paths below and the sky above. I shivered as I spotted the tall, jagged oak that everybody calls the Wolf Tree—where pagans hold rites at the full moon, according to local legend. Rain pattered on thousands of leaves, camouflaging my footsteps.

Soon I caught sight of Kiri's floodlight shining through the trees. I meant to sneak around to the street to see if the reporters were still there. But as I crept across the grass, the basement slider opened.

My breath caught. A tall, backlit figure beckoned from the opening.

This time the lights were on in the basement, and Kiri pressed a finger to her lips and led me up the stairs. "We can hang in my room. Mom's at book club, and Dad's sleeping off jet lag." Wry twist of a smile. "They never leave me totally alone anymore."

On the first floor, we tiptoed through a gigantic, sunken living room—I caught glimpses of white sofas and a glittery mod chandelier—and into a kitchen with a bay window full of hanging plants. Kiri pulled two water bottles from the mammoth fridge. She wore a fleece hoodie and shorts today, her hair twisted up and coming loose in wild strands.

Her shoulders looked tense, and she kept glancing around, as if she were an intruder and not someone who belonged here. Or maybe I was making her nervous. Did she know about the Waffle House video?

I couldn't believe everything she did was a calculated performance. I just couldn't.

Like the basement, the stairs we climbed to the second floor were

so thickly carpeted we didn't need to tiptoe. So was the upstairs hallway, with recessed lighting dimmed to a glimmer and framed abstract
paintings on either side, everything as quiet as a museum.

Kiri's room was at the far end. She opened the door and hit a
switch, and I blinked as *white white white* exploded in my eyes.

White walls. White bedspread. White curtains. White rug on the
maple floor in front of the white desk. Nothing lacy or twee, just clean
edges. No clutter, no posters, no colorful accents, no plants—even the
bookcase had only four or five books in it.

"Wow," I said, daring at last to speak as the door clicked shut
behind us. "Is all your stuff packed for college already?"

Kiri sat down on the bed. Even here she moved warily, as if she
didn't belong. "Last spring I gave most of my stuff to Goodwill. I realized I was happier without all those *things*."

She gave the word an ugly twist, as if her possessions were bugs
crawling up her arm. And then I remembered she'd said she wasn't
going to college after all.

I made a mental note to keep careful track of everything she'd told
me. I needed to be the one who felt at home in her world, the one she
trusted.

Above her desk, a framed photo caught my eye, the only interruption to the bare whiteness. It was a black-and-white three-quarter
profile of Kiri against a tree, smiling in an easy, relaxed way. Her
loose hair glowed like a halo. Behind her stood Callum, one arm slung
around her shoulders. He gazed down at her, and you could almost
see the electric spark pass between them.

Aliza had said their relationship was abusive on both sides. But
Kiri thought Callum had made her into a better person, and she did

look strong and happy in the photo, as if she'd found the place where she belonged.

"He took that." Kiri sat at the head of the bed, her knees pulled to her chest as if she were cold. "With a timer."

"He's a good photographer." It felt too intimate to claim a place beside her, but the desk chair was the only other seat, and it was way on the other side of the room. I perched myself at the bed's foot.

"He's good at everything." For a moment she didn't speak, staring down at the bedspread. Then she raised her eyes again, her arms tightly crossed, and the air between us felt different. Taut, almost humming, the way it did last night when I realized I was being followed.

"Something happened today," she said. "NBC wouldn't still be out there if something hadn't happened. I heard them talking from across the street, but I only caught a few words."

"You really can't...?" My gaze flew away from her, to the Mac laptop on the desk.

"No Wi-Fi, remember? There's the big TV downstairs, and I keep thinking about turning it on, but they might hear, and...maybe they're right."

Her parents had some nerve, in my opinion. "Right about what?"

Kiri looked straight at me, her eyes dark wells. "They say it's for my mental health. They say the lawyer advised it, too. Really, though, I think none of us wants to face it—what people are saying about me now. Who I might turn out to be."

I didn't need to ask what she meant.

Aliza didn't know the first thing about Kiri—or Katie, for that matter. Her shyness wasn't a performance; she'd always been this way. Anyway, if all she cared about was attracting sympathy, why had she come so unhinged at the Waffle House? No one is sympathetic to women who come unhinged, ever.

I needed to tell her, whether she wanted to hear it or not. I needed her perspective. "Somebody posted a video of you and Callum having a fight in a Waffle House parking lot."

Kiri's eyes widened. I could almost see her processing the info and accessing the memory—the fireworks, the questions.

If Aliza was right, and Kiri had been playing to the camera, then she must have wondered when the video would surface. She didn't give any sign of disappointment or relief, only let out a long breath and leaned back against her plain white pillows. "What are people saying?"

"That you were . . . upset."

"They're saying I'm *crazy*." She stretched a long leg, her toe poking my hip at the other end of the bed, and withdrew with a muttered "Sorry. But couples argue, right? It's normal? I guess I don't know— I've only had the one relationship."

I wasn't the person to ask, either. Just one real fight was enough to end things for Reggie and me. "Of course it's normal."

Kiri covered her eyes, as if she could remember better that way. "The thing is, with Callum, you couldn't argue. He was a blank wall. He never raised his voice. But somehow he was so good at convincing you to turn around and argue his side instead of your own."

Because he was a dick. But I didn't want to feed her my own biases about Callum; I wanted to know how *she* felt about him. "That's a smooth move," I said. "You can't fight it."

"I know! But it's so hard to explain, when other people only see what he wants them to see."

"I know what you mean. My dad's kind of like that—always trying to control the narrative." I needed to show her what we had in common, so I added something I'd never even admitted to Lore or Owen: "It kills me how much of my life I spent trying to make him like me."

Her brow furrowed. "He was your dad. Of course you wanted that."

"I wanted it even when I was older." It hurt saying it. It made me feel like a hypocrite, like a sap. "When I knew better. After I'd seen him hit my mom."

Kiri's eyes popped open. "I'm so sorry, Sam. That's awful."

"It was years ago," I said. "It only happened a few times, and then he left and he never came back, not really. Good riddance."

"Still—for you to have seen that!" She looked straight at me with the big, sad eyes that Aliza found so suspect. "You must be such a strong person."

No, I'm a fraud desperate for attention, a small voice inside me said, but the conversation wasn't supposed to be about me. "I don't think I'm strong. Not like you are."

"Me? Ha!" Kiri slipped out of bed and went over to the desk. "Not even close. I'll show you."

"Show me what?"

"What a mess I am." She opened the Mac, did some scrolling and typing, and shoved a thumb drive into the side port. "Can you use one of these?"

"I think so." Being offline certainly made life complicated.

"You might need a connector. Take this one." She extracted the drive and thrust it into my hand, along with a short length of cable. "What's on there...it's from my phone, just little notes I wrote myself every day to remember important things, starting last fall. I guess you could say like a diary. Mostly it's about him."

The diary of her relationship with Callum. My whole body came alive, my temples throbbing, and my sweaty palm squeezed the thumb drive and cable tight. "That's such a private thing. Are you sure it's okay for me to…?"

But I couldn't go on, because the truth was that I wanted to stick the drive in my old Dell and read every word on it immediately. What would Aliza Deene give for Kiri's diary? What would the networks pay? Not that I intended to sell it, or even to let anyone know it existed, but still, to *know*.

My dark secrets didn't matter to anyone, but hers did. And she was trusting me with them.

"You have to promise not to tell my parents what's in there." Kiri sat back down opposite me. "Or anybody else."

I opened my mouth.

"No, that's silly. I trust you." She was gazing off across the room. "Anyway, it doesn't mean anything; it's not evidence. It ends soon after we started our trip. He didn't like it when I was on my phone."

He didn't like it. I remembered Callum's low voice on the video, telling Kiri to wash her face as if she were a little girl. "He bossed you around sometimes, didn't he?"

"Well, it was his trip. He made the rules." She scooted forward and, before I could react, reached toward my face and tweaked a curl out of my eyes. "I like your hair. It's kind of red, isn't it?"

I shook my head, trying not to let her see how her closeness set my nerves humming. Her eyes were so big, and she smelled of some shampoo or lotion that made me think of vacations in Maine: salt spray and waves and the smooth pink inside of a shell. "My hair's dead-leaf color."

"No. No." She pinched up the curl and examined it, her face inches from mine. "It's red-brown. It's russet. I'd die for red hair. My real color's mouse-brown."

I remember. "Well, you look good as a blond," I said, trying to sound casual, though my heart thumped as she released me and returned to her side of the bed.

"My mom wants me to let the brown grow back in. She says it makes me more relatable."

I laughed because I couldn't imagine my mom saying something like that, not even if I'd emerged from a desert smeared with someone else's blood. "Relatable to who?"

"That's what I said. I pointed out that only she and Dad have to relate to me right now, and I asked if she thought I was going to be in a courtroom any time soon, and she said, 'It's *always* helpful to be someone people feel at ease around.'"

"Oh God." A courtroom. I'd caught a tiny flinch when she said the word, but I pretended I hadn't. "My mom barely even notices if my socks match."

"You're so lucky." Kiri collapsed back against the pillows. Something had released her inner tension—maybe it was giving me the diary. Maybe it was my laughter. "My mom notices everything. She's one of those people who always looks perfect and does the right things. She thought I was a loser until Callum came along—both my parents did."

"C'mon. Why would they think that?"

"My brother's this star who set state track records and went to Harvard Law, and I'm...shy."

Her voice dropped on the last word, and I asked, "So what?"

"Shy people don't achieve as much in life as outgoing people. They've done studies on it and everything. She used to say I'd grow out of it."

MARGOT HARRISON

"Those studies sound like junk science. Not everybody has to be an extrovert." But I *had* written off Katie in junior year because she was quiet, never bothering to look beneath the surface. Maybe I was as bad as her mom.

"Mom liked Callum so much," she said. "Even Dad did, eventually. He was their kind of people—good education, good family, good future. They thought he was a gentleman."

I pictured Callum extending a white-gloved hand to Kiri in a ballroom—and then, before I could stop myself, I saw her with the bloody sweatshirt around her waist. "He wasn't exactly who they thought he was, though, was he?"

"No." Kiri's gaze drifted away from mine. "I mean, they were right about his background and how he was raised. But he didn't want to be that person. He had different goals."

She was silent for a moment, staring into space. "He had goals for me, too. No." Her brow furrowed. "That's not right. I wanted goals, and he helped me set them for myself. I wanted to be better. Stronger. That night at Waffle House…ugh. I hate just saying the name."

"You don't have to talk about it if you don't want to," I said the way a good friend would, the way Lore would, crossing my fingers behind my back. *Please talk about it.*

"No. It's okay." She crossed and uncrossed her ankles, a frown pulling at one side of her mouth. "We weren't even supposed to stop in Oklahoma till we got to the campground. But I had to pee, and I was starving, and I saw an exit with the Waffle House sign, and I *begged* him. I said I'd be in and out in a second; I'd just use the restroom. I wasn't going to order anything—I mean, you can't get waffles to go, right?"

She giggled—high, nervous. "We had our dinner all packed and portioned, like always, because road food is junk and we were being careful about what we put in our bodies."

I remembered how skinny she'd been in the desert videos. How she and Callum counted out sticks of beef jerky. "But you were hungry."

"I'd had lunch! My body gets these carb cravings, that's all." She hung her head. "So, when I got inside the restaurant, I had to walk past people eating. Food was everywhere, and it smelled so good—maple syrup, *bacon*—and after I left the restroom, I did go up to the counter. I was going to order something to go, whatever they'd give me."

Her voice had gone very quiet, as if Callum might hear. It was so full of yearning that my own stomach grumbled, though I hadn't felt hungry till now.

And then, in a flash, I knew what had happened. "Callum came looking for you. Found you there."

Kiri nodded. I saw with a sickening jolt that her cheeks were red, her lip trembling.

Mom looked like that after Dad hit her. It didn't happen often—I can't be sure how many times, because I was only nine when he left for good. I'd hide in my room till the yelling was over, and when I came out, he was off to watch a game at the bar and Mom was making coffee. She'd make me look at her and say, "See, no harm done"—and it was true, there were no marks. She smiled with wet eyes, and I smiled back, already learning to fake it.

This is why I hate hypocrites. Because I am one, too.

"Did Callum yell at you?" I asked quietly. "Hurt you?"

"No! He never yelled, and he never hurt me. He wasn't like that!" She blinked, and tears spilled over her cheeks—just like that, the icy composure shattered. "He just took my arm and said, 'I don't think you want to be here,' and he led me outside. Which was a good thing to do, what I *wanted* him to do."

My throat tightened. My vision blurred. I saw and felt the scene as if it were happening to me: a fatherly hand on my arm. The calm tone that was actually smug, just under the surface. *(Brenna and I are going to church now, Sam. Are you sure you wouldn't rather come along than sit alone reading that murder book of yours?)*

I said, "Callum didn't even talk to you. He didn't care about your side." *I do. Only I do.*

Kiri didn't seem to hear. "It was like a switch flipped in my brain at that moment, and I went wild and denied everything. I wasn't hungry! I was strong! I could control myself! How dare he suspect me of being weak?"

The sight of her tears was a wire cinched around my ribs. I crawled across the bed and patted her shoulder, just a quick touch to remind her I was there. "Remember what I said before? You're not weak."

Kiri rubbed her eyes, but the tears kept flowing. "And then we were in the parking lot, and I was having hysterics." A faint smile. "Just like I am now."

I don't know who moved first. But somehow my arms were open and she was folding herself into them, her wet face pressed against my shoulder.

She was tense at first, but when I patted her back, she relaxed. Her body shuddered with sobs against mine as she said, "Oh God, I'm so sorry. Oh God, I miss him so much."

I said, "Shh, it's okay." I stroked her tangled hair. I smelled her ocean smell, smooth and astringent at once. I said, "You're okay, you're safe." I may even have said, *He's fine, he'll come back*, but I don't remember now.

If I did say those things while she cried in my arms, all that softness and hardness in one trembling package, it was only because I knew she wanted to hear them.

Me, I was pretty sure I knew now what kind of person Callum Massey was. And even if Aliza was 100 percent right, even if Kiri *had* done it...I was starting to understand why.

When I woke up, it was dawn, the world swathed in pearly mist from the lake.

I must have dozed off right there at the foot of the bed. Now my cramped muscles ached as I eased myself upright and looked down at Kiri.

She was sleeping in her hoodie and shorts, one arm thrown over her head. Reggie would have said, *Even mass murderers look innocent when they're sleeping*, and she probably wasn't wrong. But I remembered Kiri sobbing—*I miss him so much*—and something gave way in me.

If Callum was alive and fine out there, he deserved to rot in hell for everything he'd done to her, both before disappearing and after. And even if he wasn't, even if she were guilty, she still wasn't the scheming ice queen Aliza had described. People needed to know that.

Kiri opened her eyes. Rolled over. Spat out a strand of hair and said in a slurred, sleepy voice, "You leaving?"

"Probably should, right?" I walked over to the window and looked down at the foggy street. No vans with TV logos—it must be too early for them.

"Are you hungry?"

I turned, expecting her to invite me downstairs for cereal—but instead, she reached under the mattress and pulled out a crumpled, half-empty pack of Fig Newtons.

Stashing food. Was that something apocalypse survivors did? "No thanks, I'm okay."

She must have seen me staring, because she reddened and said, "I guess that's weird."

"Oh, I keep snacks in my room, too." *Just not under the mattress.* "I don't eat this early, though."

She rose and came to stand beside me, pointing to where the street dead-ended under the blue-gray western sky. "See the silver Ford Explorer? It's always there now, every night, and it never used to be."

I thought of the black SUV. "Who do you think it is?"

Kiri turned toward me. She'd cast off the softness of sleep, her eyes focusing hard. "I don't know. But I assume they're watching me. To see if I make any sudden moves."

"Sudden moves?" Then I realized who she meant. Warmth spread over my face as I imagined cops peering up at us from the Explorer, grumbling and sipping cold coffee.

"Like trying to run away," she said.

FROM KATIE DUNSMORE'S SENIOR-YEAR DIARY

September 2

I haven't been writing because something happened on Saturday that still doesn't feel real. I met someone!

"Someone." Real exciting, right? But what I mean is a boy. A guy. A MAN.

I was doing my usual trail run at Smuggs when I tripped over a root I should've known was there and ate it. Nothing big, just a scraped calf. But this guy came up behind me and said, "Are you okay? That looks nasty. I've got Neosporin in my pack."

Maybe I should've told him I was fine and kept running, limping or not. In the woods, you don't talk to strange guys. But . . . he was young. Maybe in college. He was way taller than me, which is technically impossible because I am a giant, or that's what every boy at my school seems to think.

Broad shoulders. Black hair. Narrow waist. Jacked arms and back—not like he worked out all the time, but just naturally rugged. Like he belonged in those woods. He smelled like a campfire, too.

He must have sensed my jitters, because he said, "I hope I didn't freak you out. I was after golden chanterelles."

I honestly didn't know what to say.

He unzipped his pack and showed me a bunch of cute little saffron-yellow mushrooms with ragged heads, resting on a folded dish towel. "They're good in an omelet, or sautéed with onions over a campfire."

My mom buys foraged mushrooms at the co-op, but I don't know anyone who actually goes out in the woods and forages them. "Are you camping around here?" I managed to get out. If he was with his wife or girlfriend, that would make me feel safer.

But maybe just a bit disappointed, because he was outdoorsy and movie-star gorgeous.

He shook his head. His eyes were keen and deep-set; I couldn't tell if they were brown or dark blue. "Nah, this is just an excursion. I live on Butternut Mountain, off the grid. This season, I cook everything outdoors."

He had a deep voice, a nice voice, the words just a little halting. Like he'd been alone awhile up there on his mountain.

I think that's why I stayed. Why I kept talking to him. If he'd fed me a line, like the sleazy "photographer" last week, I would have been out of there in a second.

"That's cool," I said. "Living off the grid, I mean. I'd like to do that someday."

He smiled at me—a gleaming-white, beautiful smile. "Someday we may all be living off the grid, whether we like it or not. I'm Callum, by the way."

And he stepped forward and shook hands, as formal as somebody in a Jane Austen novel. A gentleman.

He walked me to the top of the trail, and we kept talking. Callum comes from the DC area, same as my dad— neighboring towns, even. He's already been to college— Georgetown!—but he dropped out in junior year to climb mountains for real life experience. He and a friend summitted a bunch of peaks in the Andes. He showed me pics of them standing arm in arm in the blinding snow. They climbed icy slopes with crampons and fell into crevasses and walked for miles and ran out of food. They nearly died!

"When you're in those situations, you have to discover your own strength," he said. "You have to discover it real quick."

He looked hard at me, like he was evaluating whether I was strong or just another silly, spoiled suburban girl, and I looked away. But I wanted to show him I wasn't intimidated, so I asked, "Are you going to go back and get your degree? Don't you need one for a job?"

He said, "I'm hiding from the real world, Katie. Why do you think I live in the woods?" Then he smiled, and I realized he was being sarcastic—quoting the opinions of other people, like his parents. He knew he wasn't hiding from anything.

It's hard to explain, but though we were alone up there, I wasn't scared of him. He didn't try to touch me, even in a casual way. He asked me questions about myself, but nothing like did I have a boyfriend or did I like to party—none of the questions guys ask when they want to know if you're DTF (cringe!). He asked me about my training program, my distances and times, and when I told him, he nodded and looked impressed, like he understood about pushing your body's limits.

We compared our strength diets. He has his own version of paleo, which all has to come from within twenty miles of where he lives. He raises chickens and grows vegetables and buys beef from his neighbors. No dairy, gluten, or white sugar. The Luna Bar in my backpack felt like a scarlet A!

But Callum didn't mean to make me feel bad, I could tell. He was like a little boy who couldn't help telling me all about the things he loves.

I had to head back down the mountain, and he said he was going farther up. And then—ready for this?—I asked him for his number! Proactive Katie in the house!

When we exchanged numbers, he said, "You know, you don't look like a Katie to me. There are so many Katies."

"I'm actually Katharine, but it's kind of boring."

"There are other choices. You could be . . . how about Kiri?"

He held up his phone, and I saw that's what he'd named me: Kiri Dunsmore.

"It sounds like a name for some tiny fairy girl. Not a giraffe like me."

He frowned. "That's how you see yourself? A giraffe?"

"Um." He didn't need to know the names I'd been called in gym class. When you're six feet tall at age thirteen, people can be brutal. "I mean, I am big. I take up space."

"You take up exactly the amount of space you should." He held out his hand and shook mine again. "And you don't look anything like a giraffe, Kiri."

I wasn't sure at first, but the more the name rolls around in my head, the more I like it.

September 5

So get this. Callum Massey is a YouTube star!

His channel is all about wilderness survival and subsisting off the land. He lives in a cabin in the middle of nowhere with a goat named Parsley and chickens named Moira, Myrna, Melanie, and Miranda. We get to see him chopping wood and setting up a solar generator and mending the roof and foraging for mushrooms, just like he was when I met him. He looks straight at the camera, his eyes kind and understanding, as he explains how you can do it yourself, too.

He has more than a hundred thousand subscribers, and hundreds of people leaving comments on every single vid. A lot of them are doomsday prepper types talking about their favorite guns for defending the homestead—yikes. Then there are fans who watch the channel for his arms and abs, and they aren't shy about saying so. Some of them are practically drooling on the screen, and OMG, I wonder if that was basically me when we met. If I embarrassed myself!

Anyway, I know now he's not ever going to text me. He took pity on me because I stumbled, that's all. He's an influencer! Lusted after by all the legions of petite girls who post selfies with smoky eyes and crop tops, and here I am looking like a raccoon every time I try to apply eyeliner! He is Out of My League, and I need to stop thinking about him now. Forever. No more Callum. Deleted from my brain.

But how wild would it be if he did text me?

7

The rain had stopped, but the leaves in the park still whispered as I felt my way back along the path in the darkness. Pepper spray clutched in one hand, I walked as fast as I could, wincing when gravel crunched under a heel.

Across open grass, past the turnoff to the beach. Somewhere in the darkness loomed the Wolf Tree, though this time I could only feel it, not see it.

Finally I reached the empty parking lot to find my bike all alone in the rack. I bent to unlock it, willing my hands to stay steady. But the cold steel slipped through my fingers as if it had been oiled. And where was my key? I gripped it for an instant, only to feel its weight slide from my grasp. A clink in the blackness.

"Samara."

A deep voice spoke above me. I grabbed for the pepper spray, but I must have dropped it, too. I knelt and fumbled desperately in the high grass—but he was already there, towering over me. A tall man in dark clothes, face shadowed by a hood.

"Samara, where have you been? We need to talk."

A flashlight clicked on, casting his features into monstrous relief.

For an instant, he was Callum Massey, smiling with cold eyes—and then, with a tiny shift of the light, he was my father, still smiling. There was a scorpion on his neck.

He reached for me—

—and I startled awake, wincing at the pain in my cheek and neck, one side of my face mashed against the glass concessions counter. My phone had gone to sleep beside me.

The theater was open, but hardly anyone came to the early shows, so there were no customers in the lobby. The dream's terror clung to my brain the way woodsmoke does to your hair, though no one had ambushed me in the park when I came back from Kiri's house this morning.

I woke my phone and saw Kiri's third diary entry on the screen. Maybe reading about her first meeting with Callum had made me dream of him, though there was nothing sinister about the guy she described there.

She'd said she was giving me the diary to show me she was a "mess," and now I understood, though I couldn't judge her as harshly as she judged herself. Her gushing made me cringe a little—so high-schoolish!—but she *had* been in high school at the time. If I'd been keeping a diary when I met Reggie, it might have been just as embarrassing.

I meant to keep reading, but Maren wanted to discuss her latest breakup and drag her ex, and as soon as she went on break, a dozen people needed tickets for the four o'clock. After *that*, Lore started texting me about their new crush, an apple-cheeked girl they'd met interning on a goat farm.

Lore is ridiculous about crushes. Left to themself, they'll flail and flutter and analyze every tiny gesture endlessly. I had to deliver a stern pep talk about how when someone smiles and flirts with you there's a good chance they actually like you.

I was typing, So you'll ask her for coffee? when Owen shambled into the booth and started digging through drawers. "WD-40?"

"Have you checked the supply closet?" I hit send.

"You know that's always the first place I check." His hand darted into a drawer and came out with a spray can. "Ha! I knew Debra stashed it here."

My screen lit up with Lore's incredulous emojis, followed by We are so not even close to the point of coffee.

Why not? YOLO. Pretty funny, me telling someone else to gamble on romance when I still felt weird standing a few feet away from Owen. Reggie had dared me to hook up with him, and now I knew that kind of thing didn't work for me. It wasn't him in particular.

As for romance—I thought again of Kiri gushing over Callum in the diary, and my stomach turned over. She'd been so eager to believe everything he said, so grateful for every scrap of attention. Worshipful. If I had been that bad with Reggie, I never wanted to be again.

You did not just say YOLO to me.

WD-40 in hand, Owen left the booth and plopped his elbows on the counter in front of me. "You hear the latest?"

I typed, Said what I said, sent the text, and pushed the phone away. "Lore's being ridiculous about asking some goat girl to coffee. What latest?"

"Goat girl? Sounds very Vermonty." He slid his phone across the counter to me, a page cued up. "Check this out."

The name *Massey* jumped from the headline, and my throat tightened as if hands had closed around it. That dream had done a number on me.

"Now you're getting as addicted as I am to..." But the sentence didn't matter enough to finish, because I was reading the rest of the headline: FBI SAYS MASSEY FAMILY RECEIVED TEXT FROM MISSING SON'S PHONE.

Somewhere in the distance, Owen was still walking me through the news, but the words on the screen were more important. I swallowed the article in a single gulp, key phrases sticking in my gullet. *August 2*—when Callum's parents received a text from his phone. *Pings from cell towers*—what the FBI and ISB had been tracking since July 29. *Los Alamos, Santa Fe*—where the phone's signal was detected. But since the delivery of that single text, the signal had vanished, seemingly for good.

The text said *I'll always love you. I'm sorry.*

I gave back Owen's phone and reached for my own. When he saw I wasn't going to talk, he grunted irritably and returned to the projection booth. More texts from Lore flashed on my screen, but I didn't read them. I went straight to Aliza Deene's feed.

By August 2, Kiri was back in Vermont under her parents' strict supervision. She couldn't have brought Callum's phone to Los Alamos or Santa Fe. When the text was sent, when the phone was (presumably) destroyed, she was nowhere near it.

She hadn't lied about Callum's phone vanishing from the campsite, then. Someone had made it disappear, the same person or people who'd made Callum disappear—unless that someone else *was* Callum.

Aliza had no new video up yet, but people were leaving fresh comments on the last one.

Hear about the phone yet? Eating some crow, Aliza?

Look at the text to his folks. That's a suicide note.

No way. Too obvious. It was planted.

From a distance came the whoosh and pop of the theater's double glass doors. It was probably a customer, and I needed to get off my phone right now, but the comment section was heating up. People were second-guessing the FBI.

Why do you think the feds released this the day after the Waffle House video? They don't want the public distracted by the Kiri mess. They want to flush out the real killer.

"Excuse me?"

A deep voice. I looked up to find a young man—tall, broad-shouldered, wearing a neat polo shirt and slacks. His hair was black. So were his lashes, dipping low over a pair of velvety dark eyes that didn't quite focus on me.

His voice was velvety, too, as he said, "You're Kiri's friend, aren't you? The one she sees at night."

My throat cinched. I opened my mouth, but only a croak came out.

"I didn't mean to scare you." His lips tipped upward, but not in a real smile. "I'm another friend of Kiri's, and I'm worried about her. Would you be willing to talk—later today, or whenever works for you? We could go across the street to Panera. Plenty of people around."

He pushed a card to me across the counter, but I didn't look at it. I was watching the way his collar parted, revealing a discolored smudge just above his collarbone, as he said, "My name's Simon Westlake."

A scorpion tattoo.

We're looking at Kiri. This time, she's positioned her phone for the perfect selfie; morning sunlight shines directly on her face, and she pops against the background of pink-orange stone.

"Hey!" A wide, wide smile turns her cheekbones sharp and her face into a skull. "It's our day eighteen at Lost Village National Monument, and would you believe what a beautiful day it is?"

The camera jolts sideways to capture a wedge of blue sky, then returns to Kiri's face, which has not stopped smiling.

"*So* beautiful! Sun every day, so much sun! If this is the end of the world, it could be worse, right?" She laughs, and that's when you notice that, though her skin still glows, her teeth are a little gray. Her pulled-back hair looks greasy. "But never mind that, because it's time to get breakfast, and I have double the food now!"

Pause. The smile doesn't falter. "Not that I'd actually eat twice my share! We have strict portion sizes. We live mostly off the land and take only what we need! So anyway, I'm gonna eat some delicious rehydrated beet mush now. Nom nom. What's your favorite restorative breakfast? Tell me in the comments!"

FROM KATIE DUNSMORE'S SENIOR-YEAR DIARY

September 12

I just had an ACTUAL DATE!!!!! Better late than never, right?

After Callum didn't answer my first text, the one that just said Hi and that took me five days to work up the courage to send, I wiped him from my brain again. Tried, anyway. Then, this morning during calculus, he texted that he was coming to town for errands and suggested meeting at Panera on Shelburne Road at seven.

Mom says you should never accept a last-minute date. It shows the guy your time isn't valuable, so you aren't valuable. But I didn't ask for her advice, so ha!

I did dress down, but then I felt bad because Callum was wearing a nice collared shirt, pressed and everything, like my dad. He jumped up from the table and shook my hand and blushed. It was so adorable that I almost forgot to be nervous.

It was so surreal being at Panera—especially that Panera, where it's mostly moms and toddlers and middle-aged people playing board games. To me, everybody else was in black-and-white; he was in Technicolor.

It was also weird because Callum doesn't drink coffee or tea or soda or anything but water! I was too shaky to eat, so I asked for a salted-caramel iced latte, and when I saw that he was just having water from a plastic cup, I felt weird.

He said I shouldn't—it's not that he disapproves of other drinks, just that he doesn't "see the point."

He wasn't condescending about it. The whole time he was smiling and shooting me glances in a way that was totally flirty and at the same time like a little boy who just wants the grown-ups to notice him.

I teased him, asking him why a salted-caramel iced latte needs to have a "point," and then he got more serious and said that when he was a kid, he was overweight and inactive and hated himself. So when he was my age, he decided to turn his life around and go to the gym, and he realized he could reshape his body and mind any way he wanted. Part of that is exercise, and part of it is being ultra-conscious of everything he puts in his body and making sure it contributes to making him stronger. (Which, God knows, he is! I was practically melting looking at his arms when he rolled up his sleeves.)

So now the iced latte was tasting sickly sweet, but I didn't entirely like what he was saying, so I said, "There are different kinds of strength, though. You could be a lot heavier and still healthy"—basically quoting Coach Dever, who tells us not to fixate on our weight.

"Maybe," he said. "But with my lifestyle, you kind of need to be fit. Like the pioneers were." He told me how he has to build a fire in the woodstove to cook food, which means going out in the forest and cutting down trees and splitting them and stacking them.

I blinked away my visions of shirtless, sweaty Callum in the woods and asked why he couldn't buy cords of wood the way my parents do.

He looked at me, still with the nicest eyes a person could have, and said, "Maybe I could, but I don't want to live the way people live now. I want to live the way people will have to live in a hundred years."

Then, at last, I got it. "Because of the climate crisis."

He nodded—ding-ding-ding, I'd got something right! "I don't want to bore you," he said. "Or scare you."

But he wasn't boring or scaring me. I told him about my project last year in earth science, which involved reading all about how our civilization is unsustainable and headed for a collapse because we're too selfish to make drastic changes in our lifestyle (like, um, no more iced lattes in plastic cups, Katie!!). Those books kept me awake at night, and when I told my dad—who's CFO of a company that makes solar arrays!— he just shrugged and said the collapse wouldn't happen till we were both dead, which is so fully missing the point.

I word-vomited all that, and Callum rested his chin on his palms and listened.

Then he said, "I don't have to explain to you, then. The way I live now is because I have profound respect for the future. I don't want to ignore what's coming, whether I personally experience it or not."

Respect for the future. YES. When I was trying to explain to my dad, that's exactly what I should have said.

I looked at Callum, and it was like a current passed between our eyes. I understood him. He understood me.

"I want to see the way you live," I said. "The woodstove. The woods. The cabin."

"I want to show you," he said. "But I'm not sure your parents would like you hanging out with a guy who's a few years older than you."

He was right about that, at least as far as Dad goes. (Mom would probably be happy to see me date any human person at this point.) But they're both way too busy to notice—and anyway, thanks to them, I've got the Prius and can go where I want.

"Yeah, you're so old," I said. "Practically middle-aged."

And I did something I've never dared to do with a guy before—I touched him. Just a tap on the back of his hand, but I felt the shock wave travel up my arm.

He didn't touch me back, just sat there and looked at me, very serious. "You understand that you're beautiful, don't you?" he said. "I'm honestly not sure if you know that. It's not the flashy, self-conscious kind of beauty. Your whole face— you glow."

I blushed so hard tears came into my eyes. I'm blushing again just writing it down! I mean, I've gotten gross so-called "compliments" before, but this wasn't like that. He sounded as if the words were being yanked from some cavern deep inside him.

We're doing CrossFit together next week. I can't wait!

8

The card was damp and creased from being clutched in my palm. I held it as I stood at the crosswalk waiting for the light to change, the bike beside me, a breeze from the Saturday afternoon tourist traffic tossing my sweaty hair.

It said *Simon Westlake, Adventure Tours and Mountaineering Instruction*, with an address and phone number in Colorado and the generic outline of a mountain.

I knew now that Colorado's license plate has a mountain on it, too. It's green and white like ours, but mostly white—the exact plate I'd seen on the SUV that followed me.

Simon Westlake: mountain climber, adventurer, bosom friend and possible abductor and/or murderer of Callum Massey. Someone who had "ambushed" Kiri and talked trash about his friend. And someone who was creepy with young girls, if the story Callum had told Kiri was true.

I might not know a lot about real journalism, but I knew that when one person throws out a bunch of accusations, you can't just repeat them and act like you've done your job. You have to get a response from the person who's been accused.

Warm wind blew from the south, damp against my cheeks. The sky had gone deep violet—more rain coming, maybe a thunderstorm this time. The crossing signal beeped, cars and trucks wheezing to a halt. I stuffed the card deep into my jeans, hopped on the bike, and pedaled across the four busy lanes to Panera.

There was always another option: Go to the cops and tell them everything Kiri had told me. That would mean accepting that I would probably never see her again. I'd be cut off. But I could still make that choice and step back inside my safe bubble of bad movies and a shitty job and surfing true-crime feeds for vicarious excitement.

You don't have to do this. Maybe this fear is a gift from your gut. A few more steps, and I wouldn't be able to turn back.

I locked the bike in the rack by the entrance, then stepped into the air-conditioned chill and the babble of voices. I could have walked here, but I liked knowing I had a slightly better getaway strategy than my own two feet.

Or, if I dared, a way to follow West and see where he was staying. There were cheap motels up and down this strip.

The dinner hour was starting. Just like Kiri said in her diary, a healthy crowd of moms, kids, office workers, and board gamers, which would make it tough to kidnap someone in broad daylight.

Be normal. Go to the counter. Giant, come-hither posters showed me bisected strawberries, glistening corn chowder, iced tea in happy rainbow colors. Photos staged in a studio with aggressively inedible props.

The milk foamer roared. The sound system warbled. Voices overlapped: "Apple, chips, or bread?"

My stomach lurched. I turned to face the dining area, and there he was.

Standing in a harvest-colored booth, raising his hand to get my attention and then letting it fall, like we were on one of those awkward first dates you see in rom-coms.

Kiri had described him grabbing her arm at the rest stop. *He made me go sit in the food court.* But he was letting me come to him.

Go. I made my legs take me across the room. My head was a balloon bobbing toward the ceiling; a gentle roar rose in my ears.

I'm not bad at faking chill—Reggie used to say so, anyway. It was why Tierney was always trying to get a rise out of me; he wanted to see me sweat, but I never let him.

I wiped damp palms on my jeans, forcing myself to notice the colors of the banquettes, the clatter of dishes, the laughter from the gamers' table in the back. By the time I reached West's table, I was under control. He had his elbows drawn in and gaze lowered, as if he weren't looking forward to this conversation, either.

I sat down across from him. Sucked in a deep breath and said on the exhale, "You're the one who followed me, night before last."

"I'm sorry." Those dark lashes dropped over his eyes. "I saw you leave her house that night, and I figured you were her friend. I wasn't sure where else to start."

"You were watching her house?" My sweaty palms went cold as I realized that the whole time we'd been discussing him in the basement, he could have been out there.

West nodded, ducking his head. Seen in better light, the scorpion tattoo wasn't that sinister, the tail and pincers an almost whimsical series of curlicues. It wasn't meant to intimidate; it was something an arty dude might choose, or someone who wanted people to think he was that type.

"When I saw the TV news camped out there, I knew I couldn't

just go up and ring the bell," he said. "She never goes out by herself, does she?"

I started to shake my head, then caught myself. He was fishing for information.

He went on: "Her folks don't let her see visitors—that's why you come at night, isn't it? They don't even know you're there."

Goose bumps rose on my bare arms. "We're friends from high school. We hang out at her place 'cause it's bigger than mine. If you want to talk to her, why don't you, I don't know, text her?"

"I wouldn't know which number to use." His skin had a light sheen of sweat, too. "I'm guessing the feds took her phone."

If I hadn't been so nervous, playing clueless might have been kind of fun. "If you're her friend"—I didn't want to say Kiri's name in public—"why hasn't she mentioned you to me?"

"She didn't? That's hard to believe." There was a new edge on his voice. "When I came up and spoke to you in the theater, you did a double take."

Had he seen how scared I was? But he was clearly on guard, too, showing none of the smooth menace I'd expected. "You *followed* me. I recognized you," I lied. "You keep asking questions. What do you actually want?"

West raised his eyes. Under the dark lashes, they were almost walnut colored. "Look," he said, "I know this all seems pretty mysterious, and I'm sorry about that, too. But it would help me to know—what's your name, by the way?"

"Sam." He didn't need to know my last name.

"Sam. I know this is a weird question, but can I trust you not to pass on what I tell you to anyone but...our mutual friend?"

My heart thumped. "What, you're thinking I'd post it on all my socials?"

West flinched, and I said quickly, "She trusts me for a reason. If there's something she should know, I'll tell her and no one else."

I'd make an exception if he confessed to something dire enough. But what were the chances he'd do that right here in Panera?

West seemed reassured. He leaned toward me again. "I'd like to see her," he said. "It can be anywhere she wants, but I'd like to talk to her for a half hour, alone."

So he didn't want to tell me secrets at all. "I don't know about that." Sweat trickled down my neck as I tried to look as if I wasn't instantly rejecting the idea. Alone with Kiri, somewhere like the park, West could pressure her to change her story. He could even hurt her. "She doesn't like to leave the house."

"Please just give her a message from me. The rest is up to her." He looked wary again. "Will you do that?"

"I need to know something first." The trick, I saw now, was not activating his defenses. Not saying no outright.

"What?"

I clenched a fist under the table, steadying myself. "Before, when I said she didn't mention you, that wasn't exactly true. She told me you were Callum's best friend, and...that you didn't want her to go to Lost Village National Monument with him in the first place."

A muscle jumped in West's jaw, but he kept his gaze on me. "That's true."

"She said you told her some things about Callum—'bad' things." My voice shook, but that was okay. I wanted him to think I was an innocent kid who was worried about Kiri, my good friend who had been through a trauma. "She wouldn't say what. She just keeps protecting him, talking about how much she loves him, and...I don't think it's that simple. I want to know what she went through out there in the desert."

"I wasn't in the desert with them."

"But she said you knew things about Callum."

West plucked a raisin from his scone and placed it on the table. "Cal and I went through thick and thin. We saved each other's lives a dozen times. And, because I know him so well, I know what he puts his friends through. He likes to be the person they look up to, the person with the power to make them happy or sad or frightened." He broke off, his eyes searching me. "But you know that already, don't you?"

I did—Kiri had told me enough, even if she didn't want to dwell on Callum's manipulativeness. "You told her something else, though. Something that shocked her."

"And you're dying to know what it was?" He arched a brow. "Maybe you're wondering if I decided to blackmail my friend? Or worse?"

Yes. If West had stolen the phone from the campsite, he could so easily have sent the text Callum's parents had received, the text Kiri couldn't have sent. The supposed suicide note.

But I'd pushed him too far, and now his hackles were up. "Of course not!" I said, backpedaling. "I guess I'm just wondering why I should trust you alone with my friend when she's already under huge emotional stress. You know what else she said? That Callum told her you got creepy with an underage girl."

West's cheeks flushed hard. "I never..." Then something shifted in his face, a recognition, and he said, "Wait, you mean Arianna? But Kiri knows that wasn't..."

"She didn't mention a name." I tried for an icy demeanor, like one of the DAs on my grandma's favorite cop show when they cross-examine pedophiles.

"Well, if that's who she meant, it wasn't like that." He still wasn't meeting my eyes. "I was seventeen and Arianna was thirteen, but nothing 'creepy' actually *happened*. She had a crush, that's all. Her dad was high up in Homeland Security. I was hoping he could write me a college recommendation."

"So you encouraged this thirteen-year-old's crush?"

West's mouth twisted. "I needed the help. I'm not from a background like Cal's. I went to prep school on a scholarship, and I got a couple Cs."

I gave him a look that said *Cry me a river*, though I understood too well the fear of screwing up all your chances in life. "And none of this seems creepy to you?"

He sighed, conceding that it did now. "We exchanged a few cards—Arianna was learning calligraphy and liked to show it off. I was a kid then, too—a clueless, inappropriate kid. But that's all that happened. I swear to you, your friend is safe with me."

He didn't read like a sleazebag to me, but that didn't mean he was being honest. "I don't know. If I were her, I wouldn't risk some secret meeting without knowing *why* you want to talk to her. Can't you give me a clue?"

West sat silent, hands tightly clasped. From the gamers' table came shouts and laughter. A child whined, demanding a cookie. Outside, eighteen-wheelers roared by with remorseless speed.

My thirty was probably over. Soon people would be trickling in for the 5:45 show, but I didn't budge. I couldn't.

West spread his hands palm down on the table and stared at them fiercely, as if inspecting his nails for dirt. "Fine," he said. "I'll tell you exactly what I told her when I asked her not to disappear into the park with Callum."

My breath caught. Finally, he was going to reveal something.

"When I saw Cal in DC, he was in one of his weird, paranoid moods. He talked about wanting to leave the country and live like a nomad, and he seemed to assume his girlfriend would give up all her college plans to come with him. I wasn't sure she was up for that. So I found her at the rest stop in New Mexico, and I warned her." He clasped his hands again and pulled them to his chest. "That's all."

I could tell it wasn't. "And what did she say when you told her?"

West's mouth tightened. "That she already knew Cal's plan. She was fine with giving up her future to be with him. Being out there on the road with him, I think she lost track of what's real."

There was a look in his eyes that I didn't like: a weary, sad certainty. As if he thought he could guess what had happened in the desert, even if he hadn't been there.

"She would never hurt Callum." The words came easily to my lips—words Kiri would have wanted me to say, though I wasn't sure I believed them. "She loves him."

"Sam." West sighed. "You want the best for her. So do I. But—"

"But she *couldn't* have done it." I couldn't resist throwing the information I'd learned today in his face. "Didn't you hear about the message from Callum's phone?"

West's face went utterly blank. "Message?"

"He used his phone outside the park after he disappeared, after she was already back home. Or somebody did." *Maybe you.* "A text went to his parents on August second, saying he loved them."

The blood drained from West's face, turning his eyes into dark pools fixed directly on me. Though he hadn't changed position, I was suddenly acutely aware of the span of his shoulders and the muscles in his chest and forearms and neck, of all the things a strong body like that could do to a smaller body without even really trying.

But his words, when they came, weren't angry. Just a surprised rumble in his throat, as if he were adjusting to unwelcome information. "Shit. That's . . . not what I expected."

Before I could formulate another question, he was standing up. "You're right, Sam. She shouldn't meet me without knowing why it's important."

I hauled myself off the banquette, my whole chest vibrating eagerly with my heartbeat. *Tell me already.*

"Can you tell her what I'm about to tell you? Word for word?"

"I can do that."

West's eyes were soft and human again, and uncomfortable. "First of all," he said, "let her know that when I leave here, I plan to drive up north to the doomsday cabin. And second, tell her she was right to notice the footprints. They came all the way here with me."

"What?" I had a feeling my mouth was gaping open. Was he admitting he'd left the footprints in the campsite?

"She'll understand."

But I don't. "Are you sure? She's been through so much shit already, and now you want me to give her a coded message? You're not exactly making me trust you."

West clearly couldn't care less whether I trusted him. "If she decides not to meet me after hearing that, fine. But she should have all the facts. So please say what I just said," he added, sweeping crumbs off the table into his cupped hand. "Word for word. After that, it's her choice."

FROM KATIE DUNSMORE'S SENIOR-YEAR DIARY

September 24

Study hall. Just now in the hallway, Hayley M. tried to make me do this special fist-bump thing she started at our last practice, and when I failed the test, she whispered "Giraffe" as I walked away. Marissa and Abigail cracked up. They have NO idea how juvenile they are.

Maybe I should just quit track. What's the point? C and I are doing CrossFit again after school, and this time I swear I'll keep up with him!

Later: *OMG! Every muscle hurts. I'm lying on my bed unable to move, but that workout. Was. Amazing.*

C is so much more fit than me. He never gets tired. But when he saw me in my new workout outfit, his eyes kind of popped.

Later, when I was all sweaty, he pinched my midriff and said, "You've got a little pudge here." I didn't know what to say, but the hurt must have shown in my eyes, because then he said, "It's cute, though. I'd like to put a tattoo with my initials right there," and smiled in the sweetest way.

On the way home, I asked if he thinks I should lose weight, and he said no, I'm athletic, I'm fine, but I'm not sure he meant it. I've always felt pretty fit, but some of the girls in that class were so tiny! I'm just not built that way.

Then he asked me to come to lunch on Saturday, as if

he already knew that dinner, or any other nighttime date, would be too much, too soon. He gave me his address: 55 RR#3, Cold Springville, 51 miles northeast of here, follow the signs for Butternut Mountain and the Long Trail. I have it memorized.

9

I let West leave Panera ahead of me, pretending to head for the restroom. Then I darted to the outer glass door, pressed my back tight to the wall so he wouldn't see me if he happened to glance over, and watched him cross the parking lot.

He strode straight to a black SUV—a Grand Cherokee, it turned out—with Colorado plates. The instant he closed the driver's door, I moved. By the time he was pulling out, I was outside with the bike unlocked, swinging my leg over the seat.

It was a long shot trying to follow him anywhere, and I needed to get back to work—Maren couldn't cover for me forever. But the traffic was still bumper to bumper on this stretch of highway, four lanes of cars inching along under the angry silver sky. And he had to be staying close by—this place was Dive Motel Central. It wouldn't take too long.

When the light changed, he hung a left out of the lot. I followed him across the median, keeping a safe distance, and slid into the bike lane.

For the first two blocks, traffic was stacked so thick I almost could have passed him. Things thinned out when we coasted down toward

GE Healthcare, where the speed limit rises to forty. I considered giving up, thinking I'd lost him.

But when I reached the light at Allen Road, there was the Colorado plate, just four cars ahead of me. I was panting by that time, my face on fire and my hair soaked with sweat, but I gripped the handlebars tighter, not ready to stop yet.

West was no longer a bogeyman for me, but I didn't like how he'd ended our conversation on that cryptic message. For all his talking, the only useful thing he'd said was that Callum wanted Kiri to run away with him permanently. Then there was his strange reaction to learning about the text from Callum's phone.

When he said the footprints had come all the way here with him, was that an admission he'd been in the campsite? A threat? I couldn't possibly know without Kiri's help. But the very fact that West was giving her a coded message said they had secrets. And if they already had secrets, should I really be helping pass them back and forth?

I remembered how pissed off I'd been after watching a docuseries about an alleged murderer on trial, only to go online and read that the editor of the series had later gotten romantically involved with the suspect. How could you trust a story when the person responsible for shaping it was *part* of it?

I couldn't let myself be West's tool—or Kiri's. That was crossing a line.

The light changed. I pedaled as if the devil were after me, crouched low over the handlebars, wet wind in my face.

You're just being pigheaded. Turn around and go back to the theater before you lose your job.

That's when I saw his left blinker flash.

The red-and-white neon sign for the Pole Star Motel loomed over the surrounding car dealerships and Nepalese restaurants. It was a weird old place, with a brick A-frame lodge facing the road that looked as if it might have been pretty spiffy in *Mad Men* times.

Most of the rooms stretched behind the lodge, in a long one-story building facing the parking lot. Owen and his friends had snuck in there a few times, taking advantage of the broken window locks, and learned that each room had its own brand of ugly vintage decor.

By the time I made it across the highway and into the lot, my calves aching, the Grand Cherokee was parked opposite Room No. 17. The plaid curtains were closed.

I took a quick breather, hiding behind a minivan, and then coasted back to the intersection. I might not know what West's message meant, but now I knew where to find him.

FROM KATIE DUNSMORE'S SENIOR-YEAR DIARY

September 28

Things I did on the second real date of my entire life:

1. Drive up the steepest dirt road with the deepest ruts I've ever driven on—in Vermont, that's saying something.

2. Get lost in a thicket of trees so overgrown that Callum had to come save me and lead me to his cabin, which is so tiny and weathered that your nose practically hits the wall before you spot it.

3. Swoon over the very tight tee he was wearing under his flannel.

4. Swoon again over the way he's fixed up the inside of the cabin with a thousand adorable nooks and crannies and so many! Built in! Bookshelves!

5. Ask why the beautiful bookshelves are empty. The answer: He decided to get rid of Things. He reads—of course!—but two books at a time from the library are enough.

6. Eat a surprisingly delicious kale salad with strips of beef from cows that Callum's neighbors raised and slaughtered themselves.

7. Climb a terrifying cliff with Callum belaying me. At the top, I couldn't see a single sign of civilization until he pointed out a few distant houses. He says it's

impossible to completely escape from people unless
you go out West, or way north into Quebec. He knows
of places up there where no one would ever find you.

8. Hold a chicken named Miranda in my arms and pet her
while Callum asked me what I cared most about in life.

I admit, I gulped. It reminded me of Dad getting into those
super-serious moods where he asks me what my "life goals"
are. But with Callum, it feels safe to be honest. He's so sweet
and lighthearted and teasing, even at his most serious.

"I want to be the first woman to finish the Barkley
Marathons." I started explaining what that is—but, of course,
he already knew all about the world's hardest ultramarathon.

"You want to be strong," he said. "Both mentally and
physically. You want to survive."

"Yeah, I guess." I stroked Miranda's mottled red feathers.
She was sitting practically still in my arms, just chilling. "She's
like my cat, Hensley," I said. "He loved to cuddle with me in
the last few years before he died."

"She's old, too. Hasn't laid in four months." Callum gave
Miranda's feathers a gentle stroke, grazing my hand on the
way. "It's a sign of weakness, you know. When we aren't strong
enough to be sure we can take care of ourselves, we get
more affectionate toward others so they'll take care of us."

Was it a sign of weakness that I wanted him to hug me
right then?

"But what about love?" I asked. "Caring is human nature.
Without it, the human race just ends."

"The human race is already on its way out." But he didn't meet my eyes as he said it. He reached out to stroke Miranda again, and this time he squeezed my fingertips tight and didn't let go.

My heart was pounding hard—I thought for sure he'd lean over and kiss me, but he didn't. So I said, "I don't want to believe that's true, Callum."

"You're an optimist, Kiri." He released my hand, and then he did meet my eyes. His were so dark, so deep and full of sadness. But I knew the possibility of joy was trapped in there, and I yearned to dig deep and let it out.

One day, I wanted to say to him, everything will change. You'll have kids—probably not with me, but with somebody—and you'll be the best dad in the world. You'll love them so much. You'll move mountains for them.

"We'll just have to agree to disagree on that," he said.

10

The storm finally broke as I crossed Kiri's backyard.

Rain came in sheets, drenching me in seconds. I pounded the slider with a flat palm and then a fist, the sound lost in the downpour.

When the slider finally opened and I stepped inside, I was out of breath. The trickling down my cheeks made me feel as if I'd been crying. Kiri took one look at me, and her eyes widened as if she thought so, too.

"What happened?" Her voice was wispy.

I motioned for her to shut the slider, then to close the curtains. The window felt so exposed. "West," I said breathlessly, crouching on the mat to tug off my soaked Chucks. "I talked to him. He's here."

Kiri's eyes widened. She glanced at the slider as if West might be standing outside. "You talked to him in person? *Here* here?"

"Not here at the house. Just in Burlington."

"But *why*?"

"Yeah, I'm wondering the same." Should I tell her he'd been casing her house? "But it's him, all right—he came to the theater, and he had the tattoo. We went to Panera and talked."

"Panera?" The fright was fading from her face, but the combination of West and Panera seemed to be more than she could process. "It doesn't make sense. I only just told you about West two nights ago. Did you find him online and ask him to come here?"

"Of course not!" Indignation heated my cheeks. "Why would I do that? You made him sound terrifying!"

"I don't know!" Kiri bounced on the balls of her feet, rising and falling. "I just don't understand why *now*. You definitely didn't post anything about meeting me?"

"No!" Her sudden distrust felt like a blanket thrown over my head, hot and smothering. "I would never! Anyway, West was already here the night you told me about him. He tailed me back home on my bike. That's how he knew about me."

Her mouth opened, then closed. "Why didn't you tell me?"

"I didn't know it was him until today. I thought he was a reporter or just some creep."

Kiri turned away from me, gazing into the rain. After a moment, she said, "I know you wouldn't post anything. I'm just confused."

You think you're *confused*? I wanted to know what West's coded message meant, and I wasn't sure how to find out without crossing the line between investigating the case and interfering in it.

For now, I passed her the card West had given me at the theater—soaked but legible. "He said he's here because he wants to see you. He wants to find a safe place and time to meet."

Kiri gave the card a glance and tossed it on the floor. Then she turned briskly, walked to the far wall of the basement, and bent to pick up two free weights from a rack.

"Tell me everything he said," she ordered, doing biceps curls. "I need to know."

I scooped up the soggy card, stuck it into my pocket, and gave her a quick recap: how West had admitted to tailing me; how he'd confirmed her story about the rest stop; how he'd even confessed (sort of) to the creepy business with thirteen-year-old Arianna.

Kiri continued her exercise routine, her face expressionless. Frustrated, I added something I hoped would get a reaction: "West told me what he said to you at the rest stop. About Callum—how he was in a bad place, mentally speaking, and he wanted you to run away with him."

"Run away?" Kiri extended both weights all the way out to her sides, her arms shuddering. It hurt to watch her.

"From civilization. So Callum didn't ask you to do that?"

She lowered both weights with a little gasp. Behind us, rain battered the glass. "Do you believe what West says? That he was concerned for poor little me?"

She was being paranoid. *I* was being paranoid. The two of them had messed with my head. "I don't know," I said. "I didn't get the scariest vibe from him, but there was one weird moment—when I told him what the FBI just released."

I repeated the information about the text Callum had sent his parents on August second from the disappearing phone. *I'll always love you. I'm sorry.*

Kiri's eyes widened. "If West had Callum's phone, he could've sent that."

"Yeah. But West didn't act guilty when I told him. It was more like he was surprised—and pissed."

Kiri turned and faced the mirror on the far wall. She raised both weights over her head, her shadowy reflection mimicking her. "He could have been faking his reaction. It's not like you'd know. You're not a detective."

That stung a little, and I was pretty sure West hadn't been faking anything in that moment, but there was no point in arguing. I had to broach something I knew she wouldn't want to discuss. "Kiri, did you have any reason to think Callum didn't plan to come back from the trip?"

A hard blink. The tiniest flinch. Then her face went stony again as she got herself under control and lowered the weights to her sides. "Are you talking about suicide?"

"I don't know." But she'd thought about it, too—I could tell. After Callum's doomsday talk on their date at the cabin, how could she not? "Do you know if Callum planned to come back to Vermont after the trip? To his cabin?"

"Why are you asking about the cabin?" She set both weights down with a clunk and swung to face me, the fear back in her eyes. "Is it because you read about it in my diary? Have you been there?"

"No!" But the address was in the diary. Maybe she shouldn't have given it to me if she didn't want me to see the place for myself. "I just wondered if Callum packed up the cabin before he left. Cleared out."

"No! I don't think so. I don't know!" Kiri took a step, tripped over one of the weights, staggered over to the couch, and collapsed on it. Hid her face against her knees.

"I'm sorry." I was making things worse. I was torturing her, sending her back to the lonely place in her head, all because I wanted to know what West's message meant. And yet I was too scared to ask her.

You're not a detective. I sat down beside Kiri, wanting to touch her but not daring, trying to think of something normal and sensible to say. What would her mom's advice be? What would *my* mom want me to tell her? "You could still tell the cops about West, you know. Tell them everything and let them decide. That investigator, Emily Garza—she seems kind of smart and cool."

Kiri didn't seem to hear me. She sprang to her feet and marched to the slider, where she yanked back the curtain and peered out.

"West wants a meeting?" she said, wheeling to face me again, two tiny replicas of the table lamp reflected in her eyes. "Fine. Let's set it up."

I rose, not liking the defiant look on her face. "Really? It doesn't seem like a good idea."

"Why not? I'm not afraid of him."

"But if West is involved in any way in Callum's disappearance, then meeting him could be dangerous for you." I wasn't a lawyer, I shouldn't be giving her advice on her case, but it seemed so obvious. I shook my head firmly. "And there's something else—what he said in his message. I don't like it."

"What message?" Her eyes blazed at me.

I hadn't forgotten a single word of West's message, but when I opened my mouth, nothing came out for a moment. If telling her compromised the police investigation, I would be to blame.

It wasn't neutral. It wasn't ethical. But I had to see what she did next. For my own investigation.

I dug my nails into my palm, summoning up West's words. "He said you'd understand."

"Just tell me." Her voice was low and tense.

"West said . . . first, when he leaves here, he's going to drive up north to the doomsday cabin. And second, he said you were right to notice the footprints. They came all the way here with him."

"Footprints." She stared at me. "Like the ones I saw after Cal disappeared."

"Exactly. Is West saying he was in the campsite that night?" If so, I couldn't figure out why he had admitted it. The footprints were in Kiri's viral video; everyone was wondering who'd made them.

Kiri didn't seem to hear, only turned to the slider again. She pressed her palms against the glass, planting her feet wide, as if by getting closer she could somehow see the whole dark, rain-swept yard.

She spoke, but at the same moment lightning split the sky, washing us both in unearthly light. The thunder arrived an instant later—a throaty boom that I felt in the soles of my feet, vibrating in the house's foundation.

Water scudded down the glass in mad zigzags. When lightning flashed a second time, every drop glowed white, making Kiri a smudge against the deadly brilliance of the outdoors.

Then the window went dark again, and I saw she'd lowered her forehead against the glass and folded her arms over it. Her shoulders shuddered.

I went and touched her gingerly, the way I had last night. This time, she gave a start, but she didn't shake me off.

"What did you say just now?" I asked. "The thunder..."

Kiri turned to face me. Another lightning flash backlit her, hiding her expression, but it couldn't hide her trembling.

"I need to see him," she said. "Knowing what he knows—it's the only way I can ever be free. You can set it up. You can even be there, like a fly on the wall, if that's what you want."

Fly on the wall. Was that what she thought I was—a spy? A rubbernecker?

Though I *did* want to see what she and West would say to each other, I shook my head. Giving her the message was bad enough. "If West has something to say, he can give the FBI a statement. That's how this stuff is supposed to work."

I expected her to collapse again, to huddle up on the couch and retreat inside herself. Instead, she laughed in my face—a bitter little laugh. "You sound like my lawyer."

"Your lawyer's on your side! He'd want you to tell him everything you know about West. Maybe the cops are looking for West already. You could help—"

I stopped because she'd raised her head again, and her expression chilled me to the bone. Brows drawn down, eyes too big, mouth contorted in rage or terror or both.

"Don't mention West's name to anybody," she said. "Not a soul, Sam."

"But—"

"No." Her mouth hardened into a line. "I've told you what I want. You're the only person who can help me, and if you're not going to, I think you'd better go."

I biked home in the rain and curled up in bed with dry pajamas and wet hair. Under the covers, I hugged my knees and rocked back and forth, making myself small the way Kiri had on the couch, trying not to cry.

She'd told me to leave. If I couldn't make this terrible idea of a meeting happen, then she didn't want to see me, didn't want me meddling in her business anymore.

I wanted to shake my fists like a little kid sent home from a sleepover after a stupid argument: *It's not fair!* By seeing West and carrying the message, I'd already done so much for Kiri. If I wanted to keep her away from him, that was for her own good, not mine.

Or was it? I wondered what she could possibly want from West. *Knowing what he knows—it's the only way I can ever be free.* It didn't sound like something an innocent person would say.

Unless—maybe she hoped West would tell her what he would never tell a courtroom: what had happened to Callum. And she was willing to risk everything to know the details. Did she suspect, despite what she claimed, that Callum's last text might have been a very deliberate goodbye? That West might have helped him?

Her diary might have more clues. It might even help me decode West's message. I needed to finish it—now, tonight.

But before I could open the file, a text popped up from Owen: Hey, you ok? Meant to catch up with you earlier. Who was that big guy you woro talking to? Looked kinda sketch to me.

Warmth flooded my cheeks. It always felt a little strange when Owen acted protective, looking out for me the way a friend, a brother, a dad was supposed to do. Since we'd hooked up, it had felt even stranger than before.

Nah, he was harmless. Just some grad student wanting to buy a yearlong pass.

Then, all at once, I had an idea. I opened the diary and scrolled back a few entries to the place where Kiri had written Callum's address.

Hey, you off tomorrow too?

Owen thumbs-upped.

Of all the off-kilter things Kiri had done tonight, one of the least explainable was the accusing way she'd reacted to my simple question about whether Callum had moved his stuff out of the cabin. *Have you been there?*

If I did go to the cabin, maybe I'd find out why.

I opened Maps and typed in the address. It was up north in the sticks, about an hour away.

Want to take a trip with me?

FROM KATIE DUNSMORE'S SENIOR-YEAR DIARY

November 19

I just drove home at 1:00 AM at 70 mph through the woods, crying half the way and smiling the other half, and I'm not even sure if I'm crying or smiling right now. I'm such a freaking mess.

We had dinner at Callum's cabin finally, a real dinner, and everything started out so perfect! I mean, he doesn't have crystal champagne glasses or anything, but there was a toasty fire and a yummy stew, and he was waiting on me and telling me about using foraged purslane and being so sweet. And then I ruined it.

This whole time, I've been waiting for him to mention his YouTube channel and his following. I figured he knew I knew—hello, Google!—but that he'd talk about it when he was ready.

Then, like an idiot, I asked if he was going to do an episode about foraging, which he's informed me is actually supposed to be called "wildcrafting." And he just stared at me.

"So you watch my channel? When exactly were you going to tell me?"

It was dim in the cabin, and his pupils looked so big, flat and black. I started babbling, backtracking, and he cut me off: "There's a reason I don't date fans. They're voyeurs. They fantasize about surviving, but the vast majority of them will spend their lives staring at their phones."

After reading his sweet responses to fans' comments, it was a shock to hear how he really thought of them. I tried to tell him that he inspired people to be better. But he just shook his head and said, "I thought you were different."

Just typing those words, I'm crying again because his voice was so cold all of a sudden. Like we were a million miles apart sitting at the same table.

I explained that I actually never saw his channel before I met him, so I was not a crazed fan. He just sat there and ate, not even looking at me. When I ran out of words, he got up and opened the woodstove and shifted a log and closed it and sat back down and said, "So you're really not a fangirl? You're not a clout chaser?"

"No!"

"Then you should know that that stew you're eating? That's Miranda."

It took me a second to understand, and then I dropped my spoon. Stew splashed in my face.

Usually I say hi to all of C's chickens when I come over, and Miranda gets special pats because she's the oldest and weakest. But tonight I'd arrived when they were already roosting, so I hadn't seen them.

I said, "No. You wouldn't."

Cal looked straight at me. "Do you want to know the difference between a survival groupie and a survivor, Kiri? A survivor isn't afraid to make necessary sacrifices."

I knew he'd hunted and slaughtered animals, but Miranda wasn't "an animal." She was part of his home. She was a character on his channel.

My stomach gurgled, everything I'd eaten coming back up. I left the table and ran to the sink because the outhouse was too far.

"Please tell me you're lying," I said when I was done. "If you really made me eat Miranda, I'm leaving right now."

That's what I meant to say, anyway. But I was shaking pretty badly. The next thing I remember, he was holding me, and he felt so warm and strong and good that I didn't pull away, though I wanted to.

"I'm sorry," he said, soft in my ear. "I wasn't going to tell you till later. I was going to say she died of natural causes. You're not ready yet for this truth."

I told him I'll never be ready to eat my friends. He said I have a tender heart, and he values that. "But if you want to be like me, if you want to be on my channel, you'll learn to slit a chicken's throat yourself—the most humane method."

We've talked a hundred times about how if you're going to eat meat, you should be willing to slaughter and butcher it, but still, Miranda. I cried, and he led me back to the table and sat me down and got me chamomile tea. He said I have to take these things slowly, I can't become a new person in a few months, but he knows I'm strong. He kept repeating that. You're strong.

Then he said something I'll never forget: "You're not just a fan, Kiri. You'll never be just a fan to me."

When I calmed down, we had a great conversation. He said he has mixed feelings about "selling himself" online, but it's the best way to spread his message. He'd actually love for me to be in his vids, but not until I'm eighteen, because otherwise it wouldn't look right. He's planning a road trip next summer to New Mexico, where there's a state park filled with ancient caves, and he wants to live out there for a month and stream episodes and show people that we can all survive a bleak future if we prepare ourselves for it.

His voice got slower and lower as he described this park, all red and orange like Mars, with thousand-year-old footprints and endless sunlight, and I almost forgot to feel sick. I was imagining us out there in the desert, making the stark choices that the desert forces on you, and I thought maybe he was right. Miranda was near the end of her life. Keeping her alive might have been cruel when, instead, she could nourish us and help us survive, too.

Just before I left, he took both my hands and looked into my eyes and said, "You could come with me. To New Mexico."

I didn't say anything back, but my heart leapt.

So happy sad mad confused. Maybe this is what being in love is. Maybe this is how you know.

11

Since January, when I had my accident and Mom stopped letting me use the car, I'd almost forgotten there was a world beyond the city. Once you escape Burlington's suburban sprawl, forest closes in and mountains ring the horizon. Blue with distance, they turn green and brown as you get closer, their flanks mottled like those of the Holstein cows in the steep pastures. If you see a town with more than two thousand people and one stop sign, there's probably a ski resort or college there.

We veered north off the main road onto a narrow one that soared and plunged and twisted.

Aside from the occasional tumbledown house hugging a hillside, signs of civilization were few and far between. Walls of tangled spruce and cedar loomed on either side, except when the road took a sharp turn and the forest fell away, revealing dizzying views of open fields that stretched to rocky crags on the horizon.

"This sure is the ass end of nowhere," Owen said, steering his ancient Legacy into a curve. "Callum must've wanted the full Vermont experience."

"Do any of your cousins live out here?" Owen likes to brag about being a fifth-generation Vermonter, not a flatlander transplant like most of us in the city.

He snorted. "My family's from the Upper Valley—no comparison. Up here is *Deliverance* country, Samara. I might have to defend you from fine young men looking for breeding stock beyond their own sister."

"Eww." There he went, talking about protecting me again. My cheeks flushed. There was a little grumble in his voice that brought back certain moments I'd been trying to forget since we collided on that stupid dare last November.

"Or maybe we'll meet some lusty maidens looking for exotic seed," I suggested. "They'll take one look at that luxuriant red facial hair of yours and—"

"Wait, wait." He was riding the brake. "I need you back on the map, navigator. The turnoff might be up here."

The turnoff was a rutted thread of dirt that led straight uphill. Twigs and rocks cracked under the tires as the car whined into low gear, the AWD working overtime. Overhead, lime-green boughs covered the streaky blue sky.

"Mr. CrossFit must have had a vehicle with an impressive transmission," Owen said.

"They got a Ford Transit for the road trip." I checked my phone. "No service again, but I think it's about two miles to the trail. We should park up the road, just in case there's . . . anyone there."

"Police, you mean?" Owen swung the wheel to avoid hitting a giant rut. "You think they'd bother to surveil Callum's place?"

"I hope not."

"I mean, I'm certainly curious." Owen steered us around a gigantic glacial boulder that had dictated the course of the road. Through a break in the trees, a valley glimmered disturbingly far below. "But is there anything in particular you're expecting to find up here?"

"I just want to see it, I guess." Scenes from Kiri's diary flitted through my mind, though I'd been too sleepy last night to finish it. Miranda the chicken, served as a stew. Kiri vomiting and Callum sweet-talking her back on his side.

If Kiri didn't want me to come here, she shouldn't have given me her diary. Or she could easily have erased the address from it. But she hadn't—perhaps because she hadn't thought of it, perhaps because she *did* want me to see where Callum had lived.

"I think we're here!" Owen braked to a crawl. "See, on the left, the hemlock thicket? I'll find a pullout."

All I saw where he pointed was a mass of dark boughs. Just past it, the woods retreated to make room for a run-down trailer, and Owen pulled off the road and parked behind some bushes. "It's okay. Nobody lives here anymore."

"How do you know?" I wondered if this was where Kiri parked her shiny new Prius when she came.

"No barking." Owen locked the car, and we started back up the dirt road together. "Folks out here have watchdogs."

The road was a tunnel, trees and undergrowth clustered so thickly that only a sickly, greenish twilight made its way through. The hollow drumming of a woodpecker echoed around us. One moment it seemed to come from my right; the next, from behind me.

"There!"

Owen pointed, and this time I saw it, too. From the thicket poked a rough-hewn post that held a battered plastic mailbox with a number taped to the side: 55.

Owen crossed the ditch in one easy stride and held out a hand to help me up the bank and onto the trail. "I don't see any police tape. The staties probably don't have the budget to hang around and run people off."

I hoped he was right. "If we meet anybody," I said, grabbing his hand, "we'll just be dumb, curious kids. Murder tourists."

"That's what we are, though, right?" Owen grinned as he lifted a tangle of prickly boughs so I could step underneath.

"No." I spoke sharply, before I could stop myself. When he looked at me, frowning, I tried to turn it into a joke. "I mean, speak for yourself. I'm a *podcaster*."

After the first few yards, the trail wasn't so bad. Maybe the cops had trampled down the foliage. Mosquitoes came in clouds, though, whining in our ears. No sooner had I slapped one on my elbow or shoulder than another one attacked my back or ankle—or was that tiny sting a raspberry pricker?

Owen smacked me on the back of my neck, just above the collar of my T-shirt, and I leapt into the air.

"Sorry! He was about to get you."

"Thanks." I tried to sound startled, nothing more.

His touch didn't bother me. How could it? We'd known each other forever, play-wrestling on gym mats when we were seven and eight. Owen's body on its own could never feel unsafe to me.

It was the expectations that came with the touch now. It was the heavy, dragging note I heard in his voice every time he reached out to give me an elbow nudge or a shoulder bump. And I edged away because I knew he might want to take things further.

Everything had changed between us in the grass of the cemetery behind the theater, on an unseasonably warm November night, and mainly what I remembered was trying to focus on the stars, hazy through the clouds, because it freaking hurt. And then it was over.

He was sweet and considerate and all that stuff, but I was as far from being in the mood as you can be.

When I told Reggie, she rolled her eyes and said good intentions are about the best you can expect from a teenage boy, and she would show me how much better it is when you're with someone who knows what they're doing.

And it was better with her—less predictable, anyway. But I still found myself focusing on cracks in the ceiling plaster and the patter of rain outside. They both kept telling me to let myself go, to lose myself in the moment, but beyond a certain point, I just couldn't do it.

Lore said that if I was demisexual, everything could change when I fell in love. Was I in love with Reggie, or just sort of with the idea of her? I honestly didn't know. Reading Kiri's diary, with all its gushing over Callum, made me wonder if sometimes love isn't even about the other person. It's about how they make you feel, who they make you think you can be.

Reggie made me feel untouchable. Callum made Kiri feel strong and beautiful. I remembered her saying, *When someone comes along and turns you into a better person . . . how can it just be over?*

And both of them were cruel to us, too, when they chose to be, building us up only to tear us down. So maybe it wasn't really love at all. Maybe Kiri and I both just desperately wanted to be *more*.

"Look!" Owen called.

A bird shrieked in the distance like a warning. Through the clinging needles, I finally glimpsed the wall of a building.

In her diary, Kiri said she couldn't see the cabin until she was practically inside it. Maybe she'd exaggerated the cabin's wildness the way she exaggerated Callum's hotness, or maybe the state police had done a number on the place.

Or someone had. As the breeze blew branches into a new configuration, sunlight shone on the rough-hewn wall. It was covered with spray-painted tags, so wild and stylized they were barely readable.

"Shit." Owen stepped past me into the clearing. "Who'd come all the way up here to tag the place? Kids?"

We walked slowly around the cabin, swatting mosquitoes and pushing away prickers and wild grapevines. It was tiny, maybe three hundred square feet, but you could tell it had been built with care. The walls and the pitched roof looked solid. It was easy to imagine smoke unfurling from the stainless steel chimney while Kiri and Callum sat cozily inside by the fire.

But the windows were broken, the tall grass still peppered with their shards. The weathered boards had been notched and hacked all over as if some furious person had taken a hatchet to them. And the walls were covered with unhinged red and black scrawl. I managed to decipher the words PARASITE and DIE and COLLAPSE and EXTINCTION and, oddly enough, RESPECT.

Respect for the future. That was what Callum told Kiri he had. It was why he wouldn't bring a child into the world or go to a supermarket or even boil water for coffee, though he seemed to have no problem adding to atmospheric CO_2 with a giant gas-guzzling van for a social-media-driven road trip.

"Kids didn't do this." A cold feeling was settling in my gut.

"Then who would?"

On the cabin's far side, we found a big pile of charred stuff, as if the vandals had heaped everything there and set it ablaze. Boards, posts, cordwood, the half-burnt jacket of a book on "primeval cooking," blackened stretches of chicken wire.

Chicken feathers, too. Once I noticed them, I saw them every-where, pounded into the dirt or floating free like cottonwood fluff, catching the light. Bile rose in my throat as I made a circuit of the tiny yard, expecting any second to stumble over the dried-out corpses of—what were their names? Moira? Miriam? Miranda?

No. Callum had killed Miranda, the old hen Kiri liked to hold and pet, and cooked her in a stew, only telling Kiri after her friend was in her stomach. And she'd come home from that dinner still half convinced he was Prince Charming.

Why hadn't she seen the giant, flashing warning signs? When we talked about the Waffle House incident, she seemed to understand what was wrong with Callum's behavior, yet she still missed him enough to cry about him in my arms.

Maybe she couldn't help it. Maybe it wasn't love so much as a kind of addiction.

From the woods behind the cabin came a crunch, then a sharp crack. I stepped closer to Owen before I could stop myself, my heart jolting. "What's that?"

"Huh?"

"Up there! Didn't you hear?"

Owen looked where I was pointing, then shook his head. "You're not used to the woods, Sam. Probably a squirrel."

How could he be so calm? Despite myself, though, I felt reassured by his big, unflappable boy-presence. That must have been how Kiri felt about Callum.

Why was she so damn insecure? Why couldn't she look beyond her fantasies of a rugged nature boy who paid her attention and recognize the opportunistic asshole who wanted to control her?

It was so easy for me to see, but I could also see that she hadn't *needed* Callum to make her a better person. Her feelings about Miranda, for instance—what one person calls weak, another calls caring.

And now, partly thanks to Aliza, hundreds of thousands of strangers online thought *Kiri* was the manipulative mastermind.

It wasn't fair, but so little is. "C'mon," I said to Owen, giving the cabin's door a hard shove.

It opened easily. Smells of rotting vegetation wafted out. "Gross," I said, raising my phone to peer into the darkness within.

Kiri had described minimalist neatness and order in the cabin. Now it was pure chaos. I saw chopped pieces of what must be furniture, more spray-painted messages of hate, and bright green mold creeping up the walls like veins full of radioactive fluid.

That much mold doesn't grow in a few weeks. Mushrooms had sprouted under the woodstove, and tall grass was poking up through a gap where the floorboards had been hacked open.

This wasn't recent vandalism by true-crime buffs or curious locals. The cabin had stood this way through a whole humid summer of growth and decay.

Callum could have done this himself. Judging by Kiri's reaction to my question about the cabin, she knew about it, though she'd pretended she didn't.

On top of a junk pile, an intact wedge of paper caught my eye. I bent and tugged out the torn half of a heavy card.

It was expensive paper, thick and cream-colored and covered with elaborate calligraphy that had clearly been done by hand. Because the sheet had been torn lengthwise, each line had only a few words: *Next month we could maybe. Would be a shame if. Don't want you to have to* ("want" was underlined three times). *So so looking forward.* At the top, a date: last December. And at the bottom: *Love you to infinity.*

Kiri hadn't mentioned sending letters to Callum, and the sign-off felt too gushy for her. To me, it looked as if another girl had been writing love notes to Callum Massey, well into his relationship with Kiri. Making plans with him.

Who?

I'd almost forgotten Owen was there when he said, "Check this out, Sam."

He was holding his phone close to a stretch of wall that had escaped the spray paint, only to be scribbled all over with a black Sharpie. The handwriting was all caps, so elongated and ethereal that it was tough to make out words.

But I didn't need to. This was writing I recognized.

"What the…?" Owen said, peering closer. He read aloud: *"Die, Callum Massey. May worms chew on your guts as you return to the earth you love so much. Traitor, chicken killer, hypocrite, weakling.* This is some twisted shit, Sam. Did this dude ever piss off, like, the Mafia or something?"

"No," I said. "The Mafia didn't do this."

I felt so tired suddenly, there in the hot, fetid cabin, that I could have lain down on the mold-ridden floorboards and gone to sleep. Outside, the bird screamed again. Branches rustled, but I knew it was only a skunk or squirrel.

In junior English, Kiri had hand-lettered an ornate label for the portfolio that we handed in together. The letters looked just like these.

12

H ey, Sam. Hey," Owen said, peering at me from under his fluffy red brows. We were stopped at a light on our way to the interstate. "Are we even gonna talk about what we saw back there?"

"What about it?"

"Just...all of it."

A love note to Callum. A hate note from Kiri, right there on the wall where everyone could see it. They had to be connected.

Would the diary explain how? She'd seemed so earnest when she gave it to me, gazing at me with those big brown eyes. But she'd lied about the cabin, saying she didn't know if Callum would return there, and I was starting to think the diary wouldn't tell me what I needed to know, either.

I said, "Let's not post any pics, okay?"

Owen hit the gas as the light changed. "Thing is, other people will. It's just a matter of time before they figure out where he lived and that it's not guarded."

"Maybe Callum's on his way back. We can't be sure." But everything about the cabin said no. The memory of feathers trampled on the ground made me shiver in the afternoon heat. If the chickens were dead, Kiri wasn't responsible—I could be sure of that much.

"You could revive your podcast," Owen said. "Do a new season on this—it's got a local angle and everything."

I wished he hadn't hit so close to the truth, because my plans seemed absurd after last night. "I was joking before. You know perfectly well the first season tanked."

"I thought it was actually pretty good."

That made me melt a little inside, and I didn't know what to say. Owen flipped his blinker and steered us into the tight curve of the on-ramp. "Sam, have you seen Katie Dunsmore again?"

For an instant, the granite rock face seemed to rocket straight toward us, and I braced myself and closed my eyes.

"Kiri." It slipped out. Had he been waiting to ask me this question the whole trip? "A couple times." It didn't seem worth it to lie. Kiri had asked me to leave, and I couldn't be sure she would ever want to see me again.

Owen gunned the engine. We zoomed onto the straightaway, the sky big and blue in every direction over the blasted granite cliffs. "Why's she want to hang out with you?" he asked.

I'd been waiting for a different question: *Do you think she did it?* "Ooh, burn," I said, trying to turn it into a joke—but it *did* burn, and the deep-down ache in my chest wasn't just about my pride or my dreams of being a real podcaster. She'd liked me. She'd trusted me.

"I didn't mean it that way," Owen said. "It's just, the two of you weren't friends till now."

"I don't think she's ever had many friends. And..." I reached for something else, something better. "I think I get her situation in a way her old friends wouldn't." *Whether she recognizes it or not.*

"Get what? Being the main character of all the news feeds? Being a possible murder suspect? I guess I just can't help worrying, knowing you're spending time with her."

That was so Owen, and I couldn't resent him for caring. "You don't have to worry."

He raked a hand through his hair, standing it on end like a cartoon character's. "But also, I'm kind of wondering if she's...I don't know, maybe using you?"

"To do what?" His words hurt, and I laid the sarcasm on a little too thick. "To hide the murder weapon for her? To help her escape?"

To carry a message. To set up a meeting. But the meeting was the first thing Kiri had actually demanded from me. Without me, she would never have known West was here at all.

"I never said I thought she was guilty!" Owen hit the button to seal the windows; we'd reached Bolton Flats and were soaring at eighty. "I just meant she might be using you for news. You said her parents keep her offline, right?"

"Right." I had misinterpreted him and overreacted. "I guess I have told her a few things."

Everything. But she had a right to know, didn't she?

Owen didn't seem to notice my discomfort. "You know what I heard this morning? Some biker dudes were camping close to Katie and Callum—badasses with criminal records. Other campers said they were making noise, throwing beer cans. One woman saw Callum shooting the shit over at the bikers' site."

Those must be Kiri's "scary bikers." A shiver of disgust pricked up goose bumps on my arms as I imagined long-haired, aviator-shades-wearing, pot-bellied guys ogling her in her shorts and tank top while Callum watched.

"So maybe the bikers offed Callum." I tried to sound breezy. "And then they rode their bikes all the way to Vermont and trashed his house before anyone missed him—is that what you're thinking? That Hells Angels could've been lurking out there with us?"

We were out of the flats; Owen lowered the windows again so that warm wind gusted over us. "I'm just saying," he shouted over the roar, "the whole thing is sketchville. Maybe you should let the cops take things from here."

"Nothing I'm doing is getting in their way." Guilt closed my throat for a second. "Anyway, why so pro-cop all of a sudden? You're the one with ACAB in all your profiles."

"I'm not pro-cop. I'm just pro you not getting sucked into something dangerous." He spoke as if each word were an effort. "I mean, it's one thing to do a podcast about a famous criminal and another thing to do a podcast about a murder suspect who's a *friend* of yours."

"A few minutes ago, you were saying I *should* do one!" A long valley plunged to our right, the houses and trees at its bottom like toys. Life looked so peaceful down there.

He didn't know a thing, and though I'd had the same thoughts, now I found myself arguing the other side: "Would it necessarily be so bad? I mean, yes, there are ethical issues. Kiri needs a friend right now, not someone who's going to splash her secrets all over. But if I just frame it as telling her story the way she sees it..."

Maybe, deep down, I was just as needy as Kiri was. Maybe that was what drew us together.

"So you know her secrets?" Though Owen spoke softly, I couldn't miss the words.

"I didn't say that!"

"You kind of did."

I didn't answer.

FROM KATIE DUNSMORE'S SENIOR-YEAR DIARY

December 26—the best Boxing Day EVER!
Or actually Boxing Night—ha! I'm just home from Cal's, and he actually told me to leave because it was getting so hot and heavy too fast. He said if we went any further, he wouldn't be able to control himself, and I guess I felt the same! <blushes>

I told him I'm 100 percent ready and I can get a prescription for the pill any time I want—it's one of the few things Mom and Dad are cool about—but he's old-fashioned about these things. He wants me to be eighteen before we go all the way AND before I go on camera with him. I can help him with setup and editing before then, but that's it. People might find out I'm underage and think he's a perv, he said, even though the age of consent in Vermont is sixteen.

Well, tonight I'm the perv, and I blame Cal. He made the vibe in the cabin so perfect, with candles and festive pine and holly hanging everywhere. We were so cozy on the couch, I felt like I was living in a steamy romance novel!

The only bad part was when he pinched my middle again and saw I'd gained a little weight, like I always do in the winter. I told him I'm in the so-called healthy BMI range, and then he asked if I've ever been 125. Which, for my height, would be a waif! Not healthy at all!

But I get it. He equates weight loss with self-control.

I didn't want to burst his bubble, so I told him I'd give it a try, just for fun, and see if I can make myself look like a supermodel. It's just a matter of willpower, right?

13

S am? Did you hear me? You could study video with Zephyra
Taub. She had this amazing anti-colonialist multimedia show at
the Firehouse last year."

"Wow." I tried to muster some enthusiasm for community college,
digging my toes into the dirt so that the giant porch swing rocked
gently in its steel frame.

Lore and I were sitting in one of the coveted swings along the boardwalk. It was a perfect afternoon on the downtown waterfront, the lake
sparkling blue and gold all the way to the Adirondacks. Everywhere
you looked were laughing girls in halter tops and little kids with dripping creemees and cyclists and in-line skaters and bright-eyed dogs.
The wrecked cabin in the mosquito-ridden woods felt like another world.

"I don't know about art classes," I said. "If I'm going to study video,
it should be web promo, branding, stuff like that."

"Do you *want* to study branding?" Lore's pale brows drew together.
They were getting way too excited about planning my academic
future, knees drawn to their chest as they consulted the CCV curric-
ulum on their phone.

At least Lore wasn't asking me about Kiri, which meant Owen

hadn't tattled. But all this talk about the future drove me up the wall. "Do *you* want to pick up goat shit? Every career has unglamorous parts."

"Farming is my dream." Lore slid their feet back to the ground, rearranging the skirt of their pretty yellow-and-black-print dress. "If you don't do something you love at least a little bit, you'll wither up, Sam. I know you."

I gazed at the horizon, where the mountains were growing purpler as the sun dropped toward them. Oh, I'd had a dream all right—a breakout podcast, a story all my own. I'd even mulled over some possible titles: *The Desert Changes a Girl. She Came Back Alone. Only She Came Back.*

It seemed so naive now, as if Kiri were a character I'd invented. But she wasn't, and the desert *had* changed her, and Owen might be right that she was using me. She'd been so angry when I refused to set up the meeting.

"Maybe I don't need college," I said. "I could take virtual classes and work freelance. I could go anywhere." Reggie had dropped out of college, and so had Callum. "Institutions are failing, Lore. These days, college is basically a fancy summer camp for people with inherited wealth."

"I got need-based aid!" Lore protested.

"I don't mean you. You worked your ass off in school. But me—I fucked up, Lore. I gotta be practical."

"You don't sound like you right now."

"Maybe this is me," I said.

"Reggie's gone, okay? You don't have to act all cool and cynical for me. I like you the way you are."

I swallowed hard, trying to think of a comeback. But Lore had scooted forward to examine some new action on the boardwalk: a young guy shouldering a camera with the WPTZ logo and clutching a windscreened mic in the other hand.

I sat up. Beside the guy stood a perfectly made-up young woman with brown hair and a floppy-bowed blouse—the reporter who'd chased Kiri into the woods on the fateful day we met.

The two of them were interviewing a girl I recognized from school. I couldn't remember her name, only her strong calves, high ponytail, and eager-to-please smile.

"Hey, that's Hayley Marquette," Lore said.

The reporter's voice rang out: "So, you were on the BHS track team with Kiri Dunsmore?"

"Yeah. Three years." Faced with the reporter's polished stage presence, Hayley looked terrified.

"Could you say that again in a complete sentence, Hayley?"

"Um. I was on the track team for three years with Katie Dunsmore."

I could feel all the impatience the reporter was hiding; she needed a good story, and Hayley was not a good storyteller. "What were your impressions of Kiri—Katie?"

"Vultures on a corpse," Lore muttered.

"Shh."

Two more track team members flanked Hayley just off-camera—offering support or trying to get into the shot, it was hard to say which. "Katie was shy, really shy. But nice!" Hayley said. "She was just one of those people who don't make friends easily."

"Antisocial." The sharper voice of another girl—Olivia something. The cameraman swung to get her in frame.

"Did she ever talk to you about her boyfriend?" the reporter asked. "Callum Massey?"

"No way," Olivia said, taking over. "Not a word. But that last semester, you could tell something was wrong, you know? She stopped going out with us after practice. She got scary-skinny."

The reporter replaced her fixed smile with a serious expression. "Do you think Kiri Dunsmore was someone who might get involved in an abusive relationship?"

Leading questions are bullshit. I bit down hard on my lip, wishing I could tell Ms. Perfect where to stick her fake concern.

Hayley nodded tentatively. Olivia jumped in again: "Well, she was kind of more of a follower type. And people like that are more likely to—"

A group of cyclists coasted between us and the news team, drowning out the analysis. I grabbed Lore's arm. "C'mon. If we stick around here, they might try to interview us, too."

"Why would they?" But Lore left the swing without protest and followed me toward the community boathouse. "We didn't really know Katie."

For an instant, I wanted to tell my friend everything—about the midnight meetings, the diary, the night in Kiri's bed, West, the cabin. I wanted Lore to know I wasn't anything like the reporter, thirsty for juicy tidbits to squeeze dry. I just wanted the full story, with all its convolutions and contradictions. Maybe I could be one of those podcasters who acknowledged their own doubts and ethical issues, constantly questioning their own narrative until they pummeled it into a deeper, richer one about storytelling itself.

But those podcasters had training and experience. And if Owen doubted what I was doing, Lore would, too.

I gazed at the amethyst curves of the mountains, where the setting sun was disappearing. "I just hate how the media turns people into stereotypes."

"Good reporters don't," Lore said. "CCV has journalism courses, you know."

"Oh yeah?" Reggie would have said that journalism was a dying field, but I didn't feel like channeling Reggie anymore. I needed something to do tonight so I wouldn't be tempted to go over to Kiri's. It was too soon.

"Can I come over?" I asked. "I want to see how big Puffball's getting."

Lore looked a little startled, then happy. "Sure, if you don't mind mac and cheese from a box."

Just like old times. We'd play with the cats while we streamed bad CW shows, I would probably end up sleeping in Lore's old scout camp sleeping bag, and in the morning, their dad would make us both waffles. I wanted nothing more.

"You can tell me about all the best radical journalism profs," I said as we walked back to the parking lot. "I want to be the twenty-first-century Lois Lane."

Lore gave me a friendly nudge. "I think you'd look great in a fedora."

FROM KATIE DUNSMORE'S SENIOR-YEAR DIARY

January 3

139

January 20

133. Carb-free meal plan and extra workouts ftw!

February 1

134. DAMN, so much for willpower. This is way harder than C claimed it would be. He says I look amazing. I think I look okay, I think I've always looked okay (for a giraffe), but I'm in it to prove something now. If he could reshape himself, so can I.

February 12

129!!!!!

February 16

Omg!!! I'm in so much trouble!

Whenever I go to Cal's house, I tell Mom and Dad that I'm staying at Abigail Schafer's grandma's cabin in Stowe. But yesterday Mom ran into Abigail's mom at the Flynn and found out we haven't seen each other outside school for months! Then Dad remembered that one of his friends had seen me with "a grown man" outside CrossFit, something he originally thought was a misunderstanding, and our family dinner became a giant shit show.

I came clean. I told them all about Cal and asked if I could bring him for dinner so they could meet him. Mom didn't seem that bothered, especially after she saw how handsome Cal is, but Dad called him a predator, and it took hours to calm him down.

It insults me how he thinks I can't make choices for myself. I'll be eighteen in a month and two weeks, and then I can go live with C in the woods and eat nothing but wildcrafted mushrooms if I freaking want to!

February 25

PHEW. Dinner went perfectly. I was a little afraid Cal wouldn't even accept the invite, but he said if he were my parent, he'd be protective, too. He wore a suit jacket and tie, and he acted like what someone would expect from a boy who went to prep school and Georgetown. He complimented everything in the house, including my dad's golf trophies and my mom's cooking. She was practically flirting with him by dessert, and he was flirting back in that sweet, meaningless way he does sometimes. Ha! Cal can charm anybody. He was also being so nice to Dad, calling him "sir" and listening respectfully to his boring stories, that I think Dad warmed up to him.

Over coffee, Mom told C she was about to buy a ticket for me to fly to France in June to visit Great-Aunt Esther.

My face went beet red, because I'd almost forgotten that Mom promised me the France trip for my last birthday. All I could think about was C's road trip to New Mexico. We've been talking about it since X-mas, researching vans online!

I couldn't look at him. I expected him to accuse me of misleading him, right then and there.

But he didn't. He started telling Mom and Dad about his own trip plans—how he'd stop in DC and then make his way out West, shooting episodes along the way, until he reached Lost Village National Monument. He didn't talk about desert survival living, just what a breathtaking site it was and how historically important, with cave paintings made by people who built an advanced civilization there in the 1300s. He told them about the German treasure hunter whose headless body was found in a canyon in the 1920s. Dad got all excited, because he'd heard the creepy story when he was a kid.

"It sounds amazing," Mom said. "The experience of a lifetime—don't you think, Katie?"

I said yes, it would be. Dad agreed.

Then C said, "I'm teaching Kiri to shoot video. She's a natural. I'll miss her when I'm on my own this summer." And at last I understood the long game he was playing. I really can be slow to catch on sometimes, just like he says!

Dad just grunted, but Mom said, "Do you really do all that shooting by yourself? It seems like you should have an assistant."

C pulled a sad face and said, "PAs as good as your daughter are hard to find."

I wanted to blurt out, Just let me go with him! You can't stop me anyway! But I've learned a thing or two from C. I kept my face neutral, maybe a little sad, as I pointed out that I could see Great-Aunt Esther another summer and they hadn't even bought the ticket yet.

"But you want to see Europe," Dad said. "You've been bugging us about it since you were twelve."

"I'm not twelve anymore," I said. "And air travel has a huge carbon footprint."

Mom looked at Dad. "It does sound like the adventure of a lifetime," she said.

I knew then that I'd won, and I'm going to New Mexico. My gaze met C's across the table, and he looked so proud—of both of us!—that I had to work to keep the wild, gleeful grin off my face.

March 18

For once, I'm excited about my birthday! Most years I don't even have a party, just dinner out with my parents, but this year will make up for all the others.

Oh, I'll still go out with Mom and Dad, and she'll give me Grandma's ruby earrings that she's been saving for me, and he'll get tipsy and tear up when he gives me the standard kiss on one cheek.

But then comes the weekend. I have permission to take a day trip with Cal! We'll drive over the border to his parents' cottage in the Laurentians, and he'll show me the "sights." That's the official story, anyway.

But his folks won't be there. I'll be the magic age: eighteen. Old enough to be in front of C's camera, or ____!?!?! I can't even write the possibilities that are running through my head! Rest assured that I'm prepared for whatever may happen. Eeee!

C says it's cute that I'm so excited, but it embarrasses me! When I want him to touch me, the craving is so bad it's like the hollowness I feel when I'm hungry. At school or in *bed at night, I see movies in my head: We're together, and it's perfect, but then he ghosts me! Or he even goes off with another girl! And then it's like this monster takes over my body, and I tear him limb from limb and spread pieces of him everywhere.*

Only in my nightmares! My therapist says it's okay to let yourself feel all the bad feelings. You have to breathe through them and welcome them. Just not act on them.

And here's the annoying part: I'm back up to 128! New rule: No more pretzels late at night; no more snacking, period! I am cool. I am focused. I am ready.

It's going to be perfect.

14

Sooner or later, West had to come back. He knew where I lived and where I worked. And he wanted that meeting with Kiri.

Biking to my shift at the Grand Nine beside long lines of lunchtime traffic, I felt a prickle on the backs of my thighs. Every black SUV I spotted made me tense. It seemed unfair that drivers were so hidden behind the midday glare on their windshields, and I was so visible.

If and when West finally did come sauntering back into my life— in the next day, hour, minute—I would tell him Kiri wanted nothing to do with him. He would just have to accept it, and then *I* would just have to accept it if she never wanted to see me again.

Last night at Lore's, chasing kittens around the den, I'd felt safe. Now, entering the theater and clocking in, I kept checking over my shoulder.

Then I was on display behind the glass counter, just waiting for the lobby doors to swing open. Before 3:30, no one bought tickets except knots of old people from the various senior centers and stay-at-home parents desperate to entertain their kids.

Sunlight turned the glass front of the theater to molten lava. I squinted to make out the dark blur of each new arrival—a group?

Good. Tall person and small person? Good. Walking hesitantly or with a walker? Good.

That meant it wasn't him.

When I saw a tall outline that read male, with a young person's springy stride, my throat went dry. But the person was slighter than West, with narrow shoulders. Ugh, Tierney Brenner.

Funny how I'd never noticed before that Dickwad didn't have broad shoulders. When I met him last year, he seemed like a regular bruiser, but now I was comparing him with West, who actually was a big, scary man.

"Well, hey there, Sammy." Tierney crossed the carpet with his usual studied swagger, oblivious to how he'd shrunk in my eyes. It was our first face-to-face since that shitty night in January, and I wished wildly that Owen were here instead of up in the projection room.

Tierney planted his elbows on the counter. "Been a while, right?"

"Hey." I didn't step backward the way he obviously wanted me to. I had no reason to be afraid of him. "Never seen you wear a suit before."

A lazy grin spread over Tierney's face. With his cropped blond curls and blue eyes and crooked nose, he made me think of a porcelain shepherd figurine that had found its way off an old lady's shelf and into a brawl. "My dad says if I'm going to start doing the rounds for him, I gotta look the part. Like it?"

The suit had a skinny hipster cut that should have flattered him but didn't. "Not really."

"Oh, you're smooth, Samuel." The grin again. He knew how much I hated it when he called me by full names that weren't mine, especially boys' names.

I think I bugged Tierney from the moment we met. He made jokes about how I was a "tomboy" or still waiting for puberty, neither of which was true. I just didn't toss my hair and flirt when he was around the way Reggie did.

"So you're doing the rounds now?" I crossed my arms, pretending I hadn't heard the comment. When Tierney's dad did the rounds of the theaters, checking on the state of the bathrooms and the fullness of the popcorn bin and whether we'd shown up looking presentable, he was tough but fair. I suspected Tierney wouldn't be.

"Yeah, Dad thinks it's time for me to step up as heir apparent." This time his grin invited me to sneer with him. He thought he was way too cool to be in the multiplex business.

"Great," I said. "Guess you earned it."

"Right? You sticking around here in the fall, Sammy, or you off to some Ivy League school?"

"Staying." To distract myself, I grabbed the dust rag and started using it on a Republic of Tea canister.

"That's a surprise. Reggie always said you were raring to get the hell out of town, just like her."

He was bored and trying to get a rise out of me. But he wasn't West. He was nothing. If I were Reggie, I could have had him under control in a second. She called it "girl magic"—the tilted head, the winsome glances through long lashes. Kiri had some of that magic, too—I'd seen it in her videos with Callum, and sometimes even when we were together. But it had never come naturally to me, and I didn't feel like faking it. "Yeah, well, apparently I'm just another hometown fuckup."

"You're in good company, Sammy girl." Tierney offered a fist bump. I didn't take it. "What's Reggie doing these days, anyway? Heard from her lately?"

Another goad. After that night in January, he couldn't possibly think Reggie and I were still in touch. "Nah. She went off the grid."

"What's up with that? Just between the two of us, Redge was always kind of a flake, right? You don't just move away and dump people."

So Reggie had been ghosting him, too. I hadn't been sure about that, and the confirmation sent a jolt of hot, vengeful pleasure through me. "Reggie was never going to stick around this dump. Not her style."

"Yeah, but the two of you, you were pretty tight. Kinda surprised you aren't still." His gaze flitted over me in a way I didn't like. "You got a girlfriend yet, Sam I Am?"

I forced my lips to make a polite screw-you smile. "Is that an appropriate workplace question, Boss?"

"Ooh, 'boss.' I like the sound of that. No, but seriously." Tierney rose to his full height, though he couldn't seem to stop fidgeting from one foot to the other. "I know you think I'm a dick, but I'm actually offering friendly advice. You need to get out of your own way, Sam. Have a spa day or whatever. Stop pining after a bitch who's not coming back."

He thought he knew everything about me—poor little abandoned Sam, stuck in her dead-end job. Rage filled me like ice water pouring into a glass—rage at him, at myself. "Fuck off, Tierney."

"Language, Samuelito!" He shook a finger at me. "What if some nice family came in here and heard you cussing?"

If you're the boss, I quit. The words were in my head, and then they were on the tip of my tongue.

Before I could say them, Owen traipsed into the lobby, panting under the weight of a box of equipment. "Hey, Tierney!"

Tierney turned to greet him. "How's it shaking, tiger?"

I drew a breath through lungs that felt hot and swollen. *Keep it together, Sam.*

"Cool cool." Owen's tone was friendly, but he could obviously tell we'd been fighting. He tossed a worried glance at me, then asked Tierney, "What's going on, dude? Nice suit."

"Rounds." Tierney raised his chin. "Dad wants you to give me a tutorial in the projection loft."

"You've come to the right place to learn the troubleshooting of crappy digital projectors, my friend." Owen ushered Tierney past the velvet rope into the back corridor, shooting me a reassuring wink.

On his way out, Tierney turned to me, this time with wide, innocent eyes. "You didn't have to lay into me, Salamander. All I'm saying is that if I got over her, so can you."

My face burned as I realized Owen had heard that. The more Tierney hung around here, the more he'd be making my work life slightly harder in a million ways—death by a thousand unpopped, tooth-cracking kernels.

"Don't worry about me, Tier," I said. "You watch yourself."

Once he was gone, I regretted losing my temper. His advice hadn't been "friendly" at all, but maybe he had a point—I wasn't as over Reggie as I wanted to be.

Leaf shadows dappled the sun glare on the plate-glass wall. The air-conditioning cycled on. From the interior corridor came the swing of a door and a snatch of jaunty music from DreamWorks' latest. Squeaky voices and superheroes—it was all we ever seemed to have at the Grand Nine, except for the occasional art movie that nobody saw.

Three little kids bounced out into the lobby, yelling excitedly about being able to fly. A frazzled-looking woman caught up with them and shooed them out the door.

I wasn't pining after Reggie. Of course, I cared about her, and yes, we'd also messed around, but she forfeited her place in my heart when she chose Tierney over me. If jerks turned her on, boning them was her prerogative; that wasn't the issue. It was how she seemed to look down on me because I didn't want the same thing.

I tried to be cool about it during our conversation just before Christmas, when fairy lights draped the booth and we'd just funneled the seasonal crowd into the new Marvel movie.

"So, is he amazing in bed?" I asked Reggie after she admitted she was ditching me for Tierney that night, keeping my tone light and teasing. She always acted like I didn't get it—like I didn't have needs, too, just different ones. "Has he been practicing tantric on you or something?"

"Sam!" Reggie choked on a piece of popcorn. "He has a nice body and he wants me, okay? It's chemical. Sometimes that's all you need to give you a warm glow." She sighed. "Maybe someday you'll understand."

I felt two inches tall in that moment. I wanted to scream at her that I was nearly eighteen and not some naive kid, but my pride wouldn't let me. Now I wondered if Kiri felt the same way when Callum told her she wasn't tough enough yet, or that she just needed to lose ten more pounds.

She might have been angry at him the way I was at Reggie, even if she tried not to show it. I remembered how she'd described her jealousy in the diary: *And then it's like this monster takes over my body, and I tear him limb from limb.* She'd also scrawled murderous messages on his walls.

A shiver ghosted down my spine. Maybe *that's* how a woman becomes a killer.

If only my thoughts would stop drifting back to Kiri. Had she been lonely last night? Or had she been busy trying to find a way to meet West by herself? At least I hadn't told her where he was staying.

As more kid-and-parent combos trickled out of Theater Two, I woke my phone.

Maybe it was fate that Aliza Deene was the first person to pop up on my feed. She was doing a live stream, tracing traffic-cone-orange liner around her eyes and reacting to the latest: A girl named Susanna, one of Callum's DC friends, said she'd seen Kiri "upset" at a party and Callum calming her down.

"What we see here is Callum struggling to manage Kiri's emotions, which are getting more explosive by the day. He doesn't understand that a histrionic personality *feeds* on the drama. Or maybe he wants to exploit her emotions for his channel. And that's his fatal mistake."

Aliza frowned, pausing in her makeup routine to peer at her own screen. "Wait, wait, are you guys talking about the so-called 'farewell text' again? Texts can be scheduled on an iPhone with a third-party app!" She paused again, reading. "Do you honestly think Callum acted like someone who was about to self-unalive? Nope. No way. This was a setup."

"You haven't seen his fucking cabin!" I said aloud to my phone. One of the moms from Theater Two gave me a look and tugged her kids toward the door.

At least not everyone agreed with Aliza's theory. **Still no body**, one person commented, **which means CM could be halfway to Costa Rica by now. No corpse, no crime.**

What about border control?

CM wasn't the type to just disappear.

He was exactly the type to just disappear, lmao.

Not if it meant leaving his gf in trouble. I've watched every ep. He has his issues, but CM is a gentleman.

Gentleman, smh, seriously?

He tried so hard with her.

This was entertainment to them, but it was Kiri's whole life. Her future. If a jury believed this garbage about her being an ice queen femme fatale, she might never see the outside of a cell again.

My cheeks burning, I waited for somebody else to post about the state of Callum's cabin. Surely we weren't the only nosy crime hounds who'd seen the damage.

I heard he owed $$$ to shady characters.

He wouldn't run away. He had the place in Vt. He was coming back. He loved that girl! She was the one trying to use him for his fame.

That was the last straw.

I switched to my anonymous shit-posting account, the one nobody knew about but Reggie, and typed: **If you saw CM's cabin in Vt, you'd know he never meant to come back.**

It was a dumb move, but I felt better the instant I posted the comment, light-headed with adrenaline. *Come at me!*

At first, I got only the standard responses whenever anybody claims to have inside intel: **BS, lol, prove it.** But then someone asked, **What did you see there?**

Cold gripped my shoulders. I zipped up my hoodie, then popped out my earbuds and hid the phone under the counter so I could sell tickets to a dad and two little girls who'd come for the 4:10.

They wanted popcorn and juice and gummy bears—"Not that box, the one with more red ones!"—and by the time they were gone, I remembered what I'd made Owen promise: that neither of us would post about what we'd seen.

But Owen wouldn't recognize this handle.

Now there was a long string of comments calling me a liar. I typed in a rush: **Whole place is trashed, and it's been that way for months.**

Furniture in pieces. Chicken feathers. Walls tagged with creepy messages.

That unleashed a flood of replies. Couldn't neighbors have done it, or thrill-seeking kids?

Wait a minute, wait a minute. That was Aliza—she was watching my thread, too. **You think Callum could have done this to his own place, back in June? What's your evidence?**

Mold. Mushrooms. Everywhere.

I'd released the kraken of curiosity, and now I watched in a helpless trance as replies covered the screen. What did the tags on the walls say? Was there drug paraphernalia? Evidence of satanism? What had happened to the chickens they'd seen in Callum's vids? Why wasn't I posting pics to prove all of this?

And then, from DodgerBlodger, the account that had mentioned Callum owing money to people:

D!3, Callum Massey. May worms chew on your guts as you return to the earth you love so much.

The exact words I'd seen on the cabin wall in Kiri's handwriting.

The chill moved over me in waves now, making cold sweat break out on the back of my neck. I stared at the screen, unable to move, as another comment from the same user popped up:

I'm still waiting to see her. She needs what I have. Remind her for me.

FROM KATIE DUNSMORE'S SENIOR-YEAR DIARY

March 31

I did IT!!!! After eighteen years, it's done!!! I'm not a virgin anymore!

Details? Why, I never would be so crude! Let's just say that the first time was kind of ugh and the second time was rainbows and sparkles and everything they say. I'm blushing so hard just thinking about it.

Cal's parents' cottage in Quebec was adorable, and afterward, we drove to these caves carved out of a mountainside. It's a place Cal loves. He kept telling me to take in the view and the sound of the waterfall, but honestly, I only had eyes and ears for him.

The one thing I kind of didn't like was how he coached me through it. He kept asking how I was doing, so patiently—which is actually great, totally great, because it means he cares about consent, and so do I, but maybe there should be a limit on how many times you have to ask? It made me feel like he thought people were watching us or something.

In the caves, though, he kept his arm around me the whole time, and then I knew he cared. I mean, he better care! Thinking he doesn't is just irrational. Why else would he be so sweet and patient with me when I'm such a mess most of the time?

When we said goodbye, I told him I loved him . . . and he said it back!

15

"Hey, Sam." Maren propped her elbows on the counter. Her cheeks were flushed, and liner made her eyes look bigger than usual. "Could I ask a huge favor?"

"Sure." Good thing she'd come to reinforce me; the seven o'clock customers were drifting in.

"Is there any chance you could stay to close for me? My mom came to town earlier than I expected."

"No prob!" Nobody liked closing, but tonight I found I didn't mind having a reason to avoid Kiri a little longer. She would ask me about the meeting, and I would ask her about the cabin, and we would fight again.

Maren's eyes glowed. "You're my savior! I won't forget this."

"Is Spawn of Brenner still being a pain in the ass?" I asked as she slipped into the booth beside me.

"Nah, Owen's got him in the projection room, telling him war stories." Maren took my place at the register, pasting a smile on her face as customers approached. "Don't let Tierney get to you, Sam. He just postures because he's insecure."

Insecure. Sure, but why were girls always making excuses for guys?

Take Callum's contingent of fangirls, armed with a million explanations for his behavior. He was secretly shy, he had low self-esteem, he was too sensitive and pure for this world. Kiri had believed his lies, too.

West, at least, saw through Callum. West had known Callum longer than Kiri had, long enough to have his number.

And West seemed to be stalking me—online now. *May worms chew on your guts. She needs what I have.* Unless it was a huge coincidence, the first comment was to tell me he'd also seen the cabin, and the second was a reminder of the meeting he wanted.

If DodgerBlodger was West, that meant he and Kiri hadn't yet found a way to meet on their own, as I'd feared. But how had he known who I was? Could he have followed Owen and me to the cabin? The live stream had ended with no more comments from him, but I kept checking my inbox.

At about seven, Aliza Deene followed me back. At 7:10, she DM'd me: **Hey, I wonder if you'd like to talk privately about what you saw at Callum's cabin? Do you have pics?**

Funny—a few weeks ago, I would have been ecstatic about catching her attention. Now I didn't reply. I didn't like Aliza's assumptions about Kiri, and all I could think about was West. The more I chewed it over in my head, the more I wanted to march right up to that motel and confront him. Get the edge and a few real answers for a change.

Maybe I could tell West that Kiri needed more information before she would meet him. If he *had* made the footprints in the campsite, he needed to say so and explain why he'd been out there—and explain the "doomsday cabin" part, while he was at it.

She'd seemed so scared the first time she told me about him. I couldn't see why the message had changed her mind, and I had a feeling she'd never give me a straight answer.

West seemed antsy. He just might be more cooperative than Kiri—or more dangerous.

I debated the idea as I worked through the seven o'clock shows, through the sunset. Cars came and went in the parking lot, headlights winking in the dusk. The plate-glass wall went black, making me feel trapped in a giant, glowing fishbowl.

Maren gathered her stuff, tossed a last thank-you over her shoulder, and left me to handle the measly traffic for a weeknight late show. I poured drinks and scooped popcorn and reminded people to watch out for the erratically squirting butter pump. I drank a black hazelnut coffee.

At ten, Owen came out front. "I'm gonna head out. You okay to close alone?"

I nodded. "Is Tierney still up there?"

"Nah, he went out the back about an hour ago. Must have a hot date."

"Somebody who doesn't think that suit looks like ass on him?"

Owen smiled, but his brow creased. "Don't take him so seriously."

Easy for you to say. "If he just stops bringing up Reggie, he can shoot his mouth off as much as he wants."

"I think he misses her." Owen pulled on his hoodie. "You haven't seen Kiri again, have you? I keep thinking about that cabin. It creeped me out."

"Nope." Not a lie. Yet.

After he left, I worked on the closing checklist. The 9:30 show in Theater Six was the only one still running when I hauled two giant trash bags out back, propping the door open behind me. It was a Czech art movie, and we'd sold exactly two tickets to it that night.

Outside, the air was cool and damp. It was a new moon, and over the tops of the white pines, the stars were brilliant flecks of mica. If Owen had been there, I would have suggested a break in the cemetery, but I didn't want to go there alone.

Behind me, a thud.

The back door had come loose and swung closed. I pulled out the master key ring and unlocked it.

That reminded me the front doors of the theater weren't locked yet. I hurried back inside to the lobby, where I found the last two customers of the night—a middle-aged couple in Birkenstocks—having an intense discussion about the Czech movie. They slipped outdoors with apologetic smiles. "Good night!"

"Good night!" I called back.

I liked closing last fall, when it meant staying late with Reggie and making the Grand Nine our personal playground, lounging in the empty screening rooms and draping our legs over the seats. Now I just felt alone.

Theater Six is way at the end of the hall, and it's not a lot bigger than Kiri's living room. The Czech movie's credits were done, the screen blank. Silence pressed around me as I swept the broom up and down the aisles.

I probably shouldn't go see West in that creepy motel. Owen was right: Nothing good could come out of this. But West still wanted something from me, and that gave me leverage I couldn't resist trying to use.

I had my back to the screen, kneeling to reach some popcorn

kernels that had fallen way under a seat, when I heard a small crash and a giggle.

Above me. In the projection room. I scrambled to my feet and peered at the square window high on the back wall. "Hey! Owen, you up there?"

The only answer was another stifled giggle—male, it sounded like.

No one was supposed to be up there after closing.

I ducked back into the lobby, snagged the key ring from the peg in the booth, and unlocked the door to the stairway that led upward. It was pitch-dark; I flipped the light switch. "Owen? Tierney? What the hell's going on up here?"

Silence.

"Don't try jumping out at me," I called as I climbed the stairs, trying to ignore a sensation of tiny insects crawling on the backs of my arms and thighs. "Jump scares are so overdone, and you're not going to make me scream!"

A small voice inside me said: *It's DodgerBlodger.*

Which made no sense. Reaching the top step, I found the switch that illuminated the projection loft's two flickery fluorescent panels.

The room was a jumble of hulking projectors, looping wires, power strips, soda cans, and dust-coated movie swag. "Come out, come out, wherever you are!" I kept my voice steady, though blood rushed in my ears.

From the back of the room, someone yelled, "Boo!"

I screamed—the sound felt ripped from my lungs. I darted back to the door. And then, with my hand on the knob, ready to flee, I watched with a different kind of horror as Tierney reared up from behind one of the projectors and sauntered toward me, a nasty grin on his face.

Behind him, Maren crouched in the shadows. When she rose and came out, too, she looked like a high schooler who'd been caught making out behind the bleachers, her head hanging and her shirt untucked and half-buttoned.

"I'm sorry, Sam," she said, while Tierney stood with his arms crossed, smirking. "We didn't mean to scare you. We bumped into something, that's all."

Her hair was a mess, her lipstick smeared. The sweet story about seeing her mom had all been a front for hooking up with Spawn of Brenner.

Is this why we make excuses for assholes? It was a drumbeat in my head. Because we want to hook up with them? Or is it more than that— that we think they can give us something we can't give ourselves?

I turned and jogged back down the stairs without a word. Both of them followed me—Maren still apologizing, Tierney smug and silent.

"Out," I said when we reached the lobby, pointing at the glass doors. By then, my voice was more or less steady, but I still felt the vibration of that scream in my throat. "Unless you're closing up?"

He had heard me scream. He had *made* me scream. Something hardened and sharpened inside me, and I wanted to ram that smugness down his throat.

Not that I was going to do anything about it. All I could do was stand there.

They left—Tierney still with that languid strut, Maren practically skittering outside as she tossed some last excuses at me. Through the glass wall, I saw them pause and exchange what looked like a few awkward words. He touched her arm. She pulled away, drawing into herself. Then they went their separate ways across the parking lot.

My pulse still pounded as if I were back in the shadows of the projection room. An iron band seemed to be tightening around my forehead. I woke my phone and stared at Kiri's last diary entry, the only one I hadn't read.

It was time to do something. Time to take back control.

THE LAST NOTE IN KATIE DUNSMORE'S DIARY

June 6, Cape May

I don't know why I write these notes to myself, honestly. It's been so long since I even bothered.

When I was little, I used to pretend I had a sister who was older and away at boarding school. My diary was my imaginary letters to her. I told her all the things I couldn't tell Mom or Dad—how I worried that I wasn't pretty or fast or smart enough, and no one would ever love me.

But I don't need an imaginary sister anymore. Someone does love me! He loves me so much that he wants to be with me forever, just the two of us.

Omg, right?? Is it too soon? A red flag at the very least? But sitting on this beach on the edge of the continent, waiting for our big drive west, with the sun on my face and the surf lapping my toes—I want to say yes to being with him forever.

I should have said it when he asked me, the night of graduation. But something stuck in my throat, and I could see the disappointment in his eyes. I'm not the person he hoped I was. I'm not really free.

The past few months have been such a wild whirl: buying the van and fitting it up, planning the route, and getting supplies. Graduation. The cabin. I barely had a second to write. And when I did take a break, my whole brain was full of him. Writing a diary seemed like something I'd outgrown.

Now, though. On the road, space opens up in your head.

He doesn't like me to be on my phone—I'm only writing this now because he's on a walk down the beach. So when we're not talking, all I do is watch and think.

There's so much to see and feel! When we drive at night, with the groaning of the semis and the glow of reflective strips and the stink of gas in the humid air, I feel like we're going deeper and deeper into a dark canyon, and we'll come out the other end transformed into people who are beautiful and new.

Dad said a funny thing in the driveway just before I left. He held my face for an instant, and he said, "Katie, remember that every boy is just a boy." I wanted to laugh, but—

He's coming! Gotta go.

16

I didn't turn left, toward home and Kiri's. I swung right on the nearly empty highway and pedaled furiously toward the Pole Star Motel.

Anger kept my legs pumping and blood roaring in my ears as pools of streetlight passed over me. I was sick of being dicked around, sick of guys who treated women like shit and women who let them. *He doesn't like me to be on my phone.* Who made Callum God? Who gave him the right to control what Kiri did?

She did, that was who. She should have listened to her dad—even the most special person is just a person. Lore had kept telling me the same thing about Reggie, more or less, and I'd refused to hear it.

The motel's sickly white neon glowed through the dark, but the tall windows of the lodge were black except for one light in the reception area. I rode straight back through the lot to the place where I'd found the Grand Cherokee before, where the main motel building rose on a small hill. It was luminous white, with steps leading up to a porch that ran along a line of numbered doors.

The parking space at No. 17 was empty. Blackout curtains were pulled over the window, no light visible.

He had to be here! Disappointment was a stab to my gut, a metallic taste in my mouth, followed by a dizzying sense of deflation. I pedaled a circuit of the lot, searching for the Colorado plate. There was a Grand Cherokee, all right, but it was from New York.

Where could he be? Restaurants closed at nine. A downtown bar? Stalking Kiri again?

I propped the bike against a railing and marched up the steps to No. 17. Took a deep breath and knocked.

The cheap door rattled under my fist, making me flinch. I waited.

Then I tried again, wincing at the impact on my knuckles. Insects keened quietly in the grass.

The adrenaline had drained away, leaving me with a cold pit in my stomach. Even if West were here, he clearly wasn't receiving visitors.

Maybe it wasn't him I needed, though. In Aliza's comment section, he'd claimed to have something of Kiri's, an object. If it was an object, it could be inside that room right now.

Owen had talked about sneaking into the Pole Star through unlocked back windows. No. 17 was next to the concrete alley that ran between the building's two wings, around to the back. It wouldn't hurt to check.

I tiptoed past a humming ice machine. My heart thumped, that adrenaline flowing again. *This is just plain stupid.* The back window of No. 17 was half open but small.

As I walked up to it, I knew with a strange clarity that this was how I would start my first podcast episode. Not with browsing true-crime feeds, not with meeting Kiri, but with the moment when I walked up to this window behind a seedy motel and forced it wide enough to let me in.

The window yielded with a grating noise. The screen wasn't

latched. It was easy to shove it out of the way and hook my elbows over the sill.

I had crossed the invisible line from observing to interfering when I carried the message from West to Kiri. I'd trespassed by exploring the cabin. Now I was breaking and entering.

Or maybe I was kidding myself to think I'd ever been on the safe side of the line. From the moment I'd approached Kiri, acting like her friend, I'd been steering toward an ugly decision. Which mattered more to me: the story or her?

She might not want me to be here, but here I was.

I boosted myself over the sill and dropped into the darkness. The room had an odor I couldn't quite place: bleach mixed with something mustier. Woodsmoke?

Maybe West had been camping on his way here. The space felt vacant, but I had to be sure before I looked for a light switch, so I pulled out my phone.

The flashlight showed me empty twin beds with a lamp on a table between them. The bed on the left was perfectly made, obviously untouched. The one on the right was a tangle of sheets and blankets.

I switched on the lamp. Aggressively plaid wallpaper sprang out at me—one of those bold vintage design choices Owen had mentioned. When I managed to look away, I spotted a black duffel bag on top of the oak bureau.

It wasn't zipped. I went over and rifled through it as carefully as I could, lifting each layer of clothing in search of something—but what?

There were only sweatpants, T-shirts, boxers. The bureau drawers were empty. It took me maybe five minutes to search the rest of the place; West apparently wasn't the type to leave his stuff everywhere. A Jack Reacher paperback on the bedside table, the cover indented with a wild scrawl of overlapping letters as if someone had used it to write on. Shaving tools and a toothbrush in the spearmint-tiled bathroom.

I checked under the beds. In the closet. Along the molding above the door. Even in the toilet tank. Nothing!

Disappointment was setting in again, but it wasn't time to give up. I would wait a little longer outside for him to come back—I just couldn't let him know I'd been in here. Heading back to the window, past the slept-in bed, I saw something I'd missed before—a sheet of paper tacked to the headboard.

It was folded in half. A note for housekeeping? A tip? I pulled it free and opened it.

Facing me, handwritten in tall, spiky letters, were two words. And then I could guess what someone might have written on the book cover:

SEE YA.

17

I took the note with me when I left. On the back was printed info about the motel's pool hours and continental breakfast.

The pit in my stomach was deepening. West hadn't cleared out of the room, so who was saying *See ya* to him? It wasn't Kiri's handwriting.

I still didn't know why she'd reacted so strangely to West's message about the footprints. And after what I'd seen in the cabin—the evidence of her rage at Callum—I had to find out.

She'd said I was the only one who could help her. When she made me leave, it was only because we disagreed on what kind of help she needed.

That was the memory that propelled me back on the highway to Queen City Park Road. Past home, where I checked for but didn't see the Grand Cherokee. Past the ghost freeway and the deserted water treatment plant, through the park, all the way to Kiri's.

This time, I slipped around the dark side of the house to scope out the street. The Grand Cherokee wasn't here, either, though an NBC van was.

I darted back out of sight, into the backyard—where I found Kiri sitting on the deck in the starlight, her bare feet in the grass.

I opened my mouth, but before I could say a word, she jumped up and ran straight to me. Her long arms wrapped around me and squeezed me tight.

I couldn't breathe. I'd been worrying about her since I left her two nights ago, and here she was, her own breath coming warm and fast and a tendril of her hair brushing my cheek.

She drew back, holding me at arm's length. "I was scared you'd never come back."

"I'm back." She wore a black T-shirt and jean shorts, not her usual light colors. Her nearness gave me such a jolt that for a second I couldn't think of anything else to say. Then I grabbed both her hands and said, "I wasn't sure you wanted me to come. Have you seen West yet?"

I expected her to tense at the mention of his name, but she only shook her head in a weirdly giddy way. "We can talk about that later. I want to get out of here!" Her whole body seemed to vibrate as she squeezed my hands back. "C'mon. This house—it's killing me second by second."

I didn't resist as she tugged me across the backyard and uphill into the park. Her grip was strong, her exposed skin and hair glowing in the starlight. I half expected to see tiny sparks rise from the fine hairs on her arms as we fought our way through the undergrowth to the path.

She was still barefoot, and the gravel made her wince as if she were walking on hot coals. But she only laughed, as if the pain tickled her, and ran on ahead. "Come on, Sam! Keep up!"

I jogged after her, panting, through leaf-dappled light and pools of darkness. Kiri moved as deftly as if she had night vision. Last time I'd seen her, she'd been staring into the storm, paralyzed with terror. Now she seemed able to fly.

She'd lied to me last time, too, pretending she didn't know what had happened to Callum's cabin. She'd given me an ultimatum but no explanations, and that needed to change.

"Do you come here a lot at night?" I asked between gasps, catching up with her. The stars blazed fiercely among the tree branches.

"Oh no! I'm scared to come alone. I've always been scared." She darted ahead of me again, her laughter ringing out like a bird's stubborn cry. "I need you here! I was so afraid you hated me forever!"

"Of course I don't hate you!" I wanted to talk about what had happened last time, but I also didn't want to. Her giddiness was infectious. "You're the one who told me to leave."

"Forget about that! I was just surprised; I didn't know what I was saying." She veered off the path toward one of the cliff overlooks. Below us, the lake was a great stirring grayness cut off by the curve of the bay.

"So, about this meeting—"

"Where do people jump off the cliff?" she interrupted, gazing downward. "You've done it, right? You said there's a safe place."

It was just up the path. "But we shouldn't jump when it's dark," I said, though lots of kids did.

"Buzzkill. Show me!" She was full-on running now, legs a blur against the pale gravel. "If you don't, I'll just jump anywhere!"

She swerved toward the cliff again, and I grabbed her hand and yanked her backward. "You don't have a death wish, do you?"

Kiri didn't pull away from me. I felt her blood pulsing frantically just under the skin. "Like you think Callum did?" I shook my head, and she went on, "I don't want to die, I just don't want to *think*. This is a Burlington rite of passage, isn't it? If I don't do it now, I might miss out forever."

"We don't even have swimsuits." But she sounded serious, so I led her up the hill to where a big oak loomed against the sky. From there, a steep trail wound down along the cliff side to a ledge that jutted about forty feet over the deep water.

I kept stumbling over roots and rocks in the dark, and Kiri helped me up. By the time we reached the ledge, she was the one leading the way.

"It's not that high," she said, peering between cedar trunks down to the gently roiling water.

"High enough." I didn't mention that there was also a seventy-six-foot cliff nearby.

For a moment, I thought Kiri might change her mind after seeing the drop. Then she reached up and tugged her shirt over her head. In a flash, her shorts were off, too.

"Wait!" I yelled, but she didn't seem to hear. She took a few strides back and ran straight at the cliff edge.

My heart lurched as her long body arced outward. For a split second, she seemed to hang suspended in midair, arms over her head and toes pointed, an outline against distant city lights. Then she was falling, a pale streak against dark water, and then she was a splash of white foam.

"Kiri!" I ran to the edge, breathless and dizzy with terror. The splash had faded. The lake was calm. "Kiri!"

Her blond head broke the surface. "It's cold!" she shrieked. "Oh my God, that felt so good!"

Limp with relief, I grabbed a cedar for support. "You should have warned me first!"

"Sorry!" She backstroked easily in the deep water, tipping her head to look up at me. "C'mon! You have to do it, too!"

No, I don't. Yet somehow I knew I did. "You scared me half to death!" I said, stalling.

She did a neat surface dive, waggled her toes in the air, and emerged again. "Chicken!"

"Stop that! No peer pressure!" But I was laughing. If I'd jumped with Reggie, I could do it with Kiri. I unlaced my sneaks and yanked off my shorts and T-shirt. "We'll have to hike back up for our clothes, you know."

"Worry about that later!"

Worry about everything later. I walked to the edge of the cliff and looked down, toes gripping the stone. But no—you had to take it running, the way she had. That was the only way to be sure you wouldn't land in the shallows.

Stop being so uptight, Reggie whispered in my head. Then I remembered I'd already committed a crime tonight, breaking into the motel room—nothing uptight about that. A wild giggle rose in my throat, and I stepped back to the tree line, drew a deep breath, and ran.

I tried to keep myself straight with feet together, an arrow aimed at the lake, but I could feel myself tilting. The stars blurred above me. The air whistled in my ears. The water rushed up to meet me, smacking my thigh and forearm, *ouch*, and next came a shock of cold.

The momentum pulled me down, down until my toes grazed the bottom. It was soft clay and tangled eelgrass—nothing to push against. I flailed and kicked, my lungs aching, and fought my way back up until my head popped free of the water.

Kiri was right beside me. "Are you okay?"

"Yeah!" But I was gasping. I treaded water, trying to get my breathing under control. Part of me couldn't believe I was still alive.

She hooked her elbow through mine—her larger, athletic body supporting me. "You hit the water so hard."

"I'm okay. Really!" Right then, I wasn't embarrassed to lean on her.

Her hip grazed mine, both of us nearly naked. Heat rose in my chest, scary and a little pleasant at once.

Now that I definitely wasn't drowning, I was surprised at how okay I really did feel. The wind had been knocked out of me, but so had other things—doubt, fear.

The water temperature was starting to feel comfortable. She released me—a relief, but also a bit of a disappointment—and I rolled on my back and looked up. The sky was spangled with stars I could swear I'd never seen before: some bold and brash like gems, some delicate like freckles, some fine as dust.

Beside me, Kiri drew in her breath. "Over there! Make a wish!"

I caught the tail end of the shooting star, a bright fleck zipping across the sky to vanish on the horizon. "I don't believe in wishes."

"Silly!" She shoulder-bumped me. "How can you not believe in wishes? Don't you ever wish for anything?"

I remembered breaking into the motel room and having the sudden inspiration about how to kick off my podcast. It was a kind of wish, but not one I could tell her about. "Let's go up before someone steals our stuff."

We saw another shooting star while we climbed back to the top of the cliff. It crossed my mind that if I were Tierney, or probably even Owen, I would have strained my eyes through the dark to get a better look at Kiri in her underwear. But her presence was like a light in the dark, a magnetic charge on my skin, and that was more than enough.

When we reached the ledge, we flopped down and caught our breaths. Kiri said, "When we met in the park, and you scared me by fooling around on the edge of the cliff—that's when I knew I wanted to spend more time with you."

I gulped a guilty laugh. "Why?"

"I thought you were a daredevil, like...him. He was always daring me to push my limits." A pause. She stretched out her long legs. "I guess I miss it."

"My friend Reggie, she was like that, too," I admitted. "When I met you in the park, I was trying to act like her. Everything scary I've ever done, she dared me to."

"You were scared to talk to me?" There was an odd softness in Kiri's tone.

I laughed. "Of course!"

"But you didn't seem like it. So maybe you're braver than you think."

Maybe I was. Or maybe it was the easy trust in her voice, or the safety of the darkness, that made me ask what I did next: "What happened to the chickens, Kiri?"

Kiri's head snapped toward me. "Chickens?"

"Callum's chickens. At his cabin."

"Miranda? We ate her. You read that in my diary, right?" A strange, harsh laugh. "Is that what you're talking about—my diary?"

I'd been dreading this conversation, but it had to happen. "No, I went to the cabin yesterday. Just like you told me not to. But you also didn't delete the address from your diary, so I can't help wondering... *Did* you want me to? Did you want me to see all that?"

Kiri drew in a sharp breath. Crickets chirped rhythmically from the woods behind us. After a moment, she said, "Of course I didn't want you to."

"I..."

"But I guess you did."

For the first time, I became aware of my whole right side stinging from the impact with the water. The cold must have numbed me. Still I pressed on: "So maybe now you can help me understand the end of your diary. Callum never planned to come back from the road trip, did he?"

Kiri drew her knees to her chest and hugged them. "No. But he didn't want to die—he was going to cross the border into British Columbia and disappear. He wanted me to come with him to Vancouver Island."

I want to do it, she'd written in her diary. *I want to say yes to being with him forever.* I'd thought maybe he'd proposed marriage or living together—something normal.

"Why would Callum disappear?" I kept my voice neutral.

"He said it was time to leave the world behind and get serious about survival."

"And this 'doomsday cabin'—is it a real place?" It was the least threatening way I could think of to ask her about West's message. "On Vancouver Island, for instance?"

Kiri sighed. Then she rose, bent gracefully to pick up her shorts, and started dressing. "What happened at the cabin—Cal called it a potlatch. It's an Indigenous tradition where you destroy a bunch of stuff to show everybody how little material things mean to you. He sold Parsley—the goat—to a cheesemaker, but he did want to slaughter the chickens."

I shuddered, reaching for my own clothes. "Did you?"

"I told him that was cultural appropriation, and then I put the chickens in the Prius and drove them to the farm down the road where he got them. The farmer was nice. She was happy to have a few more laying hens."

So there was a happy ending for the chickens, anyway. I scrambled to my feet, feeling self-conscious now as a cool breeze hit my skin, and pulled my shirt over my head. "But you were there for this potlatch thing? You helped him do it?"

"I guess." Kiri's laugh was nervous, as if her strange bravado were draining away, leaving her as anxious as she'd been during our earlier conversations. "Cal wanted to make it look like he had badass enemies after him. When he got settled in Canada, he'd weave it into the narrative of his brand—being on the run. He said we could be an outlaw power couple like in *Natural Born Killers*, only without the killing."

Drea Flint and her boyfriend had been obsessed with that movie, too. That sure hadn't ended well for them. "So Callum planned to keep posting videos? How was he supposed to disappear, then?" If anyone would try to reconcile being famous and being invisible, it was Callum Massey.

"I don't know. He stopped talking about it because I told him I needed time to decide. I really wanted to go to college." Another sigh. "But I helped him trash the house, because he said his fans would find it and post pics and it would be legendary. It was the least I could do."

Now was the moment to ask. I couldn't let it slip by. "I saw what you wrote on the wall. With the Sharpie."

But she wasn't listening to me. Her head had whipped halfway around, and she was scrutinizing the woods behind us. "What was that?"

"Where?"

"Shh." Her gaze stayed on the tree line. "I thought something was moving."

Nothing looked to me like it was moving but the gray blurs of cedars and maples, their crowns shifting in the breeze. "You're not used to the woods," I said, remembering what Owen had told me yesterday.

"I used to be. All this time in the house, it's been messing with my head."

We walked back through the park in silence, shivering in our damp clothes. Every time a twig cracked, our heads swiveled as one.

"Why did you ask if I'd seen West?" Kiri asked. "Have you?"

I shook my head.

"Are you sure? That he's not still following you, I mean?"

"I haven't seen him or his Grand Cherokee." I didn't feel ready to tell her about the *See ya* message, since I'd also have to tell her how I'd found it. "Look, I keep thinking about West's weird message. The doomsday cabin and the footprints. Why do you think he'd tell you that he made those prints in the campsite?"

"I don't know!" But she said it too quickly, her voice high with discomfort. "Maybe that's not what he actually..." She broke off. "Look, Sam, did it scare you seeing the stuff I wrote about Cal on the walls?"

It was a sudden change of subject, but I was glad to get back to that. "Yeah. I guess it did."

"Did it make you wonder if I could have done something to Cal?"

Katydids trilled from the long grass. "Yes," I said, then remembered the card I'd found. *Love you to infinity.* "Was there another girl? Is that why you were pissed at him?"

"A girl?" Kiri sounded genuinely confused. "No! There wasn't any other girl that I know of. I was pissed because I didn't like his plan to trash the cabin—it was wasteful. And he *asked* me to write creepy stuff on the walls, so...I let my feelings out. If it bothered him, he didn't say."

We turned off the path into the woods, heading for her backyard. Someone's distant porch light bobbed through the darkness. "If I were you, I would have been pissed at Callum for a lot of reasons," I said, remembering everything I'd read in the diary.

I waited for her to defend Callum. But she said, "I wish I were more like you, Sam. You don't let anybody push you around."

"Me?" I had to laugh, thinking of everything that had happened today. I'd let Tierney provoke me not once but twice. Aliza Deene's theories had pissed me off and so I'd told the world about the cabin. "I don't think you know me that well."

"You wouldn't have fallen for Callum, though." She spoke in a small voice. "Everybody looks up to him. People think I wasn't good enough, or maybe I resented him for being perfect, and so I had to...to..."

"Everybody does *not* think that." Never mind Aliza Deene and her followers. "Anyway, Callum isn't some untouchable, perfect ideal. He was—is—human."

"But if he wasn't perfect, then there wasn't any *point*." She seemed to be shrinking into herself.

"Point to what?"

"I don't know. Everything. Do you think I'm stupid to say that? After reading my diary—after finding out how much I let him change me—do you think I'm stupid?"

I held back the tree branches so we could step onto her lawn. "I'm not the one to judge. I did the same thing with Reggie sometimes— put her on a pedestal. People make mistakes." *But we don't have to keep making them.*

"I guess so." Paused on the edge of the lawn, Kiri rubbed her cheek with the back of one hand. "It's just—I feel like everybody's closing in on me. They think I'm a horrible person. No matter what I did or didn't do, they won't let me go."

I wanted to throw my arms around her and say it would all be okay. I wanted to touch her in the easy, reassuring way she'd touched me in the lake. But I didn't know how to start. "You're telling the truth. *I* know that."

Not something a reporter or podcaster would say to a subject. Just something I wanted to believe right now.

It was a relief to return to the warmth and comfort of the basement den. I tossed my backpack on the sectional while Kiri flicked on the TV—a *Friends* rerun with the volume low.

"I thought you didn't watch TV."

"I started last night. It keeps me company. But only the old sitcoms. I stay away from news channels. Sam…"

She bent and slid something out from under one of the couch cushions. Her face was suddenly as stiff and solemn as a marble statue, and I knew there was something she hadn't told me.

"Today I found this tacked to one of the trees on the edge of our backyard," she said, holding out the object to me. It was a piece of paper folded to the size of someone's palm.

I unfolded it—and instantly recognized the dark, spiky hand-writing, a perfect match for the *See ya* note I had in my pack.

This one said: IF YOU'RE WILLING TO GO NORTH, FINALLY, MEET ME 8/14 AT HIGH NOON, WHERE THE ECHOES FLY LIKE OWLS.

"West." He was lurking around the park. He was in the motel room. The handwriting had to be his, and he could have written the *See ya* note to tack to another tree, wherever they were supposed to meet, if she didn't show up there before he headed out.

"So he still wants that meeting with you," I said, my heart sinking. Maybe that was the reason for her strange excitement tonight. When West saw I wasn't going to help, he'd found a way around me. "But where's this place with the echoes? And what does he mean by—"

I stopped, because Kiri clearly wasn't listening. She was staring at the TV behind me, violet light flickering on her face.

I turned to look, too. And the breath left me—all at once with a hard jolt, the way it had when I hit the water.

It was a news break. Above the logo of a Plattsburgh TV station, the flashing lights of police cruisers illuminated a desert landscape.

A woman's voice said: "These are images from a little earlier tonight in Lost Village National Monument, New Mexico, where the National Park Service reports they've discovered human remains in a crevice at the foot of a cliff wall. This was just about a mile and a quarter from the spot where Vermonter YouTubers Callum Massey and his girlfriend, Kiri Dunsmore, had their campsite in July."

18

Birds were singing everywhere, warbling and trilling, so loud they might have been trapped inside my skull.

I groaned and opened my eyes to the flicker of television light. Beyond the muted flat-screen, gray dawn shone through the curtains. I bolted upright on Kiri's sectional, throwing back the blanket she'd given me last night. A gray hump on the middle section was her.

The station was playing a cheery morning show, but all I saw in my mind's eye were the orange-red rocks, the flashing lights, and the serious-looking reporters who kept saying the same thing:

Human remains found in the desert.

Transported to the medical examiner. Still unidentified.

Bile rushed into my throat as I swung my bare feet onto the carpet. I was so tired, and I needed to think, and I couldn't do it with her beside me.

I'd wanted to ask so many questions last night, but the set of Kiri's shoulders told me that if I tried, she might fly apart—scream at me, shove me out the door. Or worse, she might dissolve into wordless, unending sobs.

And I wouldn't be able to comfort her, because I couldn't be sure what she was grieving. Until I knew whether the remains were Callum and how he had died, I couldn't be sure of anything.

So I sat beside her in the dark room and waited patiently, close enough to feel the shiver of her indrawn breath. She flipped through the news channels, stopping whenever we reached that same desert scene. Once I heard her sniffle, and I reached for her hand and clasped it. She didn't pull away, but she didn't meet my eyes, either.

My clothes still smelled of the lake. How could a night begin so well and go so wrong?

As I stood up, Kiri raised her head. Her hair was wild, her eyes red-rimmed. "Wait," she said. "Not yet."

"Your folks will be up soon."

"I need to give you something!" Again she slid a hand under the couch cushions, and I braced myself for some new find as unsettling as the note West had left her.

Kiri clutched whatever-it-was in her hand. "Sam, remember last night, when you said you could tell I was telling the truth?"

"Yeah." But when I said that, I hadn't known there was a body in the desert—a body that would soon be identified. A body that could lead to an arrest.

She must have seen the hint of doubt on my face. "I need to know if you still think I'm not a bad person, after you know what really happened out there. But you have to know everything."

What she handed me was a stack of paper, but the minuscule handwriting on it was Kiri's own. Pages from a notebook, folded into a tight packet about the size of a wallet.

"This is the rest of my diary," she said. "I kept it on me, always, so he wouldn't find it. It was hidden in the back pocket of my shorts when I walked out of the desert. Nobody's ever read it but me—and now you."

I stared at the pages. Words leapt out at me, sloppy and urgent—
diary, phone, snit. I wanted to open it, and I was afraid of what I'd find
inside. *You have to know everything*, she'd said. But now, with a corpse
recovered from the desert, those words rang sinister.

"I can't promise you anything," I said after a moment. "About how
I'll react."

She nodded as if she'd expected that. "It doesn't go all the way to
the end anyway. Tonight, when you've read that, I'll tell you the rest."

**VIDEO POSTED TO
CALLUM MASSEY'S CHANNEL
ON JULY 25 AT 9:10 PM**

Strips of neon pink glow over a desert horizon, mingling with tatters of cloud, all of it so bright that we can't see much of anything else.

Kiri speaks off-camera: "Check out the sunset! How's this for staying on-brand?"

Cut to a blurry, upside-down view of the landscape as Kiri walks with the phone. A campfire winks in one corner.

Cut to her face with firelight throwing every feature into relief. Her eyes are dark pits as she says, "I know I need to start hiking out, just like he told me to, even if there's nothing to go back to. If I stay here, I'll end up a pile of bones. Or like the German who lost his head."

All of a sudden, she smiles—goofy, childish. "I'm so silly, right? Running around like a chicken with her head cut off. Poor Miranda. I didn't want to forgive you for that, but I did, and then we went to those caves for my birthday, and the echoes flew all around us like owls, and I knew I loved you. Even if the world's ended, I do want to walk out of here alive. I do."

FROM KIRI DUNSMORE'S DIARY

JUNE 8, DC

Well! Apparently it's not a good idea for me to write a diary on my phone. It could be hacked. Or maybe I'd get in a snit and suddenly decide to send the whole thing to Dad or Mom or a friend (ha, what friend?), and then our privacy would be compromised. People might know exactly where we're going and what we're doing.

<u>His</u> privacy would be compromised.

I can't be trusted. I'm overdependent on my phone in general, like so many girls. Worse, I posted a selfie on the beach that was from an unflattering angle. I just don't understand brand management. So this afternoon he took my phone away.

It's not permanent. Of course. I'm learning how to use the phone only when it's really necessary, how to post Intentionally, and when I've mastered that, he'll give it back.

Fine. But I needed my phone at the party, and it wasn't fair to leave me staring at the freaking wall.

I didn't want to go anyway, but Cal said this might be his last chance to see his friends, ever, and he needed me to be there so they could be dazzled by my beauty. Always with the compliments. This time I didn't smile back at him.

We drove to the huge house of some girl named Susanna who went to private school with C. Her house was perfect. So was she. I felt like a dirty troll that crawled down from Vermont.

They all sat on an outdoor terrace drinking microbrews and smoking special organic weed, both of which Callum and I couldn't do because substances blunt your survival reflexes. They talked about people they knew from school. Another perfect girl ran up and grabbed C's hand and whispered in his ear, and they disappeared together.

I sat there and watched the sunset, pretending I didn't care, until finally a guy sat down with me. It was C's best friend, West—I was finally meeting him.

West seemed cool at first. He has big brown eyes that you could vanish into, and when he asked me questions about my life, I got the sense he wanted to know the real me, not just me as "Cal's girlfriend."

Some of the questions were a little weird, though. He asked why I wasn't eating the party food, and whether it's tough on me how C likes to control every aspect of a shoot. He asked how I'm getting home after Lost Village National Monument. So apparently he knows about C's plan to disappear, which I didn't expect. I thought it was our secret.

When C came back, I worried he'd think we'd been flirting, but he didn't seem bothered. On the way home, though, he said, "I'd be careful with West. When we were in high school, this creepy thing happened between him and this thirteen-year-old girl, my neighbor. He sweet-talked her because he wanted her to steal things for him. He would've gone to juvie if I hadn't talked to the girl's parents and saved his ass."

I said I couldn't believe he hadn't warned me about West sooner, and why would he lie to protect someone like that? We kind of got into an argument. C kept saying that nothing really happened, and the girl just made a big deal out of it because she had mental issues, and anyway, she's twenty years old now, so who cares?

Well, I care. As I listened, I started having this nagging feeling that C might not be telling the entire truth. I've seen him lie in his videos—he's good at it. He says that lying online is different from lying to people you love, it's "creative fictioning for engagement," which apparently is fine.

Apparently.

Now he's out running, and I'm in his old room in his parents' house. I found this empty notebook and tore out a bunch of pages so I can keep writing without my phone. So there!

The more I think about what we did to C's cabin, the more his whole plan feels wrong. I keep waiting for him to say it's just a stunt to get more subscribers to his channel, or some kind of loyalty test for me.

If you love someone, you should be willing to drop everything for them—family, college, future. You should <u>always</u> believe they're telling the truth.

I hope C's just testing me. Maybe the phone thing is no different from when he asks if I want to stop at McD's or Burger King and of course I say no, always no.

I still wish he hadn't taken the phone away. I wish he'd trusted me and let me control it so I could show him how little I really need it when I have him. I feel like we're climbing the same mountain and he's always ahead of me, but I'll reach his altitude eventually! I don't want him to leave me behind.

The thing no one tells you about being in love is that sometimes it makes you the loneliest person in the world.

19

Want to lay bets on when they arrest her? I'm guessing today.

    Nah. Takes at least 24 hrs for the ME's report to come in.

I wasn't even listening to Aliza's monologue anymore, just reading the comments. A three-hour-old post already had nearly five hundred of them.

They won't need the ME report if they found a kn1fe stuck in his chest.

Was there a kn1fe missing from the campsite?

They need to be thorough for probable cause. Anyway, they're watching her. It's not like they'll let her go anywhere.

I shouldn't be reading strangers' uninformed opinions when I had to finish the diary. Kiri had as good as told me I didn't know the whole story yet, and whether she was guilty or innocent, her words were the only route to the truth.

But the Grand Nine was unexpectedly busy—by our standards, anyway. Every time I picked up Kiri's secretively folded packet of papers, a new customer drifted in. Then Lore texted me some videos of Puffball going wild with a new toy, and then Maren came by to have a heart-to-heart about last night.

I told her again that she had nothing to apologize for, that I understood acting on impulse. But her cheeks flushed, and I realized with a sinking sensation that she hadn't just been hooking up with Tierney, at least not in her mind. She liked him.

"I keep telling myself it's just a rebound thing," she said. "But maybe there's something actually there, you know?"

My nod must not have been convincing, because Maren added, "Last night, I told him to stop being a jerk to you. I honestly think he's still a little jealous because Reggie liked you so much."

Jealous? Reggie had ditched me without a second thought. But Maren looked so earnest that I thanked her for trying.

After the fifth or sixth interruption, I finally gave up and started scrolling on my phone, because comment sections were easier to read in bite-size pieces than Kiri's diary was. Then, of course, I couldn't stop, mesmerized by the parade of accusations and speculations. And then it was time to sweep the theaters after the first show.

I was cleaning Theater Three when someone started yelling out in the lobby—a man's voice with a raw edge. Though I couldn't make out words, I could almost see the veins bulging in his neck.

Occasionally a customer makes trouble. Maren was selling tickets alone, so I dropped the broom and jogged back to her.

But it was only Tierney, looking like he'd been on a bender. His eyelids were red and crusted, and he leaned on the counter as if he didn't trust himself to stay upright. Maren had her arm around him and was making soothing noises.

"What happened?" I asked, not especially wanting to know.

Tierney opened his mouth and emitted a grating laugh that made me wince and sounded like it hurt him, too. "Got carjacked last night. They knocked me out and took the Range Rover."

"Shit," said Owen, who'd also come running in response to the noise. Our eyes met, and I saw a rivulet of sweat trickling down his neck.

Maren bent over her phone. "I'll call the police, and then we're taking you to the ER. You might have a concussion."

Owen helped Tierney into a chair. "Do you have a headache? Or feel nauseous?"

Tierney kept his burning, angry gaze on me. "This little bitch. It's all her fault."

"Of course it's not!" Maren said.

"Well, it happened right here in the parking lot, like two minutes after you left me." He gave her a meaningful glance that Owen probably caught. "I go to open the door of the Range Rover and *bam*!" He mimed a blow to the back of his own head. "That asshole ambushed—ambushed me! Next thing I know, I wake up in the woods zip-tied to a fucking tree."

"Sam didn't knock you out." Maren looked as if she were wondering whether he might have a traumatic brain injury.

"I didn't say that."

"Then who? Was it one person, or multiple?" Owen asked.

"One. Real big dude, *huge* dude, but I didn't see his face." Tierney lurched to his feet, throwing off Owen's restraining arms, and brandished his hands at me. "Check this out, Sammy. You satisfied?"

What was he talking about? I stepped closer—and flinched at the sight of angry red ligature marks on his wrists. "How'd you get away?"

"Sawed the ties with a rock. Took me all night." His bloodshot blue eyes were murderous. "When I finally got out of those woods, I realized I was up in the sticks, halfway to the border. That creep has my phone, so I had to hitchhike back here."

Owen patted Tierney's back. "You're lucky to be alive, man."

"No shit." Tierney glared at me. "I could be chained up in a basement right now. *You* don't care, do you? Look at that stone face."

Owen looped an arm around Tierney's waist and guided him out of the booth. "We're gonna take a drive, okay? Just a nice, peaceful drive to the hospital."

"Can you describe the guy who did it?" Maren asked in a panicky voice. "I should probably tell them all the—"

Tierney broke free of Owen and came toward me in two staggering strides. Close up, I could see dried blood in his hair and a tremor at the corner of his mouth. "Who is he?" He spat out the words, fists forming at his sides. "Your dad? Your brother? Your boyfriend? You really want to see me hurt, don't you? Just because of Reggie?"

The floor pitched gently, and my mouth went dry. "I don't understand."

Tierney's gaze stayed on mine, glassy with fury. "'You leave the little redhead alone from now on.'" He made a sound like the beginning of a laugh or a sob. "That's what he said to me—the only thing he said before he left me out there in the dark. And then—"

He hurled something at me—a crumpled piece of paper like a spitball. "That was pinned to my fucking jacket. You must know what it means."

Owen got a long arm around Tierney and steered him toward the door, whispering calming things in his ear. I stood where I was, frozen, until they were outside.

Then I picked up the crumpled paper and unfolded it.

The spiky handwriting was sickeningly familiar.

TELL SAM TO DO EVERYTHING HER OLD FRIEND ASKS HER TO. ONLY WAY SHE'LL EVER KNOW THE TRUTH.

FROM KIRI DUNSMORE'S DIARY

JUNE 15

So busy all the time now. So tired. I guess I thought a road trip would be this leisurely thing, but it's the opposite. We shoot every day, and then one of us edits while the other drives, and before we know it, it's sunset and we have to find our campground for the night.

I guess this is what West meant when he kept asking me whether I can "keep up with" Cal. He must have been tired all the time, too. But he doesn't understand C the way I do. C is still a little boy inside, a boy whose parents spoiled him but didn't truly love him—which is why he needs everything just right, for everyone's praise. That's why he doesn't trust anyone to love him as much as they should, and that's why I show him over and over again that I can and I do love him, every day.

Sooner or later, he'll believe me.

JUNE 19

We have a new game. We aren't allowed to say more than a couple sentences to other people—servers, tourists, gas station attendants. We have to pretend that civilization has already collapsed and we're focused on our own survival and nothing else. Any of them could decide to kill us for our supplies.

Sometimes when he's not looking, I break the rules. Avoiding other people makes me jumpy.

JUNE 23

There is a gaping, gnawing pit in my stomach. It comes and goes; some days are fine. Not today. I'm in the best shape of my life, I look good on camera, and when I stand in the magic light (always magic light! Hurry, don't miss the magic light!), he tells me, "You're legendary." But the pit does not go away. Or maybe there's a gerbil in there, gnawing on my intestines. I'm getting enough daily calories and nutrients. We have a spreadsheet of our nutritional needs. I should be fine.

JUNE 25

Feel SO much better today! Like I ditched my shy, mousy childhood self when I flushed the sugar and carbs out of my body. I'm not scared anymore to gun it on these long, flat highways. I can control the van. I'm weightless and flying!

JUNE 26

We look at our phones together at 9:00 PM sharp, after we've built the fire. That's the rule. The rest of the time, they stay together in the glove compartment, on the honor system. But today we got separated at a rest stop, and I glanced around the side of the building and saw him standing back there tapping on his phone, totally breaking the rules.

So maybe he has his weak moments, too, that he hides because he wants to set a good example for me. I wish he'd be more honest, but knowing he's not perfect doesn't make me love him less. Just the opposite! I wish he felt safe being his flawed, human self with me.

JUNE 28

I'm getting exponentially better on camera! (I was such a disaster at first.) I smile at all the invisible viewers out there and say we're having the adventure of a lifetime. C says there are lots of comments about how pretty I am, but he won't show me because some of them, predictably, are from gross guys. He doesn't want me to feel unsafe.

JUNE 29

My favorite part of each day is cuddling by the fire. It makes everything worth it.

I feel like I've aged ten years since graduation. Being out here, driving across blistering hot Texas with the man you love, you get to know all sides of him. We might as well be an old married couple.

I haven't brought up the phone incident, but it makes me smile inside. Sometimes I wonder, though: If I can love his weaknesses, why can't he love mine?

JULY 2

Almost passed out today. I had to do a one-minute narration on camera in front of this place called the Sands Diner (classic roadside Americana, he said), and I kept messing it up.

I repeated the script, I swear, thirty times, and he wouldn't let me wear a hat, so the sun shone in my eyes, and suddenly my stomach went all swimmy and my knees buckled and I had to sit down.

I wanted to go again after he gave me some water and a PowerBar, but he said he'd just use the best take. Ugh. I wanted to get it right.

JULY 5

We talked to so many strangers yesterday, breaking the rules; if this were a real postapocalyptic scenario, we'd be dead. The pit was gaping inside me, and there was a Waffle House. Let's not get into it.

Talked to Mom last night, and she said I look great in the vids—"So mature!" Did <u>she</u> survive the apocalypse, then? I hope so. We'll be in Lost Village tomorrow, and Vermont is a million miles away. I can't wait to stay put for a bit—travel is exhausting!

JULY 6

Tomorrow we'll leave the van to hike all the way to the campsite, toting our gear in two trips. It's stinking hot, but I don't care because this is the strangest, most stunning place I've ever been! It's like the surface of Mars, everything red and grainy as if it's been decaying for millennia. You can see paths worn in the rock by the Pueblo peoples who lived here in the 1300s. The cliffs are full of little round caves where they made drawings. Lost Village really was a village once—or even a bustling city!—but now it's empty, just sand and rocks and wind and junipers and the enormous, burning sky.

I'm so glad now that I didn't listen to West when he showed up at the rest stop yesterday. He can say what he wants. But would he really come all the way from his summer job in Flagstaff just because he's worried about me? No. He hates (or likes?) C too much, and he wants to come between us.

Everything he said could have been a lie.

West isn't strong enough to survive the collapse. He doesn't understand literally anything.

20

The comments went on and on:

This thing is open and shut. Can't believe anyone ever thought the girl who was covered in his BLOOD is innocent.

I hope they put that b1tch away forever.

She'll plead emotional abuse and get a suspended sentence.

Callum deserves justice.

Callum was an abuser and she was a fame whore. They deserved each other.

I raised my head to glance around the deserted lobby. From Theater Three came the muffled boom of a supervillain's superweapon trying to destroy the world. My heart vibrated with it, and my head buzzed with something more than exhaustion.

All this time I'd been telling myself West didn't seem like the violent type, even if he had been out there in the campsite. Now he'd carjacked Tierney and damn near killed him, and he'd done it to send me a message. *Tell Sam to do everything her old friend asks her to.*

He had to mean Kiri. But West had already arranged the meeting himself—tomorrow at noon, "where the echoes fly like owls"—and

I couldn't see why he needed me at all. What he'd done to Tierney sickened me, and I hoped Kiri would feel the same way.

Where the echoes fly like owls—what did that even mean? A place in the park? There was something naggingly familiar about it.

I grabbed my phone and searched Kiri's first electronic diary, but nothing about echoes or owls came up. So I found the videos that she'd posted from the desert and watched them again in order.

When I reached the end of the one she'd posted at sunset on July 25, my heart leapt into my throat. She was speaking the very words:

"We went to those caves for my birthday, and the echoes flew all around us like owls."

Something squeezed tight in my chest. *I know where it is.*

A man came up to buy a ticket for the 4:30 Czech movie, and I had to smile and sell it to him. It hurt to act normal. Outside, the sun muscled its way through the clouds and poured down on the plate glass.

When he was gone, I retraced my thought process. Where had Callum and Kiri gone on her birthday? His parents' cottage and some caves, both in Quebec.

Canada. Across the border. That was where West wanted to meet her—in another country, out of the FBI's jurisdiction.

I propped my elbows on the counter and wrapped my arms around myself, chills washing over my shoulders and down my spine.

Whatever exactly they'd done in the desert, West wanted to escape with Kiri, and he hoped she wanted the same. Maybe he'd stolen the Range Rover so he could cross the border in a car that wasn't linked to him. But if so, why hadn't he just picked Kiri up and taken her along? Too tricky to arrange? Too dangerous?

Must be. And that was why he needed me—why *they* needed me.

Kiri had no intention of being arrested. That was why she'd been so weird and giddy last night. Even before she heard the news about the body, her plan was set. And I was a piece of that plan—a plan that, if I went along with it, would make me a criminal myself.

Dread swept over me in waves. There was never going to be a podcast. There never could have been one. The closer I got to the case, the less I could see the whole story. And if I did emerge knowing everything, I would be too compromised ever to tell it.

Tears blurred my vision, and I closed my eyes and put my head down on the counter. Behind my eyelids, I saw Kiri splashing, laughing, skipping through the midnight park as if she were invincible. Had any of that been real, or was it all part of her strategy to draw me so close to her that I couldn't tear myself away?

"Sam. Hey, Sam!"

A voice cut through my roiling thoughts, painfully familiar. It couldn't be her, not after all this time. Not now.

But then I opened my eyes, and there she was.

"Sam! You sleeping on the job now?"

Reggie. Her mouth was a little too glossy, her smile a little too wide.

FROM KIRI DUNSMORE'S DIARY

JULY 9

I keep meaning to write, but we're always together now and I'm just so tired. The gaping pit isn't the problem—I think the desert burned all my hunger out of me.

Which is lucky, because from now until August 1, when we leave here, we live off our supplies and the desert. No restocking. I don't feel optimistic about surviving on prickly pears, so we just have to make the dehydrated mush and grains and jerky last.

I wish C wouldn't leave me alone by the fire like this. I don't trust it to keep cougars away. He heard there's a spring over by the bikers' campsite, so he went there to get water.

The bikers creep me out. There's this girl with them—maybe my age—wearing scruffy cutoffs, and when we met, she stared at me with the deadest eyes I've ever seen. Maybe she was born after the apocalypse and has never known a world where you don't need to survive.

C says I need to drop all my oppressive value judgments if I'm going with him to Canada.

Which I am! I don't know when I decided, but when I think about going home, my stomach clenches up. Even if I went back and Burlington were somehow still there, I would be waiting for the disaster that brings it all down. I feel so much safer out here where I don't have to wait. I live in the after-times now; I can't go back to the before.

The red dirt has turned my whole body a faint bronze color, and I could swear there's sand _under_ my skin.

I know the world hasn't ended, of course. Lol. I'm not losing my mind. But to know that C was somewhere in the wilderness without me and I could never see him again, never ever, except maybe on his channel like I was just another fan— I wouldn't survive that.

He says he'd never find a replacement for me, but I know he would. People are drawn to C.

The girl with the bikers, for instance: Her eyes didn't look dead when they focused on him. They looked hungry. Just thinking about that, I feel the pit open inside me again.

Come back, C. When I finish writing, I'll close my eyes and count—to 100, maybe 200, just to be sure. When I open my eyes, you'll be back.

And I won't think about what happened to the treasure-hunting German that German's Gulch is named after. Some people say this place is cursed, but C says it's the crucible where we're being reborn.

I'll count to 300. I won't think about headless treasure hunters. When I'm done, C will be back.

21

W ell," I said, "look what the cat dragged in."

Reggie's hair was its natural black with a swoosh of cherry red now. She wore a midlength, conservative skirt with her halter, and the nose ring was gone. Her wiry body hadn't changed, and neither had her bright, restless gaze—eyes like silver pinballs, always moving.

I expected her to lob a comeback at me. That was how we used to communicate: in friendly insults. But instead, she seemed to shrink a little. Then she said, "Could we maybe go out back to the cemetery? It's been a while, and I just...wanted to touch base."

"Sure thing! I'll just get Maren to take the redge." I flashed her a plastic smile as if she were a customer. This was starting to feel like the worst day of my life, but the last thing I wanted was for Reggie to know how much she'd hurt me.

So I texted Maren—Owen was still with Tierney at the ER—and led Reggie out through Theater One, doing my best to ignore the angry pounding in my temples.

She sat down where we always used to: beside the leaning tombstone of Ezekiel Martinbank, b. 1841, d. 1863, where two cedars met to cast a funereal twilight. "Oh my God, memories," she said, not meeting my eyes. "I feel like I never left."

Her wistful tone made something lurch inside me, as if our hearts were connected by a live wire. "Well, you did leave," I said gruffly. And then, "Are you back because you heard what happened to Tierney?" It seemed weird that Owen would have called her, but I couldn't imagine why else she'd come.

Reggie stared at me. "No. What happened to Tierney?"

My chest tightened again. I explained as quickly as I could, leaving out all the parts that had to do with me.

Reggie's eyes opened wide. When I was done, she said, "I can't believe it! Well, I mean, that Range Rover is practically an invitation, but poor Tier. We were the ones obsessed with true crime, and he's the one a true crime actually happened to."

"I know, right?" I raised my chin. Two could play at the game of being too cool to care. "So, if you're not here for him, then why are you here?"

Reggie was looking at me now, her eyes glistening in a way I couldn't interpret. "I've been meaning to visit ever since I came back to Vermont for the summer. I have an internship at Spruce Peak Performing Arts Center."

"Nice," I said neutrally. So she'd been in Stowe all summer, forty minutes away, and hadn't even texted me.

"It's great, yeah. I might go back to school for theater tech. I wanted to come sooner, but I just…" She dropped her gaze again. "I feel so bad."

"About what?" I was starting to hate the jaunty fakeness of my voice. But if I showed even a hint of weakness, then we would snap back to the way we'd been before. Just like Kiri and Callum: Reggie climbing that mountain and me desperately trying to keep up.

Kiri's words from last night came back to me: *But if he wasn't per-fect, then there wasn't any* point. In her diary, she'd written the exact opposite: that she didn't love Callum any less for not being perfect, and that she wished he could love her weaknesses the way she loved his. What had changed between then and now?

Had she killed Callum because he wasn't perfect? Because they couldn't forgive each other for being human?

"Sam." The throb in Reggie's voice sounded pity-adjacent, and it made me tense. "I don't mean to come back and stir things up. You look like you're doing great. But I've been wanting to apologize for ghosting you, and for everything shitty I did leading up to that."

I grabbed a button on my flannel shirt and twisted. It was an effort to make my voice come out in a DGAF tone: "Ghosting me? I thought I was the one who ghosted you."

"I don't know anymore!" Reggie cleared her throat, and I could tell that my refusal to react was frustrating her. "All I know is that I behaved like a trash fire of a person that night at Tierney's. I mean, you were seventeen!"

She sounded so pearl-clutchy and unlike herself that I couldn't help snapping back, "Sheesh, I could handle myself! Anyway, you're only two-and-a-half years older."

But, as memories of that January night flooded back, an oily sick-ness spread out its tendrils in my stomach.

We were at Tierney's downtown condo that night; Reggie had moved in with him after her own lease ran out. I'd only come over because Tierney was out at some bar, but by the time he returned, I'd had a bunch of tequila shots and was feeling too good to care. I lay back on the couch, and Reggie stroked my hair. When Tierney sat down at the foot of the couch and started massaging my ankle, I didn't pull away.

Next thing I knew, Reggie was whispering in my ear, telling me that Tierney's fantasy was a threesome with us. It was such a ridiculous idea that I laughed. And then there was no more whispering, just all of us laughing about what a terrible idea it was and how none of us could possibly want it—except that, when Tierney stepped out to take a leak, Reggie informed me he actually did.

I could barely focus my eyes. But I heard every word she said, her breath hot on my cheek: "Why are you suddenly acting like a scared little girl, Sammy? Every time I dare you to do something, you get so uptight. It won't be bad, I swear."

I tried to remind her that I'd followed through on her other dare, the one about Owen, and regretted it. But I couldn't seem to form words, so I told myself maybe she was right, a threesome was no big deal. Sometimes you gotta do things just for the experience—wasn't that the moral of half of her wild stories?

She started kissing me, and that felt good. Too good. Then another hand clamped down on my arm—Tierney's—and I jumped up like I'd been electrocuted. The room swayed around me.

Reggie was saying, "Sam, Sam, wait," in her sweetest voice, but I grabbed my coat and shoved my feet into my boots and staggered out the door without closing it. Frigid air knocked the breath out of me, sobering me up—I hoped so, anyway—as I raced to the car, dodging icy puddles. I didn't start crying until I was behind the wheel, which was also when I realized I wasn't at all sober, but by then it was too late.

I plowed into the streetlight; I did the cops' song and dance. Reggie sent me four texts that night, all of which I ignored. When I returned to work three days later, I found out she'd quit—no notice or forwarding address. Later I heard from Tierney via Owen that she'd moved back to Massachusetts.

Now Reggie hunched up her knees under her skirt and wrapped her arms around them. She looked so small. "Owen told me about your accident. I'm glad you didn't lose your license—or hurt yourself."

I shrugged, still trying to pretend none of it mattered, but it was getting harder. "Yeah, well, Mom doesn't lend me the car much anymore. I've been building glutes of steel on that damn bike, believe me."

Reggie drew in a sharp breath. "Everything I said that night—"

"Don't worry, I was so trashed I barely remember."

"*I* remember. I said horrible things, Sam, and I didn't mean them. I used our friendship to try to make you do something you didn't want to, and that was beyond fucked up."

Her voice was so miserable that I couldn't help looking at her. Her face was contorted, too, as if she actually regretted saying those things.

"So, why?" I knew I shouldn't ask—it was taking the bait—but I couldn't help myself. "If you didn't think I was pathetic, why...?" *Why make me feel that way?*

"Why do you think, Sam? Because I was in a bad place." Reggie's eyes clouded over. "I wanted to keep Tierney happy so I could keep a roof over my head, and I felt like I'd made a mess of my life since I dropped out of college, working at that crappy theater, and you—you had so many choices still in front of you. You made a whole podcast!"

Without thinking, I reached across and touched her arm. "You know that podcast was crap, and I gave up on it before I even met you."

"But you had hope. You had plans."

I let my hand fall, but she reached out and clasped it. After a moment, she looked back up at me, her eyes still shiny with tears. "I know that sounds weird—it does to me, too. But you looked at me like I was the baddest bitch that ever bitched, and I liked that. I wanted to be the person you saw."

A sob convulsed my throat. I wanted to squeeze her hand, but I didn't let myself. "I was in high school. Of course you looked cool to me."

"Well, that's why I kept pushing your boundaries. I don't know what got into me that particular night—the tequila didn't help—but I wanted to tease you. I wanted to see what you would do. I wanted to . . . touch you again."

As she said those last words, she released my hand. The sudden space between us ached, but it wasn't the sickening pain that I remembered from that night in January. It was the dull throb of something healing.

"You could have explained all that instead of just ditching me," I said in a small voice. "It hurt, and coming back here to say you're sorry doesn't change that."

"I know. I never meant to ditch you, I just couldn't face you."

I drew a breath that made me light-headed. Saying the words, admitting I'd been hurt, had lifted a weight off my chest. "But you're in a better place now. Is that what you're saying?"

Reggie's expression relaxed. "Oh, God, yeah. I'm doing so much better!"

She told me about her internship, her new therapist, her AA meetings, her plans for school, the lighting designer she was sort of maybe seeing. I didn't listen too closely, but it felt good to hear the familiar rise and fall of her voice.

Kiri's dad's words came back to me—*Every boy is just a boy.* I couldn't feel angry at Reggie for not being what we'd both wanted her to be.

When she was done updating me on herself, she asked, "What about you, Sam? Have you moved on? Found somebody new?"

That stumped me. *Yes? No? It's complicated?* I stumbled to my feet, feeling as if I were waking from a dream. *Kiri. West. The awful message pinned to Tierney's jacket.* "Nah. I better go take the register again. It's getting close to six."

As we walked back, weaving among the trees and gravestones, Reggie said, "I'm glad we got to talk."

"Me too."

"I stalk you sometimes online. I'm not too proud to admit it."

"Yeah?" Maybe she meant my occasional anonymous tweets about shitty customers.

"You're deep into the whole Kiri Dunsmore thing, right?"

Her name, spoken in Reggie's voice—it sent an electric current through me, jolting every still-sleepy nerve into full alertness.

I reached for my keys, trying to act the way I had at the beginning of our conversation—like I couldn't care less about anything. "She went to BHS with me, so yeah, I'm following the case."

"I saw your comment on Aliza Deene's post. Yesterday, from your burner account." Reggie was talking too fast suddenly, as if she'd rehearsed this part of the conversation. "You said you went to Callum Massey's house and found it trashed—is that true, Sam?"

The keys slipped from my damp fingers. I bent to pick them up, black spots blossoming behind my eyes. "Did Owen tell you about that? Yeah. He and I went there together."

"Why didn't you post pics? You took some, right?"

She sounded so eager. Hungry, almost, as if she were out for Kiri's blood. She and Aliza probably wanted the exact same thing I had wanted when I first approached Kiri in the park: to get the exclusive scoop.

But everything had changed since then, and now I needed to get Reggie off the trail. No one could know what I knew.

I unlocked the door. "Just mentioning it felt wrong. Exploitative."

"No, you did the right thing! Aliza's not just out for clicks—she cares." Reggie's concern sounded faker and faker, and I felt almost embarrassed for her. Was this the real reason she'd come?

If so, I felt sorry for her, but I didn't think she was that conniving. Her apology had seemed sincere, regardless of any ulterior motive.

We stepped into the dimness of Theater One, where ads were playing at low volume between shows, and headed up the aisle, me taking long strides and Reggie hurrying to keep up.

"I actually went to college with Aliza—did I ever tell you that?" she said. "I guess she wasn't a thing yet last fall. We were dorm mates. She's sweet. Good vibes. She's studying social work; the influencer thing is just her hobby. If you sent her your pics, I don't think she'd put any pressure on you to tell her more than you wanted to. She values her sources. I could connect you."

I gave the double doors of the theater a shove with my elbow and held them open for her. Then, in the dark corridor, I turned to face her. I drew a deep breath to keep my voice steady and asked, "Did you tell Aliza Deene who I am? Did you dox me?"

"I would never, Sam!" Reggie flitted away from me. "I'm just saying, if *I* were involved in this case somehow, if *I* knew something, Aliza's the first person I'd go to."

"I wouldn't say I'm 'involved.'"

Reggie was a good person, and I had no doubt Aliza Deene was a good person, too, but clout is a powerful incentive. They might want to make me a character in their story: the sad little high school friend who spilled all of Kiri's secrets to an influencer because she was thirsty for a little fame of her own.

I was so far beyond that, though I could never let them know. So tangled up in it all that I might never get out.

In the lobby, sunlight blacked out my vision. Reggie had fallen behind me again, but she caught up quickly, her face flushed, and threw her arms around me and whispered in my ear: "Owen and I text sometimes"—she shot a glance sideways, and I saw Owen standing at the ticket counter—"and last night when I asked how you were, he told me he's worried because you're obsessed with the case. He said that you knew Kiri in school and he went to Callum's cabin with you. That's all. Don't be mad at him."

So Owen hadn't told her everything he knew—that was a relief. "I didn't know he was that worried," I said, forcing myself to sound casual.

Reggie pecked me on the cheek and stepped away. "Well, if you change your mind, I can always get you and Aliza in touch. Don't forget that."

"I won't." And then, because I couldn't blame her for being human, I reached for her and hugged her tight. "Thanks for coming."

She hugged me back. "Let's not be strangers this time."

As the glass doors snapped shut behind Reggie, I turned to face Owen. Our eyes met, and I could feel him cringing in anticipation of a nasty remark from me.

But none of this was his fault, either. He knew so little, and the important thing was to make sure he didn't find out any more.

I smiled at him, making sure the smile reached my eyes. After an instant, his own steady brown ones relaxed.

"I wish you'd told me you were texting with Reggie," I said, "but that was surprisingly fine. She seems like she's in a better place these days."

I could practically feel waves of relief emanating from Owen as he said, "She sure does."

"How's Tierney doing?"

FROM KIRI DUNSMORE'S DIARY

JULY 12

Okay, so there really isn't much you can harvest from the desert right now, or maybe I'm just a stupid pampered white girl. I mean, yes. I am. But how does he do it? How does he have so much energy, given our daily caloric intake? What's his secret, and can I cut him open and steal it? LOL JK.

JULY 15

It's tough being normal on camera. Today I tried for an impish expression—I could see it in my head—and C said I looked like someone was torturing me. The viewers out there <u>are</u> torturing us, making us perform for their amusement. They're flopped on their couches eating popcorn and laughing.

JULY 16

"You should do your eyeliner like Nat's." I don't know how that girl manages to do subtle eyeliner in this hellscape, but apparently she does. Maybe I'll just head over and ask her. That should go well.
   I wonder if she's a runaway. I wonder if her parents miss her.

JULY 17

The middle of the day is hell on earth, so that's when we sleep now. He never touches me anymore. Says I'm too sweaty.

JULY 18

Today I pretended to look for treasure in German's Gulch,
which is a deep, narrow ravine where you can see only a ribbon
of blue sky, and I got so claustrophobic I wanted to flail and
scream.

I faced the camera and said: "They say this is where the
treasure hunter's headless body was found, but I don't feel
any foreboding. I feel like this landscape is nurturing. Like I
could be reborn here."

I tell so many lies. All scripted by him, the man whose
camera makes hell on earth look like a place you'd love to visit.

Maybe West isn't the liar after all.

JULY 19

Sometimes I want to rip that camera out of his hands and
stomp on it. Maybe then he'd actually look at me.

22

Darkness, then flickers of light. Voices speaking a language I didn't understand—a man and woman, low and urgent. My body prickled all over with exhaustion, but I forced my eyes open.

I was in a large, dark room, blinking up at a bright screen. A car's headlights swept over thick forest. A man drove, while a woman placed her hand on his thigh and said words that the subtitle translated: *We never appreciate anything till it's gone.*

As I sat up, paper fluttered from my lap to the floor, and with a jolt I remembered—Kiri's diary! After sweeping Theater Six at the end of my shift, I'd sat down in the front row to finish reading it, but instead, I must have drifted off.

Now I slid out of my seat, onto my knees, and scrabbled on the floor for the pages. I couldn't lose any of them—I'd promised Kiri I would read the whole thing.

The meeting was tomorrow. Already she might be scheming up ways to join West in Canada. Whether she was guilty or not, I couldn't believe running away was her best choice—there were too many extenuating factors. She might not have been legally insane out there in the desert, but I couldn't imagine a jury convicting her of first-degree murder.

I folded the papers and hurried up the aisle, drawing glares from the handful of people who were seeing the Czech movie. I grabbed my stuff from the breakroom, clocked out, and threw a goodbye to Maren in the booth, asking her to delete the two hours of overtime I hadn't earned.

Outside, the last pink strips had faded from the sky behind the theater. For Kiri and me, though, it was still early. I would stop at home to finish the diary, maybe even catch a little sleep.

Unless—what if she planned to leave for Canada tonight? She had her own car, but would they let her cross the border?

The thought made me pedal furiously. The traffic was thin, the city buses garaged for the night. Smells of oil and humid vegetation mingled in the cooling air as the usual signs flashed past: Nissan, Northland Credit Union, Burger King, Lowe's, Dattilio's Guns & Tackle.

Stay here, Kiri, I thought, taking the swooping left across four empty lanes onto my street, hearing the edgy guitar licks of a surfer band from Molly B's. *Just a little longer.*

In her diary, she'd said she loved Callum's weaknesses because they were part of the whole package of him as a person. I could love her anxiety, her strange whims, her awkwardness, her unpredictability. But could I love her as a murderer?

In our kitchen, Mom was doing her usual pre-night-shift routine, brewing a pot of coffee that she would pour into two giant thermoses. "Hey," she said, "you're home late."

"It was such a nice night that Owen and I decided to go for creemees."

A strange look flitted over Mom's face. Maybe she could tell I was lying, or maybe she'd started shipping Owen and me again the way she used to, half-jokingly, when we were thirteen.

Then she said, "Your friend's here. I think she thought you'd be back earlier."

Reggie, here? Suddenly I was wide awake, sinuses throbbing and warmth flooding my cheeks as if I'd just drunk the whole pot of coffee by myself. Why would she come to my house—unless she suspected I'd been lying to her about Kiri?

"I said she could wait in your room if she wanted. I hope that's okay." The furrow between Mom's brows deepened, and I knew that in her usual empathic way she'd registered my alarm. "I don't know her, but we had a lovely conversation, and—"

"No, that's fine. You did the right thing." I'd never introduced Mom and Reggie, because I wanted my cool older friend to be all mine. Reggie must have turned on the charm. I grabbed two kombuchas from the fridge and kissed Mom on the cheek, reminding myself I wasn't afraid of Reggie or her judgments anymore. "Have a good shift, okay?"

She pretended to be shocked. "Who's this sweet girl, and what have you done with my Sam?"

I rolled my eyes, but I was remembering Kiri writing about never wanting to go home to her own mother. "I appreciate you. What's wrong with showing it occasionally?"

Mom raised her thermos as if to toast. "I like this mood you're in."

At the top of the stairs, the door of my room hung ajar. I braced myself and pushed it all the way open. "Hey, Redge, I'm so sorry I—"

I stopped. It wasn't Reggie sitting at my childhood desk, painted white with pink rosebuds. It was Kiri, with her long legs draped over my dinky chair and her bare toes resting less than a foot from a pile of my discarded sweatpants.

She wore an eggplant-colored hoodie with her shorts, her hair tucked up under it. And as she swiveled restlessly in the chair, her hand fiddled with something that I suddenly, disastrously, recognized.

It was one of the postcards I'd printed up to advertise my failed podcast, *The Girl Who Killed*, with a mug shot front and center. I'd placed the crosshairs of a target over Drea Flint's face, and the font practically screamed, *Step right up to the true-crime freak show!* Such an edgy design, I'd thought at the time.

"Hey, Sam," Kiri said. "I guess you're kind of into killers, right?"

23

think Kiri was trying to sound sarcastic. Cool, above it all, like I'd tried to be with Reggie today—*I can make jokes about murder!* But on the word *killers*, her voice broke. She looked away from me, and I knew she wasn't happy with what she'd found.

I couldn't blame her, but I wasn't happy with what I'd been learning about her, either. I sat down on the bed. "That's from years ago. It didn't work out. How did you get here?"

Kiri put the card down. "Went through the park. Didn't use the street." A little twist of her lips, almost a smile, to remind me that she could leave her house any time she really wanted to. "I remembered where you live from the time I drove you home."

"Even the apartment number?"

Kiri nodded. "I told you, I noticed you in school. You stood out. Have you read the rest of the diary?"

"I'm almost done."

When she met my gaze, I saw a difference in her. She was still beautiful, in her awkward way. But her eyes were darker, as if the pupils had swelled to swallow the irises. They reflected me, those flat dark eyes, while shutting me out.

She'd decided something. A pit opened in my gut.

"Your mom gave me a free palm reading," Kiri said. "She happened to mention she does them. I offered to pay, but she said no."

Had Mom recognized Kiri from the Waffle House video? She was always better with names than faces. "That's nice," I said. "What did she say?"

Kiri raised her right palm and studied it. "She said, 'You have a long way to go. And by the time you reach your destination, you'll have learned to be alone.'"

"A long way to go where?" *Canada?*

"I guess I'll find out." Kiri rose and went over to the bookcase. She ran a finger along the spines on the top shelf—fat paperbacks with black covers accented in lurid red and purple. Words glittered silver: *kill, death, blood, guilt, dark, secret.*

"It makes a good story, doesn't it?" she said. "That I killed him? Everybody likes wondering how somebody like me could do something like that."

I shook my head. The words *Of course you didn't* wouldn't come.

"Is this girl Drea Flint like me?" She picked up the card from the desk again. "I never heard of her. What did she do?"

"Lots of things. She killed men who paid to have sex with her. Her stepfather. Men who hurt her—some of them did, anyway. Not all." I swallowed hard. "Look, it's not like that. I mean, maybe it started out that way, just a little, but I can't think of you like that now. You're my friend. You're *you.*"

Kiri didn't seem to hear. "Your mom didn't recognize me," she said, sitting down again. "I guess she doesn't follow the news. Anyway, I said I was your friend Katie from school, and we talked about you, and she asked if I was a true-crime fan, too. She said you were up on every case." She wound a stray strand of hair around her finger. "You knew all about mine before we met that first day in the park, didn't you?"

Guilt strangled me. I tried to tell myself that if I'd been using her, she'd been using me, too, but none of that canceled out what I'd done. "I never told you I *didn't* know," I said. "I never lied to you."

"But you left out so much." She picked up the card again and brandished it at me: *Exhibit A*. "It's been going around and around in my head, Sam. You didn't just run into me that day in the park, did you? You were waiting for me, just like the reporters were. Stalking me."

I wanted to crumple and confess and say I was sorry, the way Reggie had with me this afternoon, but I couldn't seem to do it. "Kiri," I said, "I know Callum taught you to be paranoid. But not everybody's after you. And this stuff"—I gestured at the bookshelves—"was just a phase for me. I haven't been into it for a while."

Every word felt like a nail hammered into my own coffin, but it was better than admitting the truth. Anything was better than being the girl whose life was so pathetic that she had to force her way into someone else's.

Kiri held my glare with those new, sharkish eyes of hers. "You never liked me at school," she said. "I wasn't cool enough for you. I didn't dare text you or anything, even though I wanted to. You would have rejected me."

"That's not true." Was it?

"But now that I'm famous for possibly being a cold-blooded murderer, suddenly I'm the most interesting person you know. Believe me, I'm aware I just happen to be the main character today. Tomorrow I'll be nobody again, or worse. But right now, if you told those influencers all about me, if you showed them my diary, then you could be the center of attention. Couldn't you?"

"That's not something I would do!" If only she could have seen me with Reggie, lying like a pro. Tears of shame stung my eyes as I unzipped my backpack, grabbed the diary pages that I'd painstakingly gathered from the theater floor, and held them out to her. *Take them back, then.* "I don't just want attention. I never wanted that. This whole time, all I've ever wanted is to know your side of the story."

Kiri just gazed at me. No tears in her eyes. "So you can be the one who tells it?"

"How? I'm nobody." When I blinked, the tears wet my cheeks and spilled off my chin. Were there any words strong enough to convince her that everything that had happened between us was real to me, especially last night by the lake? Realer than my true-crime obsession, realer than the rest of my life?

"Being a nobody never stopped anybody from posting stuff online," Kiri said.

She sounded so cynical all of a sudden. But there was something she didn't know yet—I was a criminal myself. I straightened the pages with shaking hands. "Last night, before I came to your house, I went to West's motel room."

"You talked to West? But last night you said you didn't!"

"No! He wasn't there. I—well, I broke in. The window was open. All I found was this."

The *See ya* note was still in my backpack. I handed it to her.

Kiri stared at the two words, her mouth tightening, as I told her what had happened to Tierney last night while I was busy in the motel room. Now my words came more easily, because she needed to know

West was dangerous. "And there's another note—a third note, I guess, if you count the one he left for you. This was pinned to Tierney's jacket."

I handed that one over with shaking hands. *Tell Sam to do everything her old friend asks her to. Only way she'll ever know the truth.*

Reading it, Kiri winced as if an insect had stung her. But her face didn't change.

"West could have just come and told me that, but he carjacked Tierney as a warning to us both." Now that I didn't have to hold back anything, I was babbling. "Or maybe he wanted Tierney's Range Rover, so his own license plate wouldn't be recorded crossing the border. He wants to meet you tomorrow in Canada, doesn't he? That's where the echoing caves are."

Kiri pinched West's note between her fingers and tore it neatly in half. She lined up the halves and tore them in half again. "How did you know?"

"You talked about it in your sunset video. But why would West want to meet in Canada? It's not like you can…"

"Cross the border? Because the FBI is watching me and I'm about to be arrested?"

I didn't like the flippancy of her tone, as if she'd decided she just didn't give a damn. "You don't know that," I pointed out. *Or if you do…* "Look, I hope you understand how dangerous it would be for you to leave the country right now. And to meet West? After what he did to Tierney just to get his car, I don't see how you can possibly trust him."

Unless you're desperate. Because both of you know there's blood on your hands.

Kiri stared straight ahead into the shadows in the corner of the room. "Would you?" she asked after a moment.

"Would I what?"

She picked up what was left of the note and began tearing it into even smaller pieces. "The 'old friend' is me, I suppose. So would you do anything I ask you to? Would you do anything to know the truth?"

Foreboding settled in my gut. "It depends on what you're asking."

"That's not what the note said. It said *everything*."

The bed creaked, and I looked up to see Kiri settling beside me. Again I felt that sensation from last night in the park: prickling on my skin, as if she emitted an electric charge, and an answering flush of heat inside me. When she made up her mind to do something, she was powerful.

"No," I said. "I mean, I don't know. What are you talking about? Are you seriously thinking of going to Canada tomorrow?"

Kiri tugged off her hood. Her hair came loose and streamed over her shoulders like a cloak, some of the golden strands catching static electricity and wafting upward. I wanted to snag them and brush them back behind her ear. I wanted to touch the down on her cheek where it caught the light. I sat very still.

"I have a plan," she said. "I want to surprise West. Throw him off-kilter a little."

"Surprise him?" I didn't see how that would help. "Why?"

She gazed into midair. "He won't be sleeping in the echoing caves. He'll be using the cottage as a home base—Callum's parents' cottage in Saint-Aubin-Les-Pins. We were there, too, on my birthday."

Where she'd lost her virginity. "How would West get in there?"

"He'll know where they keep the spare key. He's been their guest."

A wave of her hand. "Let's go there, Sam. Now, tonight—it's not far. We could get there in the morning, before he's expecting us."

"So we surprise him, and then what?" That foreboding inside me was growing, cold and heavy. "Anyway, remember what you said before? The FBI might have you on a watch list."

"Maybe." Her voice was low and husky—tense, but not scared anymore. "That's why I need you to drive me, Sam. You have one of those enhanced licenses, don't you? Or a passport?"

"Sure, but—"

"I could ride in the trunk when we cross the border." Her eyes locked on mine, and they weren't dead anymore. They gleamed.

"Yeah, and if the border patrol searches the car and finds you, it'll look like you were trying to sneak into Canada to…"

Then I remembered how she'd run straight off the cliff last night. How her body had arced over the void. "Kiri," I asked, "is that what you want from West? Do you want him to help you…disappear?"

The word hung in the air between us. I wished I could unsay it, but it was too late. If she said yes, it was as good as a confession.

The light faded from Kiri's face, replaced by the flat, dead look again. "If you won't help, I'll find a way to do it alone. I'll take my Prius and see what happens."

"You'll look like a fugitive." I edged closer, though I knew that by saying it, I was already becoming her accomplice. "You can't cut and run. You need to trust the process."

"That's what my lawyer keeps saying." Her voice was tight. "Look, do you even have a car?"

"Mom just took it to work." But Owen probably felt bad about blabbing to Reggie, which meant he might lend me the Legacy if I asked very nicely and didn't let him know what I needed it for.

Once West set up that meeting with Kiri, he must have known exactly what she would ask me to do. If I did it, I would be breaking the law—aiding and abetting a fugitive.

My pulse throbbed in my temples, frantic and resolute at once, as I checked my phone. It was less than an hour to the border and two more hours to Saint-Aubin-Les-Pins, north of Montreal in the green and blue middle of nowhere.

"Sam." A light, quaking hand on my shoulder. "I don't want to hide in my parents' house again tomorrow. I want to *do* something."

"If you didn't do anything wrong, then you don't *need* to do anything." Too late, I realized my voice had cut like a knife. "You know what I mean, Kiri. If I do this, and it turns out . . . well, it would make me your accomplice."

"I know." She hadn't moved her hand. Her breath was a ghost of warmth against my cheek. "But you like stories, don't you, Sam? You like finding out which version of the story is true?"

Her tone was half-serious, half-teasing; it made me itch down to the base of my spine. I said, "Sometimes it's not worth it to know."

Those newly unreadable eyes gazed into mine. "Are you sure?"

I knew what she was really saying, what she didn't need to say out loud. She didn't believe the truth would exonerate her, which meant she probably wasn't innocent, and that alone should make me walk away.

But she was also right. If I didn't go with her to Saint-Aubin-Les-Pins, I might never know how the story ended. Not just the story of what had happened in the desert, but our story, hers and mine.

It might be even worse than I imagined. But I'd come too far to turn back now.

"I think I can get a car," I said.

**VIDEO POSTED TO
CALLUM MASSEY'S CHANNEL
ON JULY 26 AT 8:18 AM**

We see the clear imprint of a shoe or boot in the red dirt. Big—a man's, probably—with an unusual pattern over the instep. It makes me think of the symbol for Aries, the ram's head, with watery swooshes above and below.

"Hey, followers!" That's Kiri off-screen, sounding chipper.

But when she swings the camera up to her face, we see that her hair is a matted, stringy mess. The sun is behind her, which may or may not be why her eyes look lifeless.

"I don't think this was here before Cal disappeared." She points at the ground—the footprint. "I mean, maybe I'm wrong? Sometimes I just don't notice things—that's what he's always saying, anyway. And maybe I'm not at my most stable right now."

She giggles, a sound that grates on the ear, and then she seems to choke on it, tears welling up in her eyes.

This is the clip that people like to meme, over and over, usually as the second half of "how it started, how it's going."

"I'm a little confused about what's real, but I have a plan now," she says, looking straight at the camera. "I should just hike back, call nine-one-one, and explain everything. I'll walk into the ranger station and there you'll be, Cal, because I made a silly mistake. We both made a silly mistake, coming

out here in the first place. We need to go back to normal."
Another giggle, but this one ends quickly.

"I don't know, though," she says. "It's hard pretending."
She smiles—a horrible, blatantly fake smile that turns into a
grimace. "I know who you are now, and I'll never be fooled
again."

24

need the Legacy," I told Owen, bent over my phone in the dark kitchen.

"Why? What's going on?" He sounded bleary; the day must have worn him out, too.

I couldn't whip up an excuse. My brain was a snarl of bare, sparking wires. "I need something, but I don't want to bike this time of night."

"I could drive you. Are you sick or something?" Then things must have snapped together in his head, because he said, "Is it her? Is this about Kiri?"

I didn't answer.

Owen took a breath so deep I heard it. "This isn't good, Sam. This isn't good for you."

"She wants to take a drive in the country, that's all. To see the stars." It was a terrible lie, but I didn't have the patience to flesh it out. "It's just one night, Owen. You owe me."

It took him a moment to answer, and then he sounded cold and formal. "Do you know what they're saying about her now? Do you know what kind of danger you could be putting yourself in?"

"Owen, do you actually believe the criminal justice system protects the innocent?" I closed my eyes tight and crossed the fingers on both hands because I was pretty sure I was about to tell a lie. "And she is innocent. I know that."

"You know, huh?" After a long moment, he asked, "Have you thought about what we talked about before? About how she might be using you?"

I know she is. I don't care. "Please," I said. "I...I can't let her go by herself." And then the part I didn't want to admit, the words that felt ripped from inside me: "I care about her."

Owen was silent for a long moment. While I could have said those words to manipulate him, I had a feeling he would know how deeply I meant them.

Finally he said, "You met this girl what, a week ago? Ten days?"

"It's been a long ten days," I said.

When he spoke again, his voice was shaking. "Wherever you're going, you gotta come back, Sam. You and my ride both, promise me you'll come back without a scratch."

I promised.

I chose the remotest, most rural border crossing I knew. There would be no lines, no fancy duty-free shops, just a shack in the woods and an agent or two guarding the gate across the road.

Driving felt weird after nearly eight months of being stuck on my bike. I kept hitting the brakes too hard, and I waited for Kiri to react—Lore would have giggled or rolled their eyes—but she just sank into her seat and gazed straight ahead. With a hood hiding her hair and shadowing her face, she barely seemed there.

Soon there were no more stoplights, just pastures and woods and a sky blazing with stars. The car had smelled a little skunky when we got in, so I had the windows wide open to air it out.

As I drove, I thought of Mickey and Mallory in *Natural Born Killers*, the terrible role models that Drea Flint and her boyfriend had chosen for themselves. Whenever you tried to separate that pair, they snapped back together like magnets, leaving a bloody trail in their wake. But the point of the story (as far as there was any point) was that society was even sicker than they were. Everybody tried to use them for clout—cops, courts, and a tabloid reporter who became their accomplice so he could get the scoop. Everybody regretted it.

Would I end up like the reporter, pleading for my life? It wasn't that I was afraid of Kiri, but a dark, quiet place will put those thoughts in your head.

I thought of Kiri all alone in the desert, making her videos. *I know who you are now, and I'll never be fooled again*, she'd said—talking to the viewers, to Callum, or to someone else?

On our first night in the den, she'd told me that some part of her was still out there in the desert. I'd assumed she was talking about the trauma of losing Callum, but now I knew it was more. There's a loneliness that gets inside you and changes you, and she'd been in that dark place even with Callum by her side.

He hadn't helped her, because he couldn't love those parts of her. If anything, he'd made it worse.

When we were about a mile from the border, deep in the woods, I pulled over at the base of someone's driveway. It was just after two. "If you want to get in the trunk, now's the time."

Kiri didn't hesitate. She got out, slinging a black backpack over her shoulder.

Bushes shielded us from the road. No cars passed while I popped the trunk and we moved Owen's junk into the back seat. Kiri tossed her pack into the trunk and climbed in after it.

She laughed when she realized she would have to lie down and fold her knees to her chest—a nervous laugh that reminded me of our earlier meetings, back when I believed she was innocent. "Lucky I'm not claustrophobic."

"Are you sure about this?" I asked.

Spruce and fir trees loomed on either side of the road, cutting sharp points in a creamy river of stars. It was a forest with no undergrowth to hide busy insects, none of the usual late-summer buzzing and trilling, just silence.

Kiri curled up in the trunk. Pale strands of hair escaped from under her hood. "I'm fine," she said, voice muffled against her shoulder.

"Sometimes they search the car. If that happens, what do we tell them?"

Her eyes were shut tight, and I didn't think she'd answer, but then she said, "Tell them we're star-crossed lovers. We can't be together in a place with as much prejudice as America."

"Ha. We're from *Vermont*."

"Say we're from Alabama."

"Car's registered here." But the words stuck in my throat.

Kiri uncurled enough to look up at me. "If they find me, I'll tell them the truth," she said. "All of it. Promise. I just want this one chance."

"Okay." I sounded gruff even to myself.

Her gaze didn't falter. "Thank you, Sam."

So I slammed the trunk and went through with it.

When I spotted the lights of the tiny border station on the horizon, I started inhaling for a count of four and exhaling for a count of four. Five more minutes and it would all be over.

I lowered my speed to the required fifteen miles per hour, foot nice and steady on the pedal, and drove up to the booth. *Breathe.* I came to a smooth stop, getting the hang of that again. Put the car in park, trying not to think about Kiri huddled in the trunk.

The agent leaned out of the booth. He was working alone—a young man with a soul patch and long eyelashes, wearing a dark blue uniform.

"Hi!" I gave him a big smile. The Canadian agents tend to look a little more chill than ours, like they might be fun to hang out with when they're off work.

This one was an exception—he didn't smile back. "Where are you coming from?" His name tag said Marc Doucette, and his French accent was so subtle that it was more like a careful frame he put around each word.

"Burlington." I held out my enhanced license, which gets you across the border without having to pay for a passport. "Hey, we practically have the same last name! Mine's Duquette."

He took it. Still no smile. "And your destination, Samara?"

"Montreal. This friend of mine went clubbing on Sainte-Catherine, and the guy she was with turned out to be a total jerk, so now she needs a ride home."

Marc Doucette handed back my ID. The corner of his mouth twitched. I couldn't tell whether he wanted to smile or was just fed up with American kids coming into his country so they could party without fake IDs. "What is your friend's name?"

"Reggie—uh, I mean Regina. Regina Chen."

Marc Doucette nodded. His shoulders relaxed. His gaze wandered away from me. "And when will you and Regina be returning to the United States?"

"As soon as I pick her up." Would he put me on some list, so the US agents would expect two people back at the hour I'd specified? With a sinking feeling, I realized that someone who was rescuing her friend from clubland had no good reason to use this Podunk crossing in the dead of night. "Unless Reggie's, uh, really sick. Maybe then we'll find a room for the night." Then I shut my mouth tight, because there's no more reliable sign of guilt than overexplaining.

My eyes locked on Marc's. His showed no expression, and my throat pinched tight.

At last, he blinked. Reached for something below my sight line. For an instant, nothing happened—and then the metal gate rose silently and inexorably to make way for me. For us.

"You two girls should be careful," Marc Doucette said. For a millisecond I could have sworn that he meant Kiri and me, that he knew everything and was letting us go anyway. But then he added, "Montreal is a big city, not like Burlington. Don't sleep in your car on the street, okay?"

"Okay." I nodded hard. "Don't worry. We'll get home safely."

I waved and smiled a last time and released the car from park.

A tap on the accelerator, and we were in Canada.

The forest vanished almost the instant we crossed the border. Now I could see the whole flat landscape in every direction: fields and fences and barns and houses, each in its pool of light. Mom always says this part of Quebec reminds her of Iowa, where she grew up.

It didn't seem like a good idea to stop too close to the border. I let two miles tick by on the odometer—driving right at the fifty-kilometer-per-hour speed limit—before I pulled over just past a gigantic dairy farm, its metal silos glinting in the starlight.

I got out and popped the trunk. "Hey. We're good."

Kiri didn't spring up and bounce out of there; she lay so still. I leaned close to make sure she was breathing. But then her lashes fluttered, and she stretched and sat up.

I offered my hand to help her out, and she took it, her skin warm and a little damp, as if she'd been sleeping in the grass. Her hood came off, hair spilling down her back, as she landed lightly on the asphalt.

"That was weird." She sounded woozy. "I felt like Snow White in the glass coffin."

"I sure hope there isn't a CO leak in the trunk." I headed back to the cab. "Do you have a headache?"

"No." Suddenly she was standing in my way. "Let me drive."

I shook my head, but she said, "You haven't had any sleep, Sam." She knotted her hair and pulled up the hood again. "I'm a good driver. I won't get stopped. I know the way to the cottage."

I did desperately want to close my eyes, but I wasn't sure about letting her take control. "You didn't sleep last night any more than I did."

"I slept today while you were at work. Anyway, I want you to finish the diary." Her voice was low and a little hoarse; each syllable itched as it entered my eardrums, sending vibrations down my spine. "I need you to know everything I know."

"Why do you need that?" I didn't say what I was thinking: that all she really needed now was for me to take her to West so that he could help her vanish. Getting over the border was probably the hardest part.

She looked at me as if I weren't making sense. "I've always wanted that, ever since I came back, Sam. To tell the truth. When I got in those people's RV—the ones who gave me a ride out of the National Monument—I was just gonna let it all spill out of me. That was my plan."

Maybe it was the rural silence that made me conscious of the whooshing of my own pulse. "But you didn't do that."

A headshake. "Being in Cal's videos, smiling when I didn't want to—I guess I got into the habit of lying. 'Creative fictioning.' I opened my mouth, there in the desert, and a story came out that wasn't true. But I wasn't entirely sure *which* parts weren't true, so I just kept telling it—to the cops, my parents, everybody."

The air seemed to congeal; it was an effort to suck it in.

If Kiri saw my dread, she didn't show it. "I even believed the story myself, some of the time," she said. "Other times, though, when I was alone, I would read the diary and pieces of the truth came back. And then I wanted to tell someone so badly. I wanted to tell you."

Maybe, if only I knew the truth, I would be ready to let her go.

"Okay," I said. "You drive, and I'll finish."

FROM KIRI DUNSMORE'S DIARY

JULY 21

The pit opened today.

I slept through the afternoon as usual, and when I woke up and heard the crackle of the fire and smelled food, everything seemed fine. Then I went out and saw that it was beans again, just beans, beans, beans, and the mesa was glowing on the horizon, which meant it was almost the magic hour and time to shoot our segment, and I went ballistic. Like all of me was one big, gaping stomach.

I don't want to be this person. I don't want this person ever to have existed.

But she did exist, and she was me, and I have to write this down or I'll never get better. I have to remember every time I've slipped, every monstrous thing I've done, because every slip could be the difference between doom and survival.

I remember it in flashes like stop-motion. I screamed at him to open the safe and give me a stick of beef jerky. He said we ate the last two sticks last night.

Screaming. Hair tossing. I don't know. I may have shrieked in his face; I may have grabbed him and shaken him. And the whole time he was so calm, so beautifully reasonable.

Beautiful. Horrible.

I do remember that the sun was sliding off the side of the mesa when he said, "You could go over there." Pointing to the bikers' campsite, hidden beyond a rise covered with juniper and creosote. "I bet they're barbecuing," he said, and when he smiled, his teeth were so white. "Wouldn't you like that?"

I walked a few steps that way, just bluffing. He said, "They might want something in return, you know."

I stopped dead. "Like what?"

He said, "Don't be naive. It's up to you, Kiri. Your life. Your survival skill set. Do what you need to."

I started walking again. Honestly, at that point I was ready to do anything, no matter how filthy or degrading, just to have the taste of meat in my mouth and the fullness in my stomach. I had no thoughts in my head, just the pit saying, "Fill me, fill me, fill me."

Then I remembered him telling me, "You're beautiful." I remembered him saying, "You glow." If I kept walking, I might survive, but my glow would fade and I would be nothing again.

I stopped. I turned around.

And he was standing there, a foot from me, with a stick of beef jerky in his hand. When I saw it, my body turned to water. I could barely hold myself upright.

"I saved a few," he said, "for emergencies."

I don't even remember eating it.

I got another stick, but only after we finished our shoot. An incentive. I pasted a smile on my face and told the camera and everyone out there (no one, no one's left alive) how clean and rejuvenated the desert makes me feel every single day.

And the pit is full again. For now.

He's over at the bikers' campsite now, "checking in" and getting water from the spring. I wonder if that girl—Nat or Natalie, her name is—has to do things for her food, too.

I shouldn't judge her. You do what you must to survive. Last time I saw her she was wearing a faded T-shirt that said CIMARRON COUNTY 4-H, so I guess she once had a home, too.

She always glares at me when I see her, and I wonder if she wishes she were in my place, with Callum to protect her.

Maybe we should ask her to join us, but I don't think I can trust her. I think she knows I don't deserve C, because deep down I'm just a regular person like her, and I don't glow except when he's looking at me.

We're all alone and there's no one to help us, and I can't afford to be this weak shell of a person. This person is not me. I need to find the light inside.

25

Daylight. Green leaves. Raindrops. Blinking up at the windshield, I tried to remember where I was. Then I heard her breathing beside me in the driver's seat.

"We're close, but we need gas," she said. "I don't have any Canadian cash, but if you use your credit card, I'll pay you back."

We were parked in the far corner of a nearly empty lot surrounded by trees. Behind us, cars swooshed through light rain on a two-lane road. At the other end of the lot stood gas pumps and a low building with a snazzy sign that said DÉPANNEUR.

"That looks like it has clean bathrooms." I unbuckled myself and opened the door. "You haven't been in yet, have you?"

Kiri shook her head. Her hood was already cinched up tight, and now she pulled out a pair of shades. "If you buy something, I'll slip in behind you. Or, uh, use the woods." She pointed at the wet foliage that grazed our windshield.

"No worries," I said. "I'll cover you."

The mini-mart was clean and shiny, probably part of a chain. The woman at the counter smiled and said, "Bonjour" with a twang, and I said it back. There were gerbera daisies in a vase in the restroom.

As I returned to the counter and asked for a tank of gas and two breakfast sandwiches and two coffees (large, please!), I imagined that we were taking a normal, innocent road trip together. Hitting Montreal, furnishing our dorm rooms at IKEA (in this version of our lives, I had a dorm room), and checking out the mountains beyond the city. Later today, we would take a hike. Kiri would laugh at my panting out-of-shapeness but wait for me to catch up, every time, because she wasn't Callum. She was a kind person.

A person who hated herself. A person who had done something terrible in the desert and lied about it to everyone. A person who needed to disappear.

My stomach lurched as it all came flooding back. I had transported someone across an international border who might soon be classified as a fugitive. When they made podcasts about her, I wouldn't be the narrator. I would be cast as her accomplice, or maybe her hapless dupe.

Behind me, the bell jangled—Kiri slipping inside.

I told the woman at the counter, "That's my friend," so she wouldn't stop Kiri from using the restroom.

The woman nodded, took my card, and said in English with an accent stronger than the border agent's, "It's a nice day for a trip to the mountains. The rain will stop itself soon."

Then she went to make the sandwiches, and my stomach lurched again as I saw the display of newspapers under the counter.

Most of them were serious-looking Montreal papers with front-page photos of politicians signing bills or making statements. Not a single face I recognized. But then, off in a corner, the headline of a tabloid screamed at me:

QUI EST L'INCONNUE RETROUVÉE MORTE AU DÉSERT?

Under the words were two grainy photos, side by side. One was

Callum from one of his videos, looking handsome and dashing. The other was Kiri from the cam footage in the New Mexico mini-mart, the bloodstained sweatshirt dangling from her waist.

I dredged up my four years of high school French. *Inconnue*: unknown woman. *Morte*: dead.

My breath caught as I pieced it together: *Who is the unknown woman found dead in the desert?*

Woman. Not Callum.

I snatched up the paper and opened to the story. French words swarmed at me; I recognized a quarter of them at most. But the gist was simple: The corpse found yesterday in Lost Village National Monument was a young woman with a head wound, and her identification was pending.

My heart began to thump as if I'd just run a marathon. If the corpse wasn't Callum, who could it be? And what had Kiri lied about?

I scanned a sidebar with the heading TREMPÉ DE SANG: MAIS DE QUI? *Sang*—blood. All I could make out were Callum's and Kiri's names, the word *pullover*, and something about percentages: *23% de Callum Massey. 77% de l'inconnue.*

Pullover. Was that the sweatshirt?

"All ready!"

I stood up so quickly my vision blacked out. The cashier smiled expectantly, and I reached for the paper bag she'd prepared. Behind me, the doorbell dinged: Kiri leaving.

My first thought was that I had to tell her. This was good news, the best news! I dredged up two dollar coins from my wallet, left over from previous trips, and thrust them at the cashier for the paper. "Merci beaucoup!"

As I rushed back to the Legacy and tried to maneuver myself into the driver's seat without spilling the coffees, though, the giddy relief retreated. None of this would be news to Kiri. Whatever partial truth I'd just learned, she almost certainly already knew it.

I meant to fold the newspaper and hide the headline from her—just until I had time to decide what to do next—but I had to get the coffees safely in the holders first. The tabloid slid out from under my arm. Before I could stop her, Kiri grabbed it.

"Oh," she said, raising it so I couldn't see her face. And then, in a small voice, "Wow."

I couldn't seem to catch my breath. "You knew it wasn't him they found, didn't you? You knew all this time."

She opened the newspaper, still using it as a barrier between us.

"Who is it, Kiri?"

Pages rustled. I grabbed the tabloid and jerked it out of her hands, the cheap paper ripping. "Who died in the desert? Who's the body?"

Kiri's eyes went flat again the way they had last night in my room. "I don't know."

"You're supposed to be telling me the full truth now, remember? I read the whole diary."

She picked up the coffee and took a sip. Her face had gone marble pale and expressionless. "It doesn't change anything."

How could I be sure of that? I remembered the entry I'd been reading when I fell asleep in the theater: *I tell so many lies. All scripted by him . . . Maybe West isn't the liar after all.*

I stabbed a finger at the paper on the seat between us. "Look, if you think West killed this girl or Callum killed this girl, you can tell me! I understand how things were out there. I know you were scared of both of them."

She looked startled. "How would West have done that? He wasn't even there."

"He basically admitted the footprints were his! And in your diary you said, 'West isn't the liar.' What does that mean, Kiri? Are you talking about when you met at the rest stop and he tried to get you to leave Callum? Why did you think he was lying to you?"

"That had nothing to do with...the body." Kiri looked straight ahead at the windshield silvered with raindrops. "The thing West told me at the rest stop that I didn't want to believe—it was about this girl, Arianna Dunne. He said she was the real reason that Callum wanted to disappear."

"Arianna?" For a few seconds, I drew a blank. Then my one and only conversation with West came rushing back. "The thirteen-year-old girl that West was creepy with? What does she even have to do with Callum?"

Kiri laughed, short and sharp. "West never did anything with Arianna—that's what he told me, anyway. He lied to her parents and pretended *he* was the one sending her little notes and gifts, so Callum wouldn't get in trouble. Arianna's parents were friends of Cal's parents, see. If they'd known Cal was romancing their underage daughter, it would have been a real scandal."

The story suddenly made more sense—Callum had a history of mesmerizing young girls. I remembered the card I'd found in his cabin, with its message in careful calligraphy: *Love you to infinity.* "Arianna was into calligraphy, wasn't she? I think West mentioned that."

Kiri nodded and took another sip of coffee. Strands of hair were escaping from her hood. "Cal never actually laid a finger on Arianna, according to West. Her dad's somebody important in the government, so it made Cal feel powerful to lead her on and tease her—until Arianna's mom found out and hit the roof. Then Cal asked West to take the blame."

"Why would West do that?" But I already knew. Callum had a way of getting his friends to do things for him. "And why would Callum need to disappear if West had taken responsibility?"

"Arianna didn't like being used. She wasn't ready for Callum to be done with her." Kiri was absorbed in the story, her gaze distant. "She went along with the lie for a while, but she's twenty now, and she hasn't let it go. She keeps reaching out to Cal, and he keeps ghosting her. She saw me in one of Cal's videos and freaked. When we went to that party in DC and Callum's friend took him aside, it was to deliver a warning. Supposedly Arianna has pics of Callum and her together when she was young that are kind of...not cool. She's threatening to expose him as a predator."

Another sip. A short, bitter laugh. "Well. That's West's story, anyway. A lot of details and no proof. This whole time I've been waiting for Arianna to come forward and say something that might tell me whether the story is true or not. But it seems like she's been quiet so far."

I nodded, resolving to look up Arianna Dunne. "As far as I know. So, at the rest stop, West was trying to warn you. He knew if you went to Canada with Callum, you'd regret it."

"He said Callum was a 'vortex.' He and Arianna had gotten sucked in, and he could see I was getting sucked in, too."

Whatever else West had done, he was right about that. But we were getting away from the body in the desert.

The body. It hit me like a chilly hand clamping the back of my neck. "Is the body Arianna?"

Finally, that put some expression on Kiri's face. "No! As far as I know, she's still back in DC."

"Who is it, then?"

Her dark eyes rose to mine, and now there was a hint of vulnerability in them. "If you read to the end, you should know."

At last, I understood.

"The girl, the biker girl." The girl who had glared at Kiri and made her feel concerned and defensive at the same time. *Maybe we should ask her to join us, but I don't think I can trust her. I think she knows I don't deserve C.* "What was her name again?"

"Natalie."

It all fit together: Callum's nighttime absences from the campsite. Kiri alone by the fire, writing in her diary. It was Natalie he'd been with the whole time. "What did he do to her?" I asked.

Kiri didn't say anything for too long. Then a tear flashed down her cheek, and I picked up my coffee and realized I was trembling and put it down again. So much for keeping my cool.

The newspaper had talked about blood percentages. Callum's blood was on the sweatshirt, but so was the blood of the "unknown"—Natalie. "It's okay," I said. "You can tell me."

Kiri clamped both hands over her mouth. Sobs burst out from under them—enormous sobs that racked her body like earthquake tremors. Each of those spasms ripped at my own insides.

But I had to know the rest.

I drew a deep breath and set my hand down on her quaking shoulder. "I'm in deep, Kiri. I'm not going to turn around and walk away."

"I know. It's just...I've never put any of it in words before." She scrubbed at her face as if she were angry at it, then turned to look at me. "I wish it did happen the way they all think," she said in a low, throaty voice. Her eyes were still wet, but her lips twisted as if she'd smelled something foul. "I wish I took out a knife and stuck it in his chest. I wish I'd laughed at him as he was bleeding out, and then I'd peeled off his bloody sweatshirt and tied it around me like a trophy. I could have sawed off his head and left him in two pieces, just like how that German treasure hunter was left. Talk about viral! They would never forget me."

An icy shiver ran over me, but I didn't look away from her. "You'd never do any of those things." *I know you.*

Kiri shook her head wildly. "I just wish I hadn't been so... stupid."

She tugged off her hood and let hair stream over her shoulders. And then, in that same low voice, but with lurching breaks and swallows between the words, she told me what happened on the day Callum disappeared.

On July 23, Kiri rose from her usual afternoon nap a little early, more than an hour before sunset. Callum was nowhere to be seen. She stuck her knife in her waistband—as she always did when walking alone, in case of cougars—and set off to find him.

She searched some of their usual paths and trails until she reached the big volcanic boulder, about forty feet high, that stood guard at the mouth of the ravine where the treasure hunter's body had been found. Callum's voice wafted down from the top of the boulder, and with it, a girl's laughter.

They were in a crevice, so she couldn't see them. She climbed her way up to where they were, grabbing at juniper bushes in the steep parts. By the time she reached them, she'd heard enough to know they weren't making out. They were sharing a bag of pork rinds, playfully tossing them and aiming for each other's mouths. Natalie had just returned from the store at the park entrance with snacks.

Kiri smelled those pork rinds. Reaching the top, breathless, she swayed dizzily and thought she might faint, she wanted a taste so badly.

She had to remind herself the outside world was a wasteland. The snacks had been scavenged, not bought. There was only here and now, and Cal would come to his senses. He was lucky she'd come after him—Natalie was ruthless and untrustworthy, like most survivors. She might chuck him off the boulder just for the chance to plunder their campsite.

Kiri stabbed a finger at Natalie and shouted, "You stole our supplies! That's why we're starving!"

It made no sense—their supplies had never included pork rinds, let alone Pringles, a can of which sat open beside Callum. But it also made no sense that Callum would eat that junk, and his mouth was full. Shiny crumbs burst from his lips as he looked at Kiri and laughed. And then he and Natalie were both whooping and pointing at Kiri as if she were the best entertainment in the world.

Maybe they were stoned. Maybe, if she'd been in a normal frame of mind, she'd have gotten a whiff of it. But all she could smell was the food.

Natalie rose from where she'd been lounging on the rock and marched right up to Kiri. She was several inches shorter, but the imbalance didn't seem to faze her. She hadn't stolen a thing, she announced. Every few days, Callum paid her for a stash of snacks when she and her biker friends made a run to the store.

Callum stepped between them with his apology face on. With it came the soothing voice that Kiri had learned to dread: "Sweetie, she's telling the truth. No one's stealing anything."

Kiri screamed something at him—a chaos of words that she wouldn't be able to remember afterward, except for one part: "Then why am I starving?"

Natalie looked at Callum. Callum looked at Natalie. "Nobody's starving," he said.

Natalie said, "Drama much?"

"Oh, she's got a flair for the drama." Kiri would never forget what her boyfriend said next, turning to her: "I know I'm a shit, and it was a dirty trick. But you're just so much more *compelling* on camera when you're hungry."

In that moment, Kiri couldn't even feel angry at Callum. The gaping pit spoke from deep inside her. Instead of focusing on him, she dodged around him to grab the bag of pork rinds from Natalie's hand.

Natalie giggled as if Kiri had started a game. She darted away from Kiri and tossed the bag to Callum.

Then the two of them were playing keep-away, gasping with laughter as they threw the bag over Kiri's head. Back and forth, back and forth. The can of Pringles sat on the ground. Kiri could have snatched it. But all she saw in that moment was the bag flying through the air, garish red and yellow against the blue sky. She could already taste those pork rinds—the delicious crunch, the explosion of creamy, bacony fat. She *had* to have them.

She chased Callum and Natalie around and around the small, flattish top of the boulder, each time forcing them closer to the precipice that waited on all sides. Finally, Natalie stumbled, allowing Kiri to get close enough to snatch a corner of the bag. Natalie held on tight to her end. Kiri clung fast to the other and pulled.

"You think you're such a goddamn princess," Natalie said. Something like that. "But if he told you to jump off this rock—"

As she began the sentence, she took a step back, probably trying to widen her stance for the continuing tug-of-war. She must have misjudged the distance to the edge of the boulder, or else the loose gravel crumbled under her feet.

Either way, before Natalie could finish the sentence, she staggered into midair and fell backward, arms flailing. She let go of the bag, and so did Kiri. It fell, too—a large form and a small one, tumbling toward the red dirt just as the sun hit the horizon. Kiri ran to the edge, but the glare in her eyes kept her from seeing anything.

Then, from below, came a terrible, wet crack.

Kiri wouldn't remember clambering back down to the base of the boulder. She wouldn't remember how Callum reacted. At this point, her memory became a jarring series of stop-motion images, sometimes paired with sounds and sometimes eerily quiet.

Blood glistening on red rock. So much blood.

Telling Callum to take off his sweatshirt. Wrapping it around Natalie's head, trying to stop the flow.

Natalie's eyes, open to the wide blue sky. So unbearably still.

His voice: "You pushed her! What's wrong with you?"

Did she answer? Tell him he was wrong? She didn't know. Anyway, soon he was singing a new tune: "Can't you see she's dead? Get up! We can leave now, tonight, for Vancouver Island! No one needs to know you did this!"

Then the knife, its hilt cool and smooth in her hand.

She was going to use the serrated edge to hack up the sweatshirt and make better bandages, a tourniquet, something. But Callum wouldn't stop hovering. She'd been trying to ignore him so she could focus on Natalie. But when she glanced up at him, her heart lurched.

He had his phone out. He was filming her.

"What are you doing?" She could feel the blood already drying on her hands, arms, chest. She stepped toward him, and he didn't move away.

"I can't help it," he said. "You're amazing."

Next thing she knew, the sharp teeth of the knife were sinking into the freckled skin of Callum's upper arm. A thought floated through her head: *I finally did it.* Another thought: *Am I glowing now?*

It felt good.

And then blood, blood, more blood, nothing but blood. Gooey, tacky, awful.

Panicked yelling. His.

Blood.

Bloody hands yanking on the blood-soaked sweatshirt, trying to get it away from her—and she was shoving, hitting, clawing, fighting. It was hers now, and she would not give it up, and he was not going to film her anymore, even if she glowed. No more.

At last, silence.

The sky was mostly dark now, except for a crimson strip on the horizon.

Sand and grit stung under her fingernails. At the base of the boulder yawned a black pit—a crevice almost as deep as a cave, but not a round, human-made cave like the ones in the cliff faces. This was the natural maw of the earth itself.

She knew it was the place to put them both. They would be heavy, but she had to lay them to rest.

The next thing she remembered was walking back to the campsite, the stars cold and unsympathetic overhead. The pork rinds crunched between her teeth, almost an entire bag for her. She savored the meaty taste and the beautiful, growing fullness in her belly.

Wait, what was that behind a rock? That fluid shadow? A cougar?

She reached for the knife, but it was gone. Maybe she'd left it deep in the earth with *them*, the two nameless people who would never appear in her thoughts again. Maybe she'd simply dropped it.

She tensed, ready to defend her food supply, but the shadow melted away. She was the only predator here, her nerves singing the high-pitched song of the hunt.

She'd lost the knife, but somehow she had Callum's phone. She must have wrenched it away from him—which served him right, because he wasn't supposed to be using it, was he? They had rules about phones.

Once she reached the campsite, she sat down and gazed at the screen, a dark pool reflecting her face. Reality began to creep back. *I should tell someone. Is there anyone?*

A list of contacts glowing in the dark. A crackle, and then a familiar deep voice said, sounding tense, "Hey, Cal, what's going on?"

"West. Not him. It's me." She couldn't speak after that. There were no words for what had happened. She just needed to know there was someone else alive in the world.

West said more things—questions? Advice? None of it made any sense to her. She sat by the campfire, quaking with sobs, until she got tired of listening to him and hung up.

She ate the last of the pork rinds, tasting dried blood on her fingers. And then she got up and went on living, because she was a survivor.

She didn't wash off the blood or burn the sweatshirt. If other survivors smelled blood on her, they would see her as someone to be feared and not preyed on.

She bedded down in the cave. She made fires and food. She shot videos—and, though this made no sense, she imagined Cal watching them and being pleased with her performance as a frightened, abandoned girlfriend. Whoever was still out there watching, he wouldn't have wanted his followers to know the ugly truth—that he was a hypocrite. That she'd punished him for it.

She looked out for the bikers, but they didn't appear. The footprints made her think someone was lurking around the campsite, though, so eventually she decided to leave. She hiked to the road where a family picked her up and gave her a ride.

The family reminded her of her own family. Her old life. With them came the possibility that maybe the world hadn't ended after all, and she really did mean to tell them the truth about the bloody sweatshirt around her waist. She felt she owed it to them.

Then she imagined Callum saying, *Don't be an idiot. I don't want to be some mangled corpse in the desert. I want to disappear and be legendary.* And she opened her mouth and a fully formed lie popped out, just as if he'd dictated it to her.

That was the beginning of the purgatory she was still living in.

"That's all I can tell you," Kiri said. "It's like it happened in another lifetime, in a parallel world where our laws of physics and psychology don't apply. It all seemed perfectly natural to me at the time, but I think the hunger messed with my head. It left gaps in my memory."

The rain had stopped, the wet leaves still dripping on the windshield. It was hot in the car, almost steamy, but I didn't open a window.

"You did kill him," I said. "That's what you're telling me."

She gazed out the window. "I can't remember enough to say for sure. But I think if he were alive, he'd have come back for me by now."

She couldn't use the gaps in her memory as an excuse for everything.

So much that she'd already told me had been a lie. "You said before that you found a single call to West on Callum's phone. But that was the call *you* made, wasn't it?"

A nod. "Later, when I went over things in my head, I wanted so badly to think West killed Callum. He tried to separate us, after all! I almost made myself believe it."

I'd wanted to know how a sweet, shy girl becomes a killer, and now I did. But I might spend the rest of my life wishing I didn't.

She didn't look at me. She was a million miles away, her breakfast forgotten. I picked up her hand from where it lay between us and clasped it.

"Why haven't they found him, then?" My voice creaked like rusty hinges. "Cal?"

A tremor ran through her. "I don't know. Maybe they have and they're just not saying, to see what I'll do. Maybe he's not there. Maybe he's on Vancouver Island. I don't know!"

"But if they searched that whole crevice, the knife would be there, too, right? Wouldn't it have your prints on it?"

Another shudder. "The knife could be anywhere. I told you, the gaps…"

I knew why she wouldn't look at me. I was asking too many questions. Maybe she thought I still cared about the truth more than I cared about her.

So I stopped asking the questions I wanted answers to. I focused on the questions that might keep her safe. It hurt my brain to do it, and it hurt my conscience, but only at first.

I couldn't shed any tears for Callum. And Natalie—her death had been an accident, even if it was an awful, avoidable one. Anyway, they were both gone now.

"West must know what happened," I said. "Even though you didn't spell it out when you called, he can put two and two together. Whatever he thinks of Callum, whatever he told you before, you shouldn't trust him, Kiri. He stalked me! He tied up Tierney and left him in the woods!"

Her sweaty fingers twitched against my palm. "I'm not afraid of West." She turned to me, and her eyes had that dead look again. "I brought my mom's gun along, just in case, but I don't think I'll need it."

Just one more thing she hadn't told me. "You know how much trouble you can get in for bringing a gun across the border?"

"It's okay!" She squeezed my hand. "We're already here."

I want you to come back with me. But I couldn't tell her that yet. "Where is it?" My dad taught me to shoot his thirty-eight, so I'm not exactly afraid of guns, but they aren't toys.

Kiri's eyes had softened again, big and pinched at the corners. She needed me to be okay with this. "It's in my backpack with the safety on. Don't worry!"

"You want me to just bring you to that cottage and leave you with West? You and your gun?" I knew I sounded frantic, but I didn't care. "Kiri, it's not too late to tell everyone the truth. The whole truth—that you weren't in your right mind when you...when Callum died. You don't have to disappear."

When I thought about leaving her with West, a granite boulder lodged itself in my chest. I couldn't draw a breath. "Where would you even go?"

Her hand was motionless in mine. "Remember when West gave you the message for me about the 'doomsday cabin'? He was right, I do know what it means. It's an abandoned hunting camp, way up north in Quebec, that belongs to an uncle of somebody West and

Callum knew at school, but he's old and never there. They used it as a base for their hiking one summer and stashed supplies in the root cellar. The woods are full of game. A person could survive there for a while."

"Just you and your backpack and your gun?"

"If I have to. Yes." She looked up again, and something sparked in her eyes. Hope, maybe. "I think West would be willing to take me there."

Sun flooded the car without warning, glaring in my eyes. "Is that really what you want? To be all alone in the middle of nowhere?"

"I've always been scared of being alone." Her free hand peeled mine open, separating us. And then her fingertips were on my forearms, running up to the insides of the elbows, the gentlest tickle. "But now—well, maybe what your mom said was right. Being alone is something I need to learn. If I can survive out there by myself, then great. If I can't, then nature will take its course. It won't be a tragedy."

A hot weight gathered behind my eyes. "It will be to your parents—and . . . to me. You have to know I can't let you do that."

"Can't?" Her breath was on my cheek, her unruly hair falling into the space between us. "Or won't?"

It was a whisper. The sun shone on her face, turning her hair to molten gold. I took a strand and tucked it behind her ear, half expecting it to burn me. "I want to do everything for you. Just not that."

A little sound came from her throat, a sob or sigh of frustration. "I don't want to leave you, either. I don't want this ever to end."

Maybe she moved first, maybe I did, but suddenly there was almost no space between us. She was so close my heart thudded in my throat.

Eyes closed, I felt her lips on mine as if they were already there. The hardness, the softness, the heat of them. The tickle of her hair.

But we didn't touch, not quite. A sigh stirred the air between us, and I couldn't tell whether it came from my lungs or hers.

"I can still feel it," she said finally. "Where we jumped off that cliff—it stings on one side."

"I still feel it, too," I said as we moved apart.

The sunlight was gone, as if hours had passed. Raindrops spattered the windshield.

She looked so soft to me now, her eyelashes dark against her cheek. *How could she have…* but I wouldn't think about what had happened in the desert. Not now.

She made me want to touch her in ways I didn't normally want to touch people. And she scared me.

I didn't know what to do next, so I opened the bag and pulled out the sandwiches. "There's one for you."

"I'm starving." Kiri plucked a sandwich out of my hand. Hers were bigger than mine and graceful, the fingers tapered in a way that made me want to catch them just long enough to feel the soft tips. She took a big bite, chewed, then said, "Oh God, should I not be starving right now? Do I sound like a sociopath?"

"No." But I couldn't help thinking of the pork rinds as I took a bite of my own sandwich.

And then I asked what I'd been wondering ever since she told her story: "After everything Cal did to you, why do you act like he's over your shoulder watching and judging you, every second?" Was it just guilt that kept her obsessed with him, or was it love? "In your video, when you said, 'I know who you are now,' you meant him, didn't you? You saw the real self behind his mask. You know all that, but you can't let go of the person you thought he was before."

Kiri put the sandwich down and glanced around as if Callum

might be standing somewhere nearby. The lot was still empty except for a delivery truck by the mini-mart and a car gassing up. "You're not supposed to speak ill of the dead," she said softly.

"I know. I know." But I just couldn't take it anymore. "Look, I'm not saying your feelings are wrong. I'm just saying—you can stop punishing yourself, okay? You don't have to banish yourself to this doomsday cabin just because you think he'd want you to."

"That's not why I'm doing it." But she looked thoughtful as she picked up the sandwich again. "And he did make me a better person."

"*You* made you a better person!" *And sometimes a worse person.* I thought of everything Reggie had told me yesterday, and I knew it was as true for the two of them as it was for us.

"You gave him power over you because you wanted to be special like you thought he was, glowing or whatever." I wanted to put my arms around her and tell her she was strong in ways Callum would never comprehend, and I wanted to shake her out of sheer frustration. "But it was always you. You're not just clay to be shaped. You had power then and you have it now."

She raised her eyes to me. They looked a little glazed. "I like that idea."

"It's not just an idea." I wasn't sure she'd even been listening to me, but if there was a chance of persuading her *not* to disappear into the doomsday cabin, I had to give it a shot.

Kiri crumpled up her sandwich wrapper. "You're wrong about one big thing, though. I'm not meeting West because Cal would have wanted me to."

"You're not?"

"No." The sun came out again, turning her face to a white mask, and for an instant I could swear I saw a sly smile tug at her mouth.

"I need to see West," she said, "because I don't know where I left the knife, and there's a chance he has it. He might have hidden it in Callum's parents' cottage, if he's staying there."

The footprints, the disappearing phone—West could have retrieved the knife, too. If he had it, her fate might hinge on him.

I opened my mouth to ask questions, but Kiri shook her head. "You said you'd do what I asked, whatever it was, if I just told you the truth."

"But—"

"If he's there, I need you to wait in the car. Let me talk to him alone. Now, here's how to find the cottage."

26

We didn't talk. I drove: up green slopes, down twisty chutes with pines on either side, through a picture-perfect ski town with chalets of red-roofed stone.

When we reached Saint-Aubin-Les-Pins—basically just a mini-mart surrounded by trees and vacation homes—I glanced at Kiri. She was slumped in her seat with her eyes closed, looking so unguarded that a chill gripped the base of my spine.

Why did she have to go in alone? If West really did have the knife, he could use it as a threat to make her do whatever he wanted. Regardless of what he had or hadn't done with Arianna, I didn't like that idea.

The road wound uphill past an orchard and a pond, and there it was—a cedar-lined driveway leading to a two-story stone cottage with a red roof. Closer, the house and grounds looked neatly kept, but there were no lights on, no cars parked, and no garage.

Wasn't West here? I cut the engine, feeling relieved and disappointed at once. Kiri must have been in one of the deep phases of sleep, because she didn't budge.

I watched the cottage for a bit. The sun shone hazily down from a filmy blue sky. Birds chirped in the hedges framing the picture window. The bright red door had a shiny brass knocker. I thought of fairy tales, with their dwellings that seem deserted but are actually enchanted. Or haunted.

What if she was right, and he'd hidden the knife in there? Wouldn't now, while he appeared to be away, be the time to find out?

She'd told me to wait in the car, but if West wasn't here, all bets were off. I stepped out onto the gravel and gingerly closed the door. Kiri hunkered down in her seat, her eyelids fluttering without opening.

I left the car unlocked, the keys on the seat beside her. I would just take a quick look around.

A gravel path—tough to tiptoe on—led to one of colored slate. Seeing no signs of movement behind the lace curtains, I walked around to the back deck, beyond which stretched a tennis court. The grass was mowed, but no lawn furniture was out; Callum's parents must not have visited all summer.

I remembered what Callum's parents must be doing right now—waiting breathlessly, fearfully for news—and a wave of cold passed over me. If Kiri did disappear, they would never know what had truly happened to him.

Back at the front door, I checked for cameras. None, so I walked straight up to the door because I couldn't go back to the car without trying.

The knob turned.

My heart thudded against my breastbone. Sweat prickled on my neck. Callum's folks didn't seem like the type to leave their property unsecured for weeks or months.

But now that I'd started, I couldn't stop myself from pushing the door ever so slowly open.

No creaks—the hinges were well oiled. Beyond a tiled mudroom was a living room as expensively craftsy as everything else. The wood-stove had a white-tiled hearth painted with blue tulips and wooden shoes. There were soft white rugs and matching sofas and rocking chairs with needlepoint cushions. To my right, at the mouth of the stairs, a clock ticked in a crisp, authoritative voice.

A cry made me jump, my heart rocketing—but it was only a bird squawking outside in the hedge.

I walked as if each step might trigger an alarm. If West was camping out here, there should be some sign of him.

The hardwood barely sighed under my sneakers as I crossed to the far wall and gazed over the lawn to the tennis court and a line of cedars. Everything so peaceful.

The afghan folded on the sofa—was it rumpled? The hardcover on the coffee table, something about the Revolutionary War, with a bookmark near the end—could it be his? But no, in the motel he'd been reading a Jack Reacher novel. These digs were certainly a step up in all things.

Light glinted on picture frames, and I stepped over for a look at the Massey family photo gallery. There was Callum's dad, a dead ringer for his son but with kinder eyes. Callum's mom, with fluffy blond hair and patrician features. The parents had their arms around each other in every photo, and I hoped their bond was as strong as it looked. They would need it.

A stocky kid in a prep school uniform—was that Callum? Yes, it had to be, because here was the same kid playing tennis and hiking, skinnier in each progressive image. Here he was rocking a tuxedo, his arm around a blond girl with a corsage who looked bored. By the time he was striking a victory pose at the summit of a mountain, he was the ropy, jacked Callum the internet knew today.

Except now he was probably a corpse buried in a crevice. Did anyone really deserve that?

Maybe not, I told the itching doubt, but he had manipulated Kiri. Provoked her. Starved her. Mocked and jeered at her despair. Even now, from beyond the grave, he was pushing her toward a fate *she* didn't deserve.

Here was a photo of West and Callum together, sitting on a rough-hewn balcony with giant backpacks beside them, feet propped on a railing. They looked relaxed and happy, two friends catching a break after a long day of hiking or climbing—whichever activity you needed those big boots for.

Boots. Four soles faced the camera, looming large in the frame.

Something lurched inside me, and I remembered the many memes made from Kiri's last video: *how it started, how it's going.*

Two of the soles in the photo bore the same pattern that Kiri had seen and recorded in the red dust: the symbol for Aries, the watery lines. She'd described the print to me as a sign that an intruder had been prowling the campsite—West sneaking in to steal the phone and the knife.

But in this photo, the Aries boots belonged to Callum.

What had West said? *She was right to notice the footprints. They came all the way here with me.*

I'd thought he meant they were his own footprints, just as I'd assumed that one of the two beds in his motel room wasn't being used.

But maybe he hadn't come to Burlington alone.

Behind me, a roar ripped through the silence.

West coming back? No, this was a car starting. When I reached the front window, I saw the Legacy fishtailing so that it faced the driveway, the motor revving from reverse into drive.

"Kiri!" What was she thinking? Was she leaving me behind?

I dashed for the door, tore it open, and hurtled back up the slate path. By the time I reached the gravel, the car was already at the mouth of the driveway, turning onto the road.

"Kiri! No!" I was out of breath from my useless yelling, and Owen's car was too far away for me to catch, but I couldn't give up. I couldn't let her go. I lurched forward.

And stopped dead as a voice said behind me: "Whoa. What happened there?"

It was a voice I knew—casual, friendly, a little drawling. Not gravelly like West's. Not embarrassed.

I turned to find a tall man standing in the open doorway of the cottage, with dark hair and an unruly beard that covered most of his face. He wore indigo jeans and a crimson polo shirt and a white bandage on his right arm, and he looked sleepy and slightly annoyed.

The beard confused me, but only for an instant.

"Hey, Sam," Callum Massey said. "Nice to meet you finally. Was that Kiri?"

Before I could answer—it must have shown on my face—he shook his head and said, "Looks like she ditched you, huh? She must think I went on ahead to the caves."

27

When you hear stories of true crime, you always think that at the crucial moment you would have done things differently. You wouldn't have followed the stranger's directions just because he had a gun. You wouldn't have believed his lie that he just wanted your cash and phone. You wouldn't have let him tie you up and take you to a second location.

You'll never be a victim. You'd know better.

What you don't realize, hearing these stories, is how hard it is to adjust when life suddenly blasts you out of one reality into another. One moment, you think you're finally putting the pieces together and figuring things out. The next moment, every fiber of your being is straining toward a car that's disappearing down a road, a car that holds someone you care about too much—*where is she going?*

And then a person who should be dead is standing right there in front of you.

I didn't move. I stared at Callum, noticing in a detached way that his feet were bare, as he strode toward me up the slate path. When he took my arm, I went limp. I let him tug me all the way to the door of the cottage, which hung open.

My heart was with the car, though I couldn't hear it anymore. Where was Kiri going? Had she spotted him? Did she know?

Had the fact that he was *alive* vanished into one of those gaps in her memory?

When we reached the door, I finally found the presence of mind to grab hold of the frame. I wasn't going in there alone with him.

He let me go. Smiled in a casual way, as if we were old friends. "Don't worry. We'll catch up to her."

Off balance, I tottered backward, reminding myself that Callum had never killed anyone. "She's getting away," I said in a low voice. "She's ditching you, too, and now you'll never find her."

"What?" His smile faded for a moment, then returned—a charming smile, but with a touch of reproach in it. "No, you're all confused, aren't you? Who did you think you were meeting in Canada?"

My gaze caught on the length of white gauze wrapped around his upper arm. Was that where Kiri had stabbed him?

"West," I murmured, as if his name were a secret.

"West's out of the picture now." Again the friendly smile. "Kiri knows that. I'm the one who left her a note setting up a meeting in the caves. She must have recognized my writing."

"*Your* writing." I'd seen three notes in the same distinctive handwriting: one in Kiri's backyard, one in the motel room, and one on Tierney.

On Tierney. As the truth sank in, I took a wobbly step down off the stoop, away from him. If Callum had written the notes, then he was the one who'd ambushed Tierney, knocked him over the head, and dumped him into the trunk of his own Range Rover.

And Kiri had known he was alive as soon as she saw the note, if not much sooner. She knew the whole time she was "confessing" to me.

How was he alive?

"You look like you've seen a ghost." Callum's gaze probed my face—the alert gaze of a predator. Cords of muscle stood out on his neck and forearms. "Like you're seeing one now. I guess she didn't tell you everything."

Nothing he was doing was overtly threatening, yet my knowledge of what he'd done to Tierney was like a red alert flashing in the air between us. I took another step backward, but where could I go?

"She's not going to meet you after all," I repeated, still hearing the rumble of the car in my memory.

But then I remembered what Kiri had told me long ago—that if Callum were alive, he would have returned to help her clear her name. Now here he was. Maybe she thought that if she did meet him at the caves, she could persuade him to turn himself in.

Callum moved—a long arm reaching for me, an iron hand on my bicep—and before I knew what was happening, we were inside the cottage and the door was shut and we were standing apart again. I staggered backward, trembling so hard my vision blurred.

"Don't feel bad," he said. "I don't think Kiri meant this to happen. She probably wanted to ditch you here, a place she thought was empty, so you'd be out of her way when she went to the caves."

"She thought I'd be safe here." I had to believe that. Kiri might have gaps in her memory, all right, but she'd also done some "creative fictioning" of her own. She knew I would never let her go off with Callum, so she'd made up the story about West and the knife, then waited until I left the car to make her escape. Even her sleep must have been feigned.

"Yup." Callum folded his arms behind his head, grabbing his elbows. Stretched so that every muscle bulged against the polo shirt. "She must have told so many lies by now she can't keep them straight. But don't worry, you haven't seen the last of her. She'll be there at noon on the dot. Mind giving me your phone?"

Again, arms moved in a blur. His hand stretched toward me.

This might be the moment. *Run*. But if he was staying in the same amazing shape Kiri had, then he would catch me in a flash.

I couldn't fight or flee my way out of this. I had to figure out what he wanted.

So I took out my phone and gave it to him before he could get any closer. "Sorry," he said, pocketing it. "Gotta be careful—you're into the true-crime scene, and I don't need any postmortem pics of me out there."

My head shuddered like an over-heavy flower on its stalk. I couldn't seem to breathe when he was within a yard of me. "How did you know that about me? *You're* DodgerBlodger, aren't you?"

"Yeah, but Kiri told me about you months ago, back when we first met. She thought you were hot shit because you had a podcast about murder."

"When you met?" I couldn't seem to breathe again. "But I barely knew Kiri in those days. She didn't know about the..."

Or maybe she *had* known about the podcast. My heart sank as I thought of all the times I'd rehashed my latest episode to Owen and Lore in the lunchroom or read a true-crime paperback in study hall. Quietly, in the background, Kiri must have been watching.

And so, when we collided in the park, she knew exactly what she was dealing with. She knew I might just be obsessed enough to help her.

The betrayal hurt like the smack of the water when I'd jumped off the cliff. But I couldn't deny that I'd been trying to use her, too—at first.

"Are you okay?" Callum peered at me, head on one side. Cat with a mouse. "Based on everything Kiri and West said, I kind of expected you to be a cooler customer. You spooked West so bad he started trying to convince me to turn myself in, which pretty much forced me to ditch him and deliver the note to Kiri's house myself, which you know was risky. But I guess at the end of the day you're just a kid, like her."

"I'm okay," I said faintly. All that seemed to be left of the chill I thought I had was an icy sensation in my palms and at the base of my neck.

"But West's always been jittery," Callum said. "I had to twist his arm to come back to Burlington, and he wouldn't stake out Kiri's street—I had to do that myself. Anyway, we should get a move on if we're gonna make the meeting. Where are my shoes?"

While he put on his sneakers in the mudroom, I made myself hold a breath and let it out slowly. Every lie that Kiri had told me burned like a brand on my skin.

She had chosen me on purpose to confide in. Pretended to be shocked when she discovered my true-crime interest so that I would feel guilty enough to break the law for her.

And all for what? For Callum? If she were setting a trap to lure him into the open, she should have told me.

Maybe she hadn't dared. Or worse, maybe she still wanted to be with him. That possibility threatened to engulf me; I had to push it away.

He rose from tying his shoes and came toward me again. This time I flitted away from him, but not far.

If I was ever going to have an advantage over this man, even the tiniest one, he needed to think I was reeling, harmless, potentially even on his side. "I still don't understand. She told me you were dead."

"Kiri and her web of lies!" He crooked two fingers and headed for the door—loose, casual strides. Not worried in the least that I wouldn't follow. Over his shoulder, he said, "Did she tell you she killed me?"

"Yes," I whispered.

But inside, I knew she hadn't lied about the most important things. Every slippery, condescending word out of Callum's mouth convinced me he was the man she'd described in the diary, the man she'd finally come to know as her tormentor, not her lover.

She deserved so much better than that. I'd tried to show her that love shouldn't hurt that way, shouldn't make you feel small, but she hadn't understood. Or it wasn't enough.

Now all I could do was walk with Callum—out of the house and across the yard and tennis court. Beyond the row of cedars, hidden from the cottage, stood Tierney's Range Rover.

"Why did you have to do that to my boss's son?" I asked, not trying to hide my trembling. "He might have a concussion."

"I needed a fast car, okay? Like I said, I couldn't stick with West; he was useless. He pretended he'd set up a meeting with Kiri, but then he dragged his feet. I couldn't trust him. And this dude"—Callum jabbed a thumb at the Range Rover—"seemed like a real douchebag. That car of his was practically an invitation."

Funny how Reggie had said the same thing. The Range Rover beeped. Callum held the passenger door open for me—ever the gentleman.

That was how his groupies saw him. If I could convince him I was one of them at heart, he might let down his guard.

I got in and buckled up.

I didn't have a prayer of running fast or far enough, but maybe I didn't want to run anywhere. Even if Kiri was lost to me forever, I had to see her again.

"So you were the one who followed me?" I asked. "Not West?"

Callum chuckled, settling himself at the wheel. "I took his car keys while he was asleep at the motel. He was pretty pissed when he found out. I thought if I staked out her street long enough, I'd catch her on a run, but instead I caught you. I told West what to say when he met you at the theater. I thought suggesting Panera was a nice touch."

"And the message he gave me for Kiri? That was your idea?"

"Message? I told him to set up a meeting."

So the message about the footprints and the doomsday cabin had been West's contribution. It must have been his way of telling Kiri that Callum was with him, so she would have all the facts before agreeing to a meeting.

And Kiri had received the message loud and clear. I remembered her standing with her hands against the slider, staring out at the lightning. The news had floored her, though she'd done her best not to let me know.

Then she'd demanded the meeting. *It's the only way I can ever be free.*

"I still don't understand." I let my voice falter. "You said West wanted you to turn yourself in, but you haven't done anything! Well, except what you did to Tierney." *And Arianna*, but he didn't know I knew about that. "Why are you hiding like this, letting everyone think you're dead? Your parents must be in hell right now."

"It's not that simple." Callum cinched his lap belt, the slightest edge of annoyance on his voice. "What about Kiri? Do you think *she's* innocent? You didn't when you drove her over the border, did you?"

I stared out the window at the cedars, avoiding his gaze.

He tugged a phone from his pocket and stabbed it with his finger a few times. "I'm gonna show you something, and it might shock you. But you need to know what we're dealing with."

He slotted the phone into a dashboard holder so I could see the screen.

Red rock. Blue sky. Two backlit figures were...dancing?

No. Callum turned up the volume, and I heard wild, high-pitched laughter. The smaller figure darted away from the camera, holding something red and yellow and shiny aloft like a prize. The larger one followed her, and I heard a second voice, low and almost moaning: "Give it to me!"

The larger figure had platinum hair—Kiri.

I pressed a hand to my mouth to hide my gasp of horror as I realized that I was seeing Kiri and Natalie fight for the bag of pork rinds. I knew what was going to happen, and I couldn't stop it.

It was hard to tell what was going on, because Callum kept darting around as if he were trying to get a better angle. I couldn't miss the final tug-of-war, though. Natalie's words were muffled, the two of them a confusing tangle of limbs against the sunset, but I watched her teeter and lose her footing and fall. Kiri ran to the edge and peered over.

The footage stopped there, but my heart was racing, thudding so hard I could barely draw a breath. Callum closed the clip and opened a second one.

Now the camera was at ground level, close up on a girl who had stringy brown hair and delicate features. Dark liquid puddled under her head, staining the red rock. Night pooled in her open eyes, their last spark of watchful life gone.

Natalie. My first real glimpse of her face felt like stepping into an empty elevator shaft with nothing to grab on to, just wind whistling in my ears. When I was younger, I went through a phase of daring myself to look at crime scene photos, with their raw wounds and lifeless gazes. But this was different, because I'd also seen her death through Kiri's eyes.

In the right foreground, a figure knelt beside Natalie—shoulders hunched, hands clasped as if she were praying. Her back was to the camera, but you couldn't miss the platinum hair.

Her voice rose above the dim buzz of static. She wasn't saying anything, exactly. She was rocking back and forth and chanting the same words over and over: "You're not good enough, you're not good enough, you're not good enough."

The clip ended. I squeezed my eyes tight shut, feeling tears swell and ache behind the lids.

The engine roared as Callum started the Range Rover. We drove for a while, each breath I took sounding impossibly loud in the red-tinged darkness, until he said, "So I guess you didn't know."

I opened my eyes. I got my face under control. "It was an accident." Nothing in the video clips contradicted Kiri's story. She had just left out a little.

"You think so?" Callum scratched the side of his nose, using the other hand to steer us back the way Kiri and I had come, toward the center of Saint-Aubin-Les-Pins. "Because, to me, it looked like Kiri chased Nat right off that ledge."

"It didn't look that way to me." But you couldn't be sure, given the angle of the camera and the backlighting. A jury might see what Callum saw, especially once they'd seen the second clip, with Kiri hunched over Natalie's body and chanting those ugly words.

A jury wouldn't know what I knew: She hadn't been saying those words to Natalie. She'd been saying them to herself.

Callum asked, "Did you know about Natalie when you drove her over the border? Or did you think she'd just killed me?"

"I thought it was just you."

"And you didn't mind that?" Callum sounded amused, and maybe a touch admiring. "You figured it was A-okay that she murdered me, since I was such a bad boyfriend?"

I didn't say anything.

"She really got you on her side, didn't she? It's hard to resist those big brown eyes."

I fiddled with a loose thread on my cutoffs, winding it around my little finger until it sliced in hard. I remembered Kiri in the car this morning, coming so close I could feel her breath.

Lying to me, this whole time.

"I figured you were dead," I said, "and whether you deserved to die or not, there was nothing I could do to bring you back." And then I said the one thing that I knew would make him trust me, if anything could: "I wanted...to make a podcast about Kiri. I wanted to tell the whole story, the story nobody else could tell."

Callum took a moment to absorb that. Then he laughed—a genuine, hearty laugh—as he turned off the main road into the woods. I took note of the sign: ROUTE DE LA GROTTE DE LA CASCADE.

"Sheesh," he said. "All this for a little clout?"

I stared down at my bitten nails. "I guess that's something you'd understand. Everything you said on your channel about stripping down your life, prepping for the end of the world—did you actually believe any of it?"

I hoped to God he was wrong and Kiri wouldn't show up at the caves. I hoped she was gunning the Legacy way up north, headed for some kind of freedom. Because I didn't get the sense that Callum cared about clearing her name.

"Well, civilization *is* ending. Just maybe not in our lifetimes."

Callum chuckled. He liked thinking he had my number. "Kiri believed it more than I ever could. I would tell her something, and she would just run with it. Honestly, she scared me sometimes."

Me too. Maybe she had convinced herself she'd killed him, at least for a while. She'd told the lies she thought he'd want her to, then contradicted them with new lies of her own. The narrow road wound up, down, and around, with firs and rippling maples on both sides. I caught the flash of a creek—first on the left, then on the right.

"You look so scared now." His tone was gently amused. "You consume too much of that true-crime bullshit, Samantha. I'm not a psychopath."

And my name isn't Samantha. "Real psychopaths are actually more likely to be the victims of crime than the perpetrators," I said, reciting something Lore had told me.

"Ha, is that so?" He swung us left at a sign that said CHEMIN DE LA GROTTE DE LA CASCADE. "I'll have to tell Kiri that. The way she acted after Natalie's 'accident'—well, it certainly makes me wonder about her mental health."

"You pushed her," I said. "You made her think she wasn't good enough." *And then you filmed her in that moment and told her she was "amazing."* No wonder she was confused about what was real.

We were on a dirt road now, bumping up and down, so maybe he didn't hear me. Anyway, he didn't contradict me, only steered us into a grassy, vacant parking area surrounded by trees.

He pulled in the Range Rover and killed the ignition. "Twenty minutes to noon," he said. "It's about a mile to the caves. Lucky thing this place is too far out to be much of a tourist attraction on weekdays."

Getting out, I heard the river, farther off than before. "If she's coming, she must really love you," I said meekly, hoping it wasn't true, as I followed him to the head of a wide trail. The haze had cleared, and it was hot but not humid, the sun making shimmering green curtains of the trees.

Callum gave me that friendly smile of his. "She knows she belongs with me. She doesn't like to be alone. But believe me, I don't underestimate her anymore."

He lifted his arm so I could get a good look at the bandage, a bulky mass of gauze stretching up from his elbow. Kiri had given him more than a little gash with her knife.

"That's a nice bandage—where did you get it? I'm guessing you didn't visit the ER before you disappeared."

"You card, Sam! You're just dying to hear the whole story from my perspective, aren't you? So you can add it to your big scoop?"

I grimaced at him. After another few strides, he said more seriously, "Kiri was out of her mind after what happened to Nat—and after she saw I'd been filming everything. If I hadn't run off and hidden, I honestly think she might have killed me for real. I tried to get the knife away from her, but she clawed me like a wildcat. And I was bleeding pretty bad, so I got away and made my shirt into a tourniquet and kind of collapsed in a crevice. Spent the night there."

He sounded awkward for the first time since we'd met, as if he didn't like admitting he hadn't been in control of the situation.

"But not the whole night," I said. "You came back to the campsite, didn't you?"

"Yeah, just before dawn." Callum flicked a mosquito off his neck. "I wanted my phone, and I lucked out—she hadn't brought it into the cave with her. It was sitting right there on a stone by the firepit."

That must have been when he left boot prints. "Most people would have, I don't know, called nine-one-one. But you didn't, because you already wanted to disappear."

"Kiri told you about that?" He frowned, probably wondering if I knew about Arianna.

"West told me."

"West." He spoke the name as if West were a sweet but incorrigible child. "I thought about going back to our van and just driving it to Canada. But it was a long hike, and I'd lost some blood. So I scurried back to my hidey-hole, and I called West and told him what had happened and asked him to be my white knight and rescue me."

"And he did?"

Ahead of us, the river's burble swelled to a roar. I caught glimpses of what looked like a tall cliff rising through the trees.

Raising his voice to be heard over the torrent, Callum said, "He didn't want to. He said this was the last thing he'd ever do for me. But he agreed to drive me to a place we know up north, where a person could hide out for a while."

The doomsday cabin.

"But you never got to that place!" I yelled to be heard over what had to be a major waterfall; it grew louder with each step. The cliff loomed high above us, with dark slits like windows marring the rock face at intervals too regular to be natural. It made me think of the round cave in New Mexico, hollowed out by human beings, where Kiri had taken refuge.

"Nah. I made West take a detour!" The closer we got to the cliff, the faster Callum moved. To my surprise, I managed to keep up with him—all those bike trips to and from Kiri's house must have done me some good.

He grabbed a slender maple trunk and swung himself to face me. "Once I had my phone back, I checked out the stuff Kiri was posting on my feed. I nearly freaked when I saw new posts. I thought she might trash me to my subscribers, or just embarrass herself by confessing everything."

If he planned to vanish, why would he care what his subscribers thought? But I could guess the answer: Callum Massey would never stop seeing himself as the star of his own drama.

"But I was wrong! She wasn't trashing me. And she was going viral—pulling better numbers than I have in seven whole years!" Admiration shone on his face—this was what he valued most. "When she acted normal, a lot of viewers didn't like her. They thought she was a stuck-up princess. But when she started being weird, she was—"

His last word was lost in the roar. "What?" I shouted.

"Incandescent! She glowed."

"She was starving—that's why she acted weird. She was in pain. Out of her mind." But he wasn't wrong. I'd been fascinated with Kiri, hadn't I? Drawn in like a moth to the flame.

Callum stepped closer to me, his face turning serious. "You wouldn't know about this, Sam, but there's a certain kind of girl who's eager to punish herself, to put herself through hell because she thinks it'll make her a better person. Or maybe she thinks she deserves it—I don't know! But when a girl like that reaches her breaking point, it's kind of beautiful."

I remembered all the time I'd spent hating myself for not being cool enough for Reggie. "Kiri thought she loved you," I said.

And I'd thought I loved her. Maybe, despite everything, I still did. Not because she was "incandescent" or broken or iconic, but because she was the girl I knew from the diary—vulnerable, a little goofy, painfully sincere. She was that girl when we were in school, too, but I hadn't bothered to get to know her then. I'd passed over her as if she weren't there.

Callum had veered back toward the cliff and was practically there now, too far away to hear me. "C'mon!" he called. "Save your breath for the climb."

He headed for a door-like opening at the base of the cliff, at least twice my height. The cliff itself was the size of a four- or five-story building. The chill of the interior radiated outward, and I shivered as it touched my skin.

Callum paused in the opening, spanning it with his long arms. The rough doorway was reinforced with masonry and plaster.

We walked through it into a roundish room about the size of Theater Six of the Grand Nine, and just as frigid with no aid from air-conditioning. The green light of the woods shone through window slits every ten feet. A concrete stairwell spiraled up on the left.

The white noise of the falls seemed to come from everywhere at once; it was hard to believe we weren't underwater. Echoes bounced off the rough, natural walls, filling the space with a strange feedback that sounded like singing.

Callum liked other people to be overwhelmed. If I let the echoing caves awe me, I would give him control. So I told myself the sound was those distant explosions from Theater Three, shrunk smaller than firecrackers, and shut it out and followed him to the stairs.

Callum took them two or three at a time, not bothering to use the cast-iron railing. "Monks built this place in the nineteenth century," he called down to me. "They had a shrine here, but now it belongs to the government."

I trudged up the seemingly endless steps, my lungs starting to strain. What did Callum think was going to happen here? He'd admitted to me that Kiri had made him run for his life, yet he didn't seem worried about facing her again.

Confidence was his strength, and maybe it would again be his undoing. *She brought a gun.*

The stairs ran halfway around the cylindrical shaft to the second floor. Here, just four "windows" let in the daylight. The openings reached almost to the ceiling, but they were narrow—slightly wider than my body, I found, stepping closer to one.

Cool spray hit my face. I held tight to the masonry edge and peered down to see the massive waterfall twenty feet below. The foaming torrent surged over dark rocks until it disappeared into a churning green pool. From there, the river hurtled on, around the curve of the hollowed-out cliff and back the way we'd come. Nothing could stop it.

"Careful!"

Fingers clamped my shoulders, pulling me backward. An electric shock went through me, and I struck out without thinking—a jab of the elbow to the place where his guts should be.

Before I could connect, Callum was already stepping away from me—laughing, his hands in the air. "Easy, Sam. I just don't want to see you getting washed downstream."

Adrenaline fizzed inside me with no outlet. Hitting him would have felt good, but now all I could do was follow him up the second flight of stairs, which began ninety degrees from the end of the first. "Why can't we just wait for her at the bottom?"

"Don't you want the best view?"

Once I got into the rhythm of climbing and breathing, it wasn't so bad, and I managed to reach the third floor without being winded. The roar of the falls was a more distant echo now, static instead of something that itched under my skin.

Callum was waiting for me, his narrowed eyes gleaming in the daylight that filtered through the openings. "I'm trying to figure out what Kiri likes about you," he said. "What you give her."

So apparently my efforts to seem harmless and pathetic had been successful—cold comfort, since I wasn't sure I'd even been pretending. I trudged past him across the chamber to the base of the third stairway. "A ride across the border, I guess."

"No, it has to be more than that." A couple of strides, and he was leading the way again, taking the stairs two at a time. "Why was she so eager for you to sneak over every night? I gave her structure and goals—and attention, of course. What did you give her?"

I couldn't talk and climb; my whole body was suddenly awash in sweat, my mind blank. What *had* I ever given Kiri besides a connection to the outside world, an adrenaline rush when we jumped off the cliff, and then a way back to him?

What did I have to give anybody? Consumed by my Kiri obsession, I certainly hadn't been treating Owen or Lore too well this past week. If I came back without the Legacy, I might find myself with no friends.

"I don't know," I said.

Callum raised a finger, gazing into midair. "Shh. You hear that?"

I strained my ears, and a new sound separated itself from the roar of the falls. From below us came a faint tapping like someone climbing stairs.

Callum was beside me instantly, latching onto my elbow before I saw him move. "Just one more flight," he said, pulling.

"That could be anyone. It could be West."

"West?" His eyes widened as if I'd said something absurd. "He's probably on his way back to Arizona. When I booked, I left him a note to let him know he wouldn't have to worry about me anymore."

See ya. But West's coded message had been a private heads-up for Kiri—Callum didn't know about that. West hadn't wanted her to fall under Callum's spell, and maybe he wouldn't abandon her so easily.

Callum was tugging me with him up the final flight of stairs. The last chamber was smaller than the others, with just three openings. "Here's our view," he said, hauling me toward the one in the center.

The opening was narrow enough that I didn't fear falling by accident but wide enough to step through. Sunlight flooded it; we were well above the treetops now.

Below, a sea of green stretched to the purple mountains on the horizon, every leaf glinting in the sun. The waterfall sparkled from its chasm, which narrowed as the river twisted through the woods. The sky was cloudless, the sun directly overhead.

The backs of my thighs prickled at the height and hugeness of it, yet some childish part of me couldn't believe anything bad would happen in such a beautiful place. Not here. Not now.

Callum spun me to face him. "Listen," he hissed, leaning down so close that I finally saw the angry circles of fatigue around his eyes. "How would you like to shoot a video of Kiri and me, Sam? A goodbye video to the world that would make you viral beyond your wildest dreams?"

One part of me, the part that had ached to go viral with a podcast, said *Yes, yes, yes.* But the other part knew that Callum would never give up control of his camera to anyone. He just wanted to see how far he could push me.

I shook my head. "I'd probably end up in jail."

"Then come with us! You can ride the wave, too."

"The...wave?" He was still holding my shoulders. My whole body itched to shove him away, but with the opening behind me, I didn't dare. Then I remembered what he'd said about Kiri going viral after he disappeared. "You mean, like, her trending? What good is that? You can't keep posting and expect them not to catch you!"

"You could post for us. We'll use a VPN." His lip curled, and I knew he hadn't figured out the details yet. "We'll find a refuge and post from there, like Julian Assange."

I opened my mouth to say that he wasn't a political figure, that he wasn't *anybody*, and shut it again. Of course he fantasized about being a famous fugitive, leading the national media on a chase all over the continent.

"What if Kiri doesn't want to?" I asked. "What if she's done with all that?"

He released me. "She's not done."

The footsteps rang louder, right below us. I willed them to be a random tourist, a monk's ghost, literally anyone but Kiri. I willed her away from Callum forever.

But this choice wasn't mine to make.

A dry whisper came from my throat: "I'll come with you. But only if she wants me to."

"Excuse me?"

"I said I'll come with you." The footsteps again—slow, tentative. I wasn't sure what I was saying anymore, only that it might distract him. "I'll shoot your goodbye video—but it won't really be goodbye, will it? I could spend some time in your hideout and tape a podcast. It would connect you with your followers. You could both tell your sides, maybe throw a government conspiracy angle in there. It would be riveting."

Callum frowned. "We're better on video."

"Then I'll do that. Whatever you want."

He chuckled. "I can't tell if you're in love with Kiri or just the thirstiest person I've ever met."

The footsteps were climbing the last flight of stairs. I remembered how Kiri had run straight off the cliff, and I willed her not to embrace danger this time. *Turn around. Turn and run.*

Callum swung toward the stairs. In a flash, I saw the glitter of calculation vanish from his eyes, replaced by swelling tears. He was becoming the Cal that Kiri needed to see.

"Here's our star," he said.

28

Kiri reached the top of the steps and stood statue still. Her gaze flicked from Callum to me and back. Her eyes widened. Her hoodie was gone and her hair loose on her shoulders, except where it caught in the straps of her black backpack.

"Sam?" she said in a small voice—then pressed her fingers to her mouth, as if she'd already said too much.

"We met at the cottage." Callum draped his arm across my shoulders as if we were the best of friends. "She's been catching me up on everything. I'm so glad you came, Kiri. I wasn't sure you would."

I didn't try to pull away from him. I was focused on her.

Her eyes glistened. Her mouth twisted—into an ugly grimace. "Why is she here?" she asked, her gaze moving from me to Callum. "I left her at the cottage so we could be alone. We don't need her anymore."

We. The word stabbed the breath out of me. Her voice was colder than I'd ever heard it before. A flash of memory came to me: the two of us in the car this morning, so close to each other. Had she just been acting?

Something in that coldness must have spoken to Callum. He dropped me like a hot potato and sped to Kiri—then stopped short,

an achingly tentative expression on his face, as if he longed to throw his arms around her but didn't dare. If he was faking, he was doing it well. "I missed you," he said.

Don't fall for his bullshit!

She raised her eyes to him—they were red-rimmed but tearless. "I thought I killed you," she said in a hoarse whisper. "You shouldn't be alive."

"I know." Callum took another step, so careful. "But I've missed you so much." His voice was broken, even as he approached her with the stealthy self-possession of a cat. "I fucked up so badly. It took a shock"—he touched the bandage on his arm—"to make me see it. But I was weak, Kiri. What happened with Nat and the food—that's the proof that I'm weaker than you."

He was targeting her need for praise. He knew her so well.

"You're so full of shit!" I couldn't stop the words from bursting out, flinging them at him because if I even looked at Kiri again, I might cry. "You don't deserve her. You don't even know her!"

Run now, Kiri, while I'm distracting him. Run.

Callum acted as if he hadn't heard me. And Kiri didn't run. She slid her backpack off her shoulders onto the stone floor.

"Let Sam go," Kiri said in that cold voice, not looking at me. "She's not part of this."

Maybe Aliza Deene was right about her all along.

I tried to make her look at me. "You don't have to go with him. What happened to Natalie was an accident!"

"A jury won't believe that," Callum said. "She's already told too many lies. People want to see her punished."

Kiri knelt to unzip the backpack. I held my breath as she fumbled inside, knowing what was in there.

"If you go away with him now," I said to Kiri in a low voice, "people might never know the truth. This is your last chance to tell it. It would be fairer to Natalie—to her family. They'd want to know."

Kiri pulled out a tube of lip gloss. She rubbed it across her lips and put it back, leaving the backpack unzipped.

Disappointment crushed me, a wrecking ball to the chest. What had I expected—for her to casually whip out the gun and blow him away? But she wouldn't have brought the gun if she hadn't at least considered the possibility.

"That *is* an idea," she said, not to me but to Callum. "We could use Sam to tell our story, the real story. She could post a video of us, so people will stop saying all those awful things, and then we could go home and turn ourselves in. Neither of us really ever hurt anybody, and people should know."

"We're not going home!" Callum snapped the words. "Are you wimping out on me again, Kiri? Hoping to crawl back to civilization and convince everybody you're innocent? Sam can make us a video once we're somewhere secure."

"She's got nothing to do with this!"

"Oh, really?" Callum stepped back, away from Kiri. He looped his arm through mine with that fluid strength of his. "A couple of days ago, she posted on a true-crime influencer's feed that she'd seen my cabin in Vermont and knew things about our case no one else did. Things you probably told her."

I didn't feel the hateful warmth of his body anymore; my own had gone ice cold. "I didn't tell anyone anything important." The words came out like sawdust. "I swear I would never—"

"Oh, and another thing." Callum marched me closer to the window, back into the sunlight. It shone right in my eyes. "She's in love with you, or with the whole trending idea of you—I can't tell which. When I told her our only option was to disappear, she begged to come with us."

"I said that because you invited me to, you fucking narcissist!" His grip was hurting me now.

"I said let her go, Cal!" Kiri's voice cut through the haze of shame and terror in my head. "She's not a survivor like you—like *us*."

"So you don't want her tagging along to the doomsday cabin?" His fingers didn't loosen.

"No!" Kiri drew a ragged breath. "You're right—we can't trust her. We're the last people in the world, Cal."

Callum's fingers dug into my arm, immobilizing me. The cold spread outward from my gut toward my limbs.

"I dunno, Kiri," he said. "I mean, technically there are a few billion people left in the world, and you might want some company where we're going. This kid's annoying, but she's also kind of cute with the podcaster act. And she did volunteer."

"Fuck you." My muscles unlocked. I tried to donkey kick him, to loosen his grip, but he twisted my arm behind my back. Tears pricked my eyes. For an instant, it took all my strength not to scream.

This was how badly he could hurt someone when he wanted to.

"Stop it!" Kiri sounded alarmed now.

Callum relaxed his grip, but only so he could drag me sideways toward the opening. I tried to plant my feet, my arm throbbing where he'd pinned it. My knees buckled instantly.

"We're wasting time here, Cal." Kiri's voice was a lash, more commanding than I'd ever heard it before.

"I know," Callum said. His confidence was a python; it had its coils around me, squeezing and choking. "But," he continued, giving me another yank toward the window, "I can't trust you anymore, sweet Kiri. A few more swipes with that knife, and that would've been all she wrote. I do have that little video of you ranting at Natalie's corpse, but I'm not sure that's enough to keep you in line. Which is why—"

I didn't hear the rest. Because then he was grabbing hold of me by the right armpit and left knee, as if I weighed no more than a doll, and lifting me off the floor and hauling my entire body through the opening.

I struggled at first, but once I grasped what was happening, I went tense and still in his grasp. Callum wasn't bluffing. All he had to do was let go, and he would do it without a second thought, without regret. I knew it with every fiber of my being.

One instant, you're standing in the dimness of a cave, and the next, light is everywhere. The world lurches and swings. Up and down have no meaning. As a warm breeze rustles your hair, you know you're about to die.

Except I didn't fall, didn't move. I remained suspended between the vastness of sky and earth, a puppet caught in the puppeteer's grasp by an awkwardly splayed arm and leg. Callum was panting, his fingertips digging into my upper arm and knee, and I knew that if I budged he might lose his grip. He must be bracing his elbows on the sill, but even strong people have their limits.

The whole thing probably lasted less than a minute. I closed my eyes, and for a few endless instants I felt nothing, not even vertigo. In the distance, two voices were arguing, one higher-pitched than the other. Did she sound a little frightened now, or was I still a distraction? A waste of time?

Somewhere in there, a memory came to me: starlight glancing on the surface of the lake. The wild glint of Kiri's eyes as she tossed her clothes away. I had landed safely at the bottom of that cliff, but this time—

Without warning, I was being lifted in great, panting heaves, by fingers slick with sweat, back through the opening.

My ankle caught on something sharp. Pain whited out my vision, but I didn't make a sound.

When I hit the floor, I was free of his hands. I hadn't even felt them release me. I rolled over and pressed my palms and cheek to the stone that stank of old dust.

A shadow above me. Long hair grazing the nape of my neck.

"Not now, Kiri," Callum said, and she was gone.

It was like coming out of nitrous at the dentist's. At first, my brain refused to get a solid grip on anything except *You're alive*, and that thought was a straight shot of 100 proof vodka.

Then I realized they were arguing again. "We don't have to take her, Cal! She doesn't even know where the cabin is!"

"She knows enough! And if we let her go home, she'll have every incentive to tell the whole damn internet." His voice shook a little.

Maybe it was only from the effort of holding me suspended in mid-air. Or maybe Callum's confidence had finally taken a hit. Maybe, while I was out there, Kiri had said something that made him think she might try to stab him again the next chance she got.

He was afraid of her, and he wanted me as a hostage.

I tasted blood. The pain in my ankle was fading, but it forced me to focus, certainty sharpening to a wicked point.

Kiri's choice belonged to her, but I wasn't going to let him take me prisoner.

They kept yelling back and forth. My legs were still too shaky from fright to stand, so I curled up, knees to chest, and breathed from my core. I could feel it, pulsing like a homing beacon on the floor just a foot or two from my right shoulder.

The backpack.

"You wouldn't survive jail!" Callum was saying. "You're not built for it. You need me!"

"I don't need anyone who threatens me." Her voice was steady now, and that gave me a burst of strength.

I opened my eyes. Crept silently toward the backpack.

Their voices sliced the air above me, but the words had lost their meaning. Only one thing mattered.

Callum had his back turned to me. He hovered over Kiri, extending his hands as if he wanted to touch her but still didn't dare, giving her all his attention.

I snuck a hand through the open zipper and shoved aside soft clothing until I got my fingers around it, cold and solid and familiar. A revolver, like my dad's.

I lifted it out in a single motion. My thumb found the safety and clicked it off.

They turned at the same time—close together but not touching. The window lit one side of her face, drawing a spark from her eyes.

They would always look so right together.

I'd startled Callum, but not for long. He broke away from Kiri and came at me fast.

But I was already aiming for the middle of his body, and I squeezed the trigger.

The recoil tipped me over onto my heels, but I managed to keep hold of the gun. The sharp clap ricocheted off the walls and drowned out the waterfall. Kiri cried out, and the two echoes mingled in the air.

The shot had made Callum stop dead in his tracks. He glanced down at his chest, no expression on his face. He was backlit, and given the color of his shirt, I couldn't tell if he was bleeding.

At last, he laughed—with relief. He lunged toward me again.

I was too close to aim at him now, too unstable. I scrambled to my feet—ears ringing, ignoring the stab of pain in my ankle—and ran directly at him, slamming my whole body into his midsection like a battering ram.

He wasn't expecting that. But he adjusted quickly—pushing back, reaching for me. With my wrist bent sideways against his belly, I couldn't get a good grip on the gun. If I tried another shot, I might hit Kiri or the wall.

Using all my momentum and the advantage of surprise, I heaved him toward the window. He seized hold of my wrist, his breath hissing as he twisted my gun hand, forcing it open.

And then Kiri came at him from the side, ramming her forehead straight into his breastbone. She screamed as she ran, a cry of pure fury.

Blue sky framed Callum. He grabbed at the masonry to keep himself from falling over the low sill, but his fingers gave way. A wild smile flashed on his face—as if he couldn't believe this was happening.

"Kiri!" he cried.

The smile was gone as quickly as it had come.

"*Go.*" I pushed the word out between my teeth. I was on the edge now, too, sun in my eyes. Let him see how it felt.

"Damn!" A foot slipped out from under him. He lost his balance, the green woods swimming sickly in the background. His body fell backward, but his arms darted forward and snatched handfuls of my shirt. The woods lurched around me as I teetered over the sill, and then I was falling, too—

And then, somehow, I wasn't. Someone had latched onto the back of my shirt with ferocious strength and was hauling me back inside.

As my center of gravity shifted, I watched Callum fall into the vastness below me, his hands still outstretched. He didn't look angry, only surprised, as if he still expected the situation magically to correct itself.

I wouldn't forget that expression.

I didn't see him hit the water. I was back in the darkness, on the dusty floor. Kiri's arms closed around me, and her hair covered me like a veil as she rocked me against her chest.

"I'm so sorry," she said, her chin pressing down on the crown of my head. "The stuff I said—I didn't mean it. I just had to make him think I didn't care. I had to make him let you go."

A wave of nausea washed over me, clashing with the thrill and relief of having her close. "You lied to me. About so much." *How can I believe anything you say now?*

"I know."

I was still holding the gun, but loosely. I didn't like how close it was to her vital organs. "Let me up," I said.

It took her a moment to comprehend the words, I think, but then she did it. I clicked the safety on again, put the gun into the backpack, and zipped it.

I didn't want to look out the window, but I had to. I counted five steps to get there. Behind me, Kiri said, "No."

I gripped both sides of the opening and looked down. Far below, the silvery cascade glittered in the sun. I searched for a dark spot on the rocks or in the water, something that hadn't been there before.

Then I saw a tall man standing beside the falls, on the bank, looking directly up at me. Black hair, white shirt, a penetrating gaze I could feel from here.

He survived. The thought spread an icy blanket over me, and for an instant I couldn't breathe. Then I remembered that Callum's shirt was red.

"It's West," I told Kiri as the man called to me inaudibly through the roar of the falls, motioning for me to come down. "Callum was wrong—he came to find you."

She wrapped an arm around my waist from behind, and I felt her trembling as violently as I was. "West's message—"

"I know. When he said the footprints from the desert came here with him, he meant to tell you Callum was the one who wanted a meeting." She nodded, and I went on, "But you already knew those footprints in the campsite were Callum's, didn't you? Did you *ever* think he was dead?"

Kiri released me and turned to face me. Her eyes had that distant look again. "I was so angry . . . I wanted to have done it. I thought I had until I saw those footprints, and even then, I tried to tell myself West killed Cal. There was the story I told people, and there were the versions I wanted to have happened, and there was the version I thought actually had—but that was just bits and pieces."

She'd told me a little of each of those versions—assuming she was telling me the truth now. But I wasn't ready to assume that, and I might never be again.

Before I could ask any more questions, she seized my hand. "We'll tell West what Cal almost did to you. He'll understand."

29

O n the last flight of stairs, I paused to catch my breath. The light was different from when we'd come. And then I remembered Callum saying, *I'm trying to figure out what Kiri likes about you*, and the world spun and dipped around me, as if he were dangling me in midair again. The nausea was back, pressing the contents of my stomach up into my throat.

I didn't realize that I was crying in harsh, hiccuping sobs until Kiri put her arms around me and said, "It's okay, Sam. We couldn't have done anything different."

We were holding hands when we walked straight up to West, who stood in the main doorway. I'd managed to stop crying by then, but my eyes felt raw. Kiri's were dry.

"Did you . . . ?" she asked West, angling her head toward the river.

West nodded. His eyes were deeper and darker than ever. "Downstream," he said. "Moving fast—I don't think he'll be found near here. But let's get to my car before anyone else comes along."

So we managed to communicate without ever saying the words *Callum's body*. Kiri didn't let go of my hand as we walked to the parking lot. The river rushed and burbled, and I tried not to think of the torrent sweeping him downstream.

If he'd dropped me, the body in the water would have been mine.

There were just three cars in the parking lot: Owen's Legacy, Tierney's Range Rover, and the black Grand Cherokee that had followed me home, so long ago.

When I saw it, my legs went floppy, and I didn't want to get in. But Kiri squeezed my hand and said, "C'mon."

We sat in the back seat, still holding hands, which left West alone in the front. My mind kept flitting off, like the white-gold sunlight in the corner of my eye. Only the pressure of Kiri's hand kept me there. Without her, I would have been a swallow escaping into the panting blue sky, higher and higher. There was only one real thought in my head:

I killed someone. Because I didn't want him to kill me.

West was talking about something, his brow urgently furrowed. Talking, talking. And then Kiri was clasping my hand tightly in both of hers and saying, "You're right. I can't go back."

"No!" I said, yanked back to the present. "You can't just disappear. Wasn't that what you were telling Callum? You don't have to!"

Kiri shook her head. Her eyes were so tired. "I don't care about me. But if we told them the truth about Cal, you'd be in trouble, too. Unless maybe I lied and said I did the whole thing—"

"I'm not lying about it!" If she disappeared now, she would be doing what Callum had wanted. "I have to take responsibility."

"Can you prove that you had to defend yourself?" West asked me. "Was Callum threatening your life?"

"He held her out the window." Kiri's nails dug into my skin. "He wanted to use her to control me, to kidnap her and take her with us as a hostage. He wouldn't have stopped at anything. But you're right—people might not believe that. His parents have a lot of power."

"And then there's the girl in the desert." West spoke in slow motion. "Was that Cal, Kiri? Did he kill her?"

"Yes." My voice was unnaturally loud. I brought my free hand down on top of our three clasped ones. "Callum killed Natalie." That's what we'd tell them.

"He didn't," Kiri said. "I can't lie about that."

"Fine. It was an accident, and you'll explain that."

"No," she said. And something final in her tone told me I was going to lose her.

In the distance, down the road, a motor rumbled. "We gotta go," West said, putting the car in gear.

Kiri said, "Not yet."

She slid her hands out of my grip. Her eyes gleamed, tears pooling in the corners, as she reached across me with those long arms to unlock my door and shove it open.

"You have to go back to your friend's car, Sam." Her face was dead white. "You can't be seen with me. You can't get caught up in this."

"I *am* caught up in it! I killed him!" I wasn't afraid to say it in front of West. My chest ached, as if someone had lodged a tow hook there and was pulling. I couldn't go back to Owen's car alone. My place was with her—in an interrogation room, in a courtroom, anywhere. We belonged together.

Kiri shook her head. Her eyes were dark holes. "I'm not going back there, Sam. I have to go on." A glance at West. "To that cabin in the middle of nowhere."

"No!" I didn't have logical arguments. I seized her hands again and clung to them. "If you're going there, I'm going with you."

Her gaze was far away, not focused on me. "You're going to college, Sam. You're going to have a life."

"*You* can have a life!" The motor was louder. Soon it would reach us. "Just tell the truth, Kiri! People sympathize with you, they like you—you don't need to disappear!"

Kiri stiffened and drew herself up. She said in that cold voice, the voice she'd used in the cave, "You know nobody made me go meet Callum, Sam. I wanted to. I *had* to face him. And now I have faced him, I understand something. You were right."

"About what?" I whispered.

She shrugged, but then her face softened. "I have power. I can't really love anyone until I understand that nobody can make me a better person but me."

Another wave of nausea.

"This isn't the way." Tears streaked down my cheeks. "You can't just keep running."

"Shh." She'd slid out of the car and was extending a hand to me. "Someone's here."

I looked up through my tears, expecting and almost hoping to see a police cruiser. But it was only a giant RV with a gray-haired driver, who was edging it carefully into a space.

"Please." I took her hand and let her tug me out, sobs choking me. I couldn't go back to my life, not now that I'd become part of her story. Even if I couldn't trust her, I couldn't spend my life lying. "Please. Stay with me."

Her arms folded around me. Her lips met mine, soft and alive, and her fingertips pressed hard into my back, and her hair cloaked my face. I kissed her back, wanting to stay inside the pulsing glow of her forever.

Callum was right—she was incandescent. But I didn't want to trap that glow on a screen and turn it into rising columns of numbers: views, likes, shares. I just wanted to be in the light.

"I have to go on alone from here." She kissed me a last time and stepped away.

Through the blur of tears, I watched her open the passenger door and get in. I watched West's lips move as he looked at me, and I knew he was making me promise never to say a word.

I nodded—that part was easy. When you love someone, sometimes you just have to accept what they're telling you. Callum had asked me what I could give Kiri. I hadn't been able to answer then, but I knew now. I could do what he had refused to do: I could let her go.

I cried as I walked to Owen's car. I didn't watch as the Grand Cherokee pulled out, didn't wave to her—couldn't. I had to get out of there before the old couple in the RV had time to notice any details about us, because there was no telling when or where Callum's remains might surface.

I didn't look back until I was behind the wheel, and by then the Grand Cherokee was a speck in the distance. It was too late to gun the motor and race after them.

Kiri wanted me to have a life, and now I had to figure out what that would be.

30

On the day of the first snowfall, I thought I saw her again.

It was a slow day at the Grand Nine, and I had my laptop at the ticket counter so I could type up my transfer application to Emerson. My journalism prof was a reporter moonlighting as a teacher, and she said I needed a school where I could join the staff of a good student paper and learn from the ground up.

I was working on the essay:

Like many people of my generation, I grew up fascinated by sensationalist stories I found online. I didn't think it mattered how you got the story as long as it was a good one. But...

Here I was supposed to say what I'd learned so far. That I liked the stability of having an ethical code to follow. That every choice you make about how to tell a story affects someone. Every quote needs a context. Every statement needs a source.

My gaze drifted from the screen to the plate-glass front of the theater, now white with whirling snow. Wind tossed sheets of it at the glass and spun it in circles. I could almost feel the cold flakes stinging my cheeks.

She was out there somewhere in the wilds of Canada. Was she

trudging through a snowstorm right now, cold and alone? Was she hunting game or splitting logs to keep herself warm?

On September 2, I had received a postcard with a Colorado postmark. *Got our friend settled. She can't stay here for good, but I think she'll be fine for the winter.* No signature, but I knew it was from West.

When I remembered Kiri, I saw her with shorts baring her long legs, a sheen of sweat on her skin. My gaze fell to the screen again, and I switched tabs and typed her name into the search bar.

My finger hovered over the return button, but I couldn't seem to bring it down.

A car drove up and parked in the lot, snow churning in its headlights. The driver's door opened. Wind whipped long, platinum-blond hair as a girl got out.

I stopped breathing.

She was tall with broad shoulders, and she pushed the snow-damp hair out of her face with delicate fingers. She stood a little hunched beside the car, as if she were self-conscious about her height.

Then a boy got out on the passenger side, and two more girls joined them from the back seat, shattering the illusion. The blond girl turned to speak to her friends. Her face was wide and ruddy, her brows almost auburn.

Not you. Never you.

They brought the chill into the lobby with them, talking and laughing about a UVM hockey game, brushing snow from their coats and scarves. The girl who wasn't Kiri reached the counter first, and I smiled and she smiled back and asked for a ticket to Marvel's Thanksgiving release and a medium popcorn.

I swiped her card and printed out her ticket. Behind me, explosions echoed softly from Theater Three.

I handed her the paper sack. She'd unbuttoned her coat to reveal a baggy sweatshirt that said ADDISON COUNTY 4-H.

She must have noticed my expression, because she frowned. I shook my head: *Never mind.*

I sold tickets and popcorn and Pepsi and kombucha and Keurig coffee to her three friends, and all of them disappeared into the theater, leaving me alone again. The snow still pelted down, turning blue as twilight fell.

I'd remembered something, or thought I had. And now it wouldn't let me go.

I unzipped the interior pocket of my backpack and slipped my hand way inside until I found a tightly folded packet of notebook paper.

Kiri's diary. I knew I should burn it, or at least find a safer place for it, but I couldn't seem to make that final sacrifice.

Keeping one eye out for customers, I unfolded the papers on the counter and shuffled through them until I found the entry I thought I'd remembered: *Last time I saw her she was wearing a faded T-shirt that said* CIMARRON COUNTY 4-H, *so I guess she once had a home, too.*

Colors suddenly seemed a little brighter and sounds sharper, as if a voice had woken me from a deep sleep. All this time I'd been waiting for news that Natalie's body had been identified and returned to her family. But the bikers had disappeared without a trace, taking any knowledge of her with them. If other campers had noticed her, they hadn't come forward. No one knew enough to connect the Jane Doe to her origin. I hadn't thought I did, either, until now.

Her T-shirt could have been thrifted. But…I cleared the search bar and googled Cimarron County. It was in Oklahoma.

My prof would have told me to call the FBI hotline, but I knew I'd never do that.

I texted Reggie: Hey, you in class?

Nope, rehearsal. We'd got into the habit of texting now and then, usually about random stuff like shows we were binging. What's up?

My hands trembled so hard I had to keep retyping. You still in touch with Aliza Deene?

Sure, why?

The screen swam before my eyes. Was I doing the right thing? But whatever Aliza had said about Kiri, Natalie didn't deserve to be remembered as an anonymous corpse found in the red sand. She deserved to go home to the people who loved her.

Tell Aliza that the girl found in Lost Village National Monument was named Natalie, and she could be from Cimarron County, Oklahoma.

When I hit send, a weight lifted from my chest. Wherever Kiri was, I knew she'd understand what I was doing.

Reggie sent me a strip of exclamation points, followed by a question mark.

Outside, the snowfall was thinning as dusk advanced. I remembered how the UVM student's bright hair had flashed as she stepped out of the car, and I remembered the magnetic closeness of Kiri in the summer heat, and I hoped she was somewhere safe and warm as night darkened.

I had my essay to finish now and my own stories to tell.

I wrote: Just pass that on to Aliza. No names. She'll know how to check it out.

**TRANSCRIPT OF VIDEO POSTED ON
JANUARY 28 BY ALIZA DEENE OF
MURDER MOST F**KED UP**

So, on the six-month anniversary of Callum Massey's disappearance, what do we even know?

We know that Callum was an emotional abuser and very possibly a pedophile. Don't come for me in the comments, Cal stans! You can choose not to believe Arianna Dunne if you want, but she's consistent and credible, and those pics of her with Callum when she was thirteen are just freakin' creepy. I think it was brave of her to come forward and talk about every way he screwed with her head, and yeah, I'll die on that hill.

Were the BPD and the FBI negligent in Kiri's case? Hells, yeah! Burlington is only an hour from the Canadian border—get a clue, cops! It was way too easy for her to slip away. Would she have made a break for it if she weren't guilty of something? Doubt it!

But do we know she was guilty of murder? We don't, friends. In case you've forgotten, we have exactly one body.

Her name was Natalie Tobin, just nineteen years old. A girl who used to have a room full of mystery novels and horse figurines; a girl who ran away from home when she was seventeen, headed for LA, and never came back. A girl who died in a fall, a girl whose blood ended up mingled with Callum's on that sweatshirt. We'll never know why.

I'm proud of the role I played in bringing Natalie's remains home, but this isn't about me. It's about Natalie. It's about the anonymous tipster who helped me ID her. It's about Arianna, who was courageous enough to let us know what kind of person Callum Massey was and why he would want to disappear. And it's about Kiri.

Kiri, honey, if you're alive out there, I wish you'd come back and face the music. I know I haven't always said the nicest things about you, but that was before Arianna came forward.

Not all of us think you're guilty. Some of us want to hear your side.

Acknowledgments

True crime is a fraught subject, for good reason—one that has always made me feel fascinated and queasy in equal measures. I want to thank everyone who helped me navigate the quandaries of exploring our culture's fascination with murder stories in *Only She Came Back*.

My wonderful agent, Jessica Sinsheimer, saw the potential in the story and supported it steadfastly. Liz Kossnar helped me dig deeper into the characters and themes with her transformative editing. Jenny Kimura made the book's multimedia aspect come alive on the page, and Peter Strain took my breath away with his haunting imagery. Many thanks also to Kelley Frodel, Jake Regier, and the whole team at Little, Brown Books for Young Readers.

Thank you to my coeditors at the newspaper *Seven Days*, especially Dan Bolles, Elizabeth M. Seyler, Pamela Polston, Carolyn Fox, and Mary Ann Lickteig, for helping me find the time I needed to write this book. Local journalism matters, and we prove it every week.

Burlington is a great town, and I hope its citizens will forgive me for occasionally fudging its geography. Thank you to Josh Hallmark of *True Crime Bullsh*** for giving me insight into the work of a true-crime podcaster.

Thank you to Nicole Lesperance for the early read and to Dayna Lorentz, Rachel Carter, Jennifer Mason-Black, Jesse Q. Sutanto, Marley Teter, Grace Shim, Ellie Marney, and Elizabeth Bonesteel for the ongoing support. I'm endlessly grateful to all the readers I've met on BookTok who dished with me about fake diaries, like *Go Ask Alice*, while I was creating Kiri's diary.

ACKNOWLEDGMENTS

Eva Sollberger, thank you for being my fearless companion in consuming true-crime media and for giving me Lily, my small but fierce resident cougar. Dad—you were never shocked when I asked ghoulish questions as a child. Mom—you're the sweetness and light I need to balance things out. Love you all.